CAROUSEL

I hope you enjoy reading this as much as I have enjoyed writing it

Raj

RAJEEV RANA

AuthorHouse™ UK Ltd.
1663 Liberty Drive
Bloomington, IN 47403 USA
www.authorhouse.co.uk
Phone: 0800.197.4150

Published by AuthorHouse 6/21/2013

ISBN: 978-1-4817-9865-5 (sc)
ISBN: 978-1-4817-9864-8 (hc)
ISBN: 978-1-4817-9866-2 (e)

TABLE OF CONTENTS

"*Fuck!* Look at the time! Tanya will kill me!"

Rajesh dived into his Porsche Boxster and tore out of the drive, leaving two streaks of scorched rubber strewn across the immaculate paving. "Thank God Dad left early," he whispered to himself, knowing full well how his father would have reacted if he had witnessed his reckless attempt to make up lost time.

But time was of the essence. He had to get from Gerrards Cross to the heart of Southall – a journey of twenty-five minutes. And already he was fifteen minutes late! Not a good start. *Tanya hates being kept waiting,* thought Rajesh. He floored the accelerator and raced through the narrow lanes, mindful of the reaction he would get if he turned up late.

He had known Tanya since childhood. Recently things had developed into a full-blown Bollywood romance. It was packed with secret rendezvous, cultural divides, and smouldering passion. She was now the love of his life, but just lately Rajesh had begun to feel their relationship had grown distant. It was his own fault; he had been spending more and more time with his boisterous friends. Tanya despaired at their juvenile behaviour. "Wasters", she called them. So, knowing he was in her bad books, he had arranged a day out to win her over. He had planned every detail, leaving nothing to chance – a lavish lunch at her favourite restaurant, shopping at Harrods and a West End show to end the evening. It wasn't his ideal way of spending the day with such a stunning girl; an afternoon of passion was much more to his liking. But he realised that Tanya was someone who needed pampering before he could enjoy her delicate fruits. The problem was, patience was not his strong point. Rajesh wanted everything life had to offer – the cars, the girls, the clothes, the cash, *sai rah!* – and he wanted it now.

Slamming the gearstick into fourth, he controlled the speed of the car with the clutch rather than the brakes, tearing around bends, shooting over level crossings. He loved being on the edge, that intense feeling of almost losing control. For added motivation he scrolled through the options on his music system until he came to the ultimate drive track – "No Easy Way Out" from Rocky 4. Remembering the emotion on Stallone's face as he tore apart the Lamborghini in the underground tunnels, he pushed harder and more aggressively on the accelerator, taking careless risks but enjoying every second of it. This was no longer a question of being on time for Tanya; this was the thrill of driving fast and beating the clock – and he was winning.

Driving into Southall always unnerved Rajesh. Having grown up on their mean streets, he was glad to see the back of them. He had long since moved up in the world and would have cut links with the place years ago if it hadn't been for Tanya.

He cruised along Uxbridge Road, shifting down the gears before stopping at a zebra crossing. The Boxter's engine decelerated from a growl to a purr. Passers-by stared at him enviously. The car, the watch, the designer clothes – here was someone who had "made it". He gazed down the bustling street and its shops, takeaways, and mini-marts thronged with people. It was so different from Gerrards Cross, with its upmarket delicatessens and trendy wine bars. He checked himself in the rear-view mirror. A handsome, clean-shaven face stared back – a regular Hrithik Roshan, even if he said so himself! He studied his reflection for a few seconds. *Tanya's a lucky girl,* thought Rajesh.

Turning off the main road, he saw her standing in her usual place at the corner of the street. His pulse quickened. Even at a distance she exuded a fierce independence. It was a look that said "Don't mess with me". Tanya was twenty-six years old – the same age as Rajesh – slim, and smartly dressed, with glossy, shoulder-length black hair framing her pretty elfin face.

Tanya had expected Rajesh to be late; nevertheless, she was fuming when he finally screeched to a halt beside her. He buzzed down the electric window and deployed his cheeky boyish grin, as if that would excuse him for being late. Tanya stared past him blankly, barely acknowledging his arrival.

He leaned over to the passenger window, poised to assuage his guilt. "Yaar. Sorry, babe. Dad had this huge list of documents he wanted me to deal with. Couldn't get away." He knew Tanya would be happy to hear he was taking more of an interest in working with his father. She lectured him almost daily about how much she missed her own father since he had passed away, encouraging him to bridge the gap between them before it was too late.

Tanya glanced at him and found it hard not to smile. She resisted as much as she could, but the soaring butterflies in her stomach caused her willpower to crumble. His effortless charm, his breezy manner – she adored these things about him. Although they had known each other since the age of five, he was still able to cause jitters of excitement within her.

Like a mother scolding a much-loved child, she looked at him and shook her head. "I think you should buy a decent watch. That cheap crap you call a Rolex doesn't seem to be working."

Rajesh ignored the obvious bait for an argument. "Yaar, come on. Next time I'll be half an hour early and be waiting for you with a rose in my mouth. Promise! Now get in so we can eat! Or I'll get out and eat *you*! Unless that's what you want?"

She shrugged. This was the closest thing to an apology she could expect. Reluctantly she got into the car and slid the seatbelt across her nubile body. She slammed the door aggressively and tutted. "Smells like burnt rubber."

"That's because I drove like crazy to get here!"

"Don't tell me you didn't enjoy it, Raj! What was it this time, James Bond? *Knight Rider*? *Miami Vice*? Or some other sad eighties crap? When are you going to snap out of that era?"

"Actually, babe, it was *Rocky Four!* And if you must know, it's not crap! It's a solid-gold classic!"

Gripping the steering wheel hard, Rajesh revved the engine and sped off down the street. Tanya glanced at him. His face was like thunder. She knew she had touched a raw nerve; insulting his watch was one thing, but slating his music was something else. She was determined not to back down but was all too aware of his stubborn childish streak. And by the look of him, he was close to throwing his toys out of the pram! She reached into her handbag and grabbed her mobile. Discreetly typing out a text message, she kept the phone out of sight the whole time. After sending the text, she placed the bag at her feet and gazed innocently through the window, secretly hoping her attempt at humour would be enough to lighten his mood.

Seconds later, Rajesh felt his mobile buzzing inside his shirt pocket. He slid it open and smiled as he read the text: "Jaan your still the immature boy I fell for … I love u." Such sweet traits made Tanya unique, setting her apart from all the other girls he had known. He turned to her and smiled. She pretended not to notice but was straining to contain her grin. He gently took her hand and placed it on top of the gear lever, and then, with loving tenderness, he covered it with his own. He changed gears unnecessarily, each time slipping his fingers between hers. Tanya couldn't resist. She leaned across and kissed him on the lips, blocking his view of the road for a second. But neither of them cared. Time seemed stand still for those few moments. She pulled away from his lips, placed her head on his shoulder, and closed her eyes. He could smell her delicate perfume, her sweetly lacquered hair.

Rajesh kissed her gently on the forehead as he called to her. "Bhandari?"

"Yes, Pagal."

They both smiled.

Parking was always a problem around the High Street, but today *kismat* was on Rajesh's side. He was able to park right outside Madhu's. Result.

"Are we going in there?" asked Tanya.

"It's your favourite restaurant, right?"

"I'm impressed."

"Why? You've been here loads of times."

"Not with the restaurant, Pagal. I'm impressed with the fact that you actually listen to me and know my tastes."

Rajesh turned to her and said, "That's easy, yaar! You're a *pindu!* We could have gone to any Mayfair restaurant, but I know madam likes to keep it real."

Tanya leaned over and whispered in his ear seductively, "Jaan, you know you love the chilli paneer."

"That's me making the best of a bad situation." Rajesh knew that even though the restaurant was in a modest location, the food and the décor rivalled any five-star central-London joint, but he still had to show slight disapproval so he could maintain his superior image.

He always received a warm reception at Madhu's; because he was the son of a wealthy man who enjoyed throwing his money around to impress his friends, the staff treated him like royalty.

The manager came over and greeted them obsequiously, shaking Rajesh's hand and smiling falsely at Tanya. "Sir, we have a very nice table over here in the corner."

Rajesh hated the idea of being shoved into a corner – any corner. He shook his head arrogantly. "No, I want *that* table, by the window. That way I can look at her and keep an eye on my car."

The manager chuckled but was not amused; spoilt rich kids made him sick. He clicked his fingers in the direction of his staff and pointed to the table Rajesh had requested. Two disinterested-looking waiters wandered over languidly, pulled back the chairs, and gestured for the couple to take their seats.

Rajesh settled into his chair and looked at Tanya. "Right. Now we've got the drama out of the way, how are you?"

Tanya produced a half smile. "I'm okay, considering you haven't called recently to wish me goodnight."

It was true, and Rajesh felt guilty. He knew he would have to do some serious crawling to placate her. "Baby doll, you know what it's like. I was out partying with Jazz and Sunny. Those guys are insane. It takes at least two days to recover."

Tanya snatched up her serviette and shoved it into her lap. "You mean it takes two days to sober up!"

A young waiter interrupted. "Sir, would you like to see the wine list?"

Rajesh raised an eyebrow. "What! Are you kidding me! Do I look like an alcoholic? It's only midday, for God's sake! What the hell do I need the wine list for? Bring us two mango lassis and a plate – in fact, two plates – of chilli paneer while we decide what to eat."

"Yes, sir. And for you, madam?"

"You *laan!"* said Rajesh."That's for both of us!"

"Yes, sir. Very good, sir." The waiter nodded and scurried off back to the kitchen.

Rajesh sighed frustratedly. "I hate incompetence. A little common sense goes a long way. But what can you do when you're dealing with freshies straight off the boat."

"Rajesh! Listen to yourself! When did you become such a snob? Sometimes I wonder what happened to that mischievous boy I grew up with. When did you become so judgemental?"

"We all have to grow up, Jaan."

"Maybe one day you'll be judgmental about me. Remember, I am not from your world. What if your crowd thought I was fresh off the boat? How would you like that?" Tanya paused. She could see that Rajesh was distracted and no longer paying attention. She banged the table with her fist. "That's typical of you! Just because you don't like what you're hearing, you switch off!"

Rajesh karate-chopped the air. "Shush!"

Tanya was shocked. She saw Rajesh take a knife from the table and slip it up his shirt cuff. He was staring out of the window, a tense expression etched on his face. "Rajesh … what's wrong?"

Ignoring her, he reached for his phone with his free hand.

Curious, Tanya turned and looked outside. "Oh my God!" There was panic in her voice. Real panic. "Rajesh! Rajesh! I will deal with this! He's harmless! Let's not create a scene. Please, I live around here. I have to see these people every day. Let it go, baby. Please. For me."

Rajesh was oblivious to what she was saying; it was as if a switch had been flipped within him, altering his entire personality. "Who are you calling, Raj? I can deal with this." Tanya began to stand up.

Rajesh instinctively grabbed her hand. "No, Tanya. Stay here. This will end today! I've ignored this prick for too long." Rajesh switched the conversation to his mobile. "Hi, Jazz. I am at Madhu's. Yeah, yeah, in Southall … Fuck what I am doing here! Just listen, will you! Mac's outside with four guys. Vicious-looking bastards. They're waiting for me to come out." He paused for a response, his whole body pumped with adrenaline. He knew this day had been a long time coming, but he didn't want Tanya around now that it had arrived. "Okay, okay. I'll sit tight. But whoever you send, tell them to hurry. These wankers won't chill for long."

Tanya looked at him with disgust. "For God's sake! Why are you causing an international incident? We've known Mac since we were kids. Let me go outside and speak to him. This is bullshit!"

But Rajesh was in no mood to compromise. He tried to calm her, using her pet name. "Look, TanJa. Sit tight for a while. This is guy's stuff. Mac only respects the rules of the street, so let's just deal with this today and wrap it up once and for all." He beckoned one of the waiters over – the freshie straight off the boat. "Ring a taxi for my girlfriend, will you."

"Yes, sir. Is everything all right?"

"Great. Just order the cab."

"But, sir, your food is yet to arrive."

Rajesh glared at him. "Just order the fucking taxi, idiot!"

"Y ... yes, sir."

Tanya hated Rajesh's rude macho side. She rarely got to see it, but when she did, it drove her crazy.

Rajesh suddenly sprung to his feet. "You have got to be taking the piss!"

"Raj, what's wrong?"

He stabbed his finger at the window. "Look! The piss-taking fuck is sitting on the bonnet of my car!" He darted out of the restaurant and was face-to-face with Mac before Tanya could even stand up.

In a desperate panic, she shouted to the restaurant manager as she ran out of the door, saying, "Call the police ... Call them ... or they will kill each other!"

When she got outside, Rajesh and Mac were squaring up. They were both of similar height, though Mac had the edge when it came to sheer physical bulk. He had short-cropped hair and an acne-scarred face. What he lacked in the looks department he more than made up for in muscle. His four cohorts were just as ugly, a tightly packed retinue of baseball-capped, tracksuit-wearing thugs. Tanya rushed over and tried to get between them. Mac extended his arm to stop her.

Rajesh grabbed it and shoved it away. "Don't touch her!"

Mac's cronies stood to attention; as far as they were concerned, the first move had been made and everything was legal from here on in. Rajesh gritted his teeth in utter fury, but Mac simply smiled back at him. After all, this was *his* town; he was surrounded by his own people, and he was playing to the gallery. Rajesh let the knife slip from the inside of his cuff so that the blade was exposed. He gripped the handle firmly, ready for action. He was totally outnumbered but figured he could take Mac out and worry about the consequences later. The pair eyeballed each other like two ancient warriors ready for a fight to the death, both oblivious to the black Range Rover speeding towards them.

The Range Rover slammed to a stop inches from Rajesh's shoulder. The driver revved the engine to get the warriors' attention. Confused, Rajesh and Mac stared at one another, both thinking the worst, expecting the mysterious Range Rover to be reinforcements for the other. The windows of the car were heavily tinted and impossible to see into. The passenger window slid down to reveal a bulldog-type thug at the wheel. He appeared to be around thirty years old and resembled a football hooligan; he was bald, and his arms were covered in tattoos. He looked at Mac, nodding his huge cannonball head. Mac breathed a sigh of relief. He recognised him from a white East London firm he had used as a go-between when dealing with Indian gangs in Southall.

The bulldog gestured at Mac to approach the car. Mac did as he was told and walked over. The bulldog handed him a mobile phone and said, in a thick East End accent, "The boss wants a word."

Mac took the phone. "Hello ... Oh, it's you, boss." Mac winced as a torrent of abuse poured into his ear.

Relief flooded through Rajesh's body; whoever was on the other end of the phone was giving Mac a real bollocking. He smiled at Tanya to calm her down.

Mac went deathly pale. He began to stutter into the phone. "B-boss ... this is nothing to do with business ... this is personal ... the cunt's had it coming for ages." He paused for a reaction but realised he was fighting a lost cause. His bollocking over, Mac handed the phone back to the bulldog, staring him straight in the eye.

This show of defiance enraged the bulldog. For a split second he considered getting out of the car to enforce his boss's message. But just considering it did the trick, as Mac's expression changed instantly from defiance to puppy-dog deference.

"Are we savvy, Mac?" asked the bulldog threateningly.

Mac nodded. "Savvy."

The bulldog gave a sarcastic grin and spoke into the mobile. "Sweet, boss. He's got the message." He put the Range Rover in gear and glided past Rajesh, giving him a cold, hard stare.

Humiliated, Mac turned and signalled to his cronies to follow. All five of them trudged back to Mac's car. It was such an anticlimax that Rajesh felt like calling him back. Maybe now was the time to challenge him and end things once and for all. But he froze. Why tempt fate? He wasn't sure why Mac had had such a dramatic change of heart, but he had enough common sense to know when he should put his head down and ride the wave.

Mac opened his car door and looked at Rajesh. "Next time, sunshine … Next time."

Rajesh started to react, but Tanya squeezed his hand as if to say, "Leave it, babe." Rajesh nodded in agreement. Instead, he turned towards Mac and blew him a kiss. Enraged, Mac dived into his car, simultaneously starting the engine and slamming his foot on the accelerator. Smoke billowed from the tyres and he was gone.

"Rajesh? What the hell just happened?"

"I don't know, Jaan. But I am guessing it has something to do with Jazz."

She gripped his hand tightly. "I'm scared. Let's get out of here."

"Relax, babe; if something was going to happen, it would have kicked off. He obviously backed off for a reason. Let me call Jazz and find out what he knows."

"You can do that from the car. Please, Rajesh, I just want to go!"

He was desperate to keep his cool; the last thing he wanted was for Tanya to see how unnerved he was by the whole episode. "Okay, TanJa, let's go; I'll run you home and call Jazz later."

The car was silent on the journey to Tanya's house. Rajesh felt anxious. He was desperate to make a few calls to find out what had caused Mac's sudden U-turn.

"Jaan, should I drop you outside your house or around the corner?"

"No. Mum is home today. Drop me by Fairways Road and I'll walk from there."

What am I, an untouchable? He thought. "Your mum loves me, babe. What's the big deal?"

"Idiot! The big deal is, good little Indian girls shouldn't be dating naughty little Indian boys, however rich they are. Now drop me at the corner."

That suited Rajesh just fine. He wanted rid of her anyway so he could jump on the phone. Careful not to make it too obvious, he pulled over and gazed at the road ahead.

Tanya sensed he was in no mood for an emotional goodbye. "Go and clear your head. You don't need the hassle. You're better than this. Look at the sort of family you belong to. Your dad is always banging on at you about family pride and your standing in the community. How would he have felt today if he saw his precious son brawling in the street?"

"Nothing happened, Jaan," he answered wearily.

"You know what I mean, Raj. Stop avoiding the facts."

Rajesh refused to make eye contact. It was his way of saying "You're wasting your breath".

Tanya sighed with frustration. "I'm going. Listen, don't call me for a few days. I mean it. Take some time to grow up." She leapt out of the car without kissing him goodbye.

Normally Rajesh would have done all he could to prevent such a sombre parting. He knew that if a girl was upset there was only one remedy – you should hold her tight and not speak, just hold her. And the more upset she was, the closer you should hold her. Eventually everything would work itself out. But on this occasion Rajesh didn't hesitate and sped off as soon as Tanya slammed the door.

Feeling the adrenaline pumping, he hurriedly called Jazz. "Hey. What's the word?"

The voice on the other end of the line was stress city. "Shit, Rajesh! What took you so long to call? Are you all right? Tell me you're out of the hood."

"Yeah, yeah. Relax, man. I've just dropped Tanya off. I'll drive over. Where are you?"

"At the tennis club. Lick it down."

"Did you send the Range Rover? Who the fuck was it?"

"Take it easy, man. What have I told you about talking on mobile phones?"

"Jazz! You're hardly Bin Laden!"

Jazz didn't like Rajesh's mocking tone. "What's that got to do with the price of rice?"

"Meaning, who the hell would want to bug *your* mobile?"

"Brother, I am one seriously connected individual. You've just seen an example of my connections, right? So get your ass down to the club and buy me a mojito. And maybe … just maybe … I'll consider filling you in."

Rajesh was frustrated as hell at Jazz's arrogance, but he knew it was necessary to massage his friend's ego. "Word. You're the man. I'll be there in fifteen."

Rajesh loved the feeling of arriving at the Stoke Poges Tennis Club. The ambience was five-star upon entering the car park. Pulling up outside the nineteenth-century manor house always put a spring in his step. He felt relieved having left Bosnia (his pet name for Southall) behind. He was amongst his own, and it revived him.

A parking valet opened the car door and welcomed him with polite deference. "Afternoon, sir."

Rajesh ignored him. Leaving the engine running, he hurried up the ageing stone staircase into an impressive marble reception hall. The atmosphere was refined elegance, like an Edwardian gentlemen's club. He mentally undressed the blonde receptionist whilst giving her a cheeky grin. Rajesh had a weakness for girls in tennis skirts; it was one of the reasons he had joined in the first place – that and the kudos of being a member.

"Afternoon, Mr Thakral. Will you be needing your locker key?"

"No thanks, hon. I'm joining some friends on the terrace." He glanced at her perfectly shaped legs, lingering momentarily to imagine stroking her inner thigh in that pristine white skirt.

"Snap out of it, man!" Jazz said, breaking his concentration and ruining the fantasy. "You're love of pussy is going to get you into deep shit one day, bro. Even *I* won't be able to bail you out."

Jazz was standing at the entrance to the members' bar dressed in his tennis gear. He was shorter than Rajesh, thicker set, and a lot less handsome.

"Cut the crap, Jazz. What happened out there? Mac was ready to kick off, and suddenly he turned into a shit out. Who was in the Range Rover?"

Jazz put his arm around Rajesh, manoeuvring him towards the garden area. He needed somewhere secluded, somewhere quiet where they could talk openly. The conservatory was perfect.

Rajesh wanted answers. He had no time for games. "Jazz, what's the dance?"

"Bro, you don't want to know what level I had to go to today to deal with your situation."

They sat down on a wrought iron bench next to a plashing fountain. The air was cool and moist. The soft thud of tennis balls drifted through the luxuriant foliage from the nearby courts.

"Jazz, all I know is Mac was going to get knifed today. That Range Rover saved his ass."

"Shut up, fool. That Range Rover stopped you getting the crap kicked out of you in front of that precious girlfriend of yours." He tutted sarcastically. "Man, when are you gonna learn? If you lie down with dogs, you wake up with fleas. Nothing good can come of knocking around with that girl. She'll drag you down and hold you back. You shouldn't have even *been* in Southall today."

"Kill the lecture, Jazz, and stop slating Tanya. Just tell me the score."

"I'll tell you the score! I'll fucking tell you the score! Mac only fears and responds to one guy, right."

"Who?" Rajesh's patience was starting to wear thin.

"Regan."

"Which Regan?"

"Joey Regan!"

"What are you talking about, Jazz? Why would a gee like Regan have anything to do with a piece of shit like Mac?"

"Fool, even dons like Regan need foot soldiers on the street. Mac did a few one-twos for him recently, and now he is on the payroll."

"*What!* Mac's connected to Regan! Great! That's fucking great! As if Mac wasn't cocky enough, now he has East London's biggest gangster on side."

"Relax, bro." Jazz pulled out a Cohiba cigar, bit off the end, and lit it up. A band of thick blue smoke enveloped his podgy face.

"What are you doing, man? You can't smoke here. The whole damn club is no smoking."

"I said relax. Ain't nobody gonna say shit to us. We're with the heaviest party around." Jazz didn't really enjoy cigars, but they gave him a sense of importance – a kind of Mafioso vibe.

"What's that supposed to mean? And who was in the damn Range Rover?"

"That was Regan's right-hand man. The guy's an absolute psycho."

"Why the hell would Regan's man get Mac to back off?"

Jazz tilted his head back, exhaling a ring of smoke and watching it rise towards the conservatory's glass roof. "To be honest, bro, I can't work that one out myself. I called a few doormen we know in Southall that look after the night clubs in Mayfair. Next thing I know I've got Regan's PA calling me asking me to confirm who you are, where you're from, and what the problem is. I explained the score. He said he'd take care of it and told me not to call anyone else. Fifteen minutes later, you call and tell me it's all good."

Rajesh hated mysteries. "Why the hell would Regan's man be so interested in helping me out, especially if Mac is working with them?"

Jazz smiled. "All I know is, you're one lucky *ghandu.* Somebody somewhere is looking down on you."

"Have you still got the number stored from the guy who called you?"

"Yeah. I think so. He didn't call off a private number. Why?"

Rajesh sat forward in his chair. "Right, give me your phone."

"You're not planning on calling him, are you? Are you fucking nuts! This is Joey Regan we're talking about."

"Just give me the phone!"

Jazz looked at him in disbelief. "You don't learn, do ya. This is not your plastic gangster stuff; this is the real thing."

Rajesh had a mocking look on his face. "Grow some balls, Jazz. It's good to keep people like this on side. Now give me the phone."

Jazz was pissed off big time. Rajesh had always been a spoilt brat. *Well, fuck him. Let the brat learn the hard way.* He tossed him the phone.

Rajesh went to the last-received-calls screen. "Is this the number?"

Jazz couldn't believe it; only an hour ago he'd bailed Rajesh out of a potential beating, and now here he was trying to play the hero! Shaking his head in disbelief, he got up and walked back into the club.

Rajesh stared at the phone. He knew that if he could establish a link with someone like Regan, nobody would dare mess with him again. But he also knew it was akin to selling his soul to the Devil. Regan's firm was as ruthless as they come. Drugs, prostitution, armed robbery – you name it, they controlled it. Still, they *had* helped him out, so the way he saw it, the least he could do was call and show his appreciation.

Eventually he pressed Call. His heart began to pound. How should he address this person? Would he even know who Rajesh was?

"Yeah? Speak."

Rajesh responded nervously. "H … hello?"

"Who the fuck is this?"

"It's Raj Thakral. You arranged for some assistance today in Southall."

"Who? What the fuck are you going on about, kid?"

"Today, in Southall, you sent someone in a black Range Rover."

"Oh, you're the kid from Gerrards Cross. The one who had a run-in with a prick called Mac."

"Yeah, yeah. That's right. I just wanted to call and say thanks."

"Don't thank me, kid; it was the boss's orders."

"Boss? Do you mean Regan?"

"That's *Mr* Regan to you, son, and don't you fucking forget it!"

"Sorry, I meant *Mr* Regan."

"You learn fast, kid."

"Well, I just wanted to say thanks. Can you please pass that on to Mr Regan?"

"Funny you should say that. The boss has asked to see you, so I guess you can tell him yourself."

Rajesh went pale. His stomach turned over. "Why does Mr Regan want to meet me?"

"That's for him to know and you to find out. This your number?"

"No, it's my mate's, Jazz – the guy you spoke to earlier."

"Right. Text me your number and somebody will call you in a day or so to let you know about the meet. And listen, kid; don't fuck this up. The boss is not a forgiving man, so don't be late."

"Okay. But can you let me know what the agenda is for the meeting is?"

"Agenda? Agenda? You prick! You're not meeting a divorce lawyer! This is the boss we're talking about! If he wants to meet you, then that's what's gonna happen. I'll put it this way: you can either drive yourself or I'll put you in the boot of my car and drive you across town myself. Either way, you'll be there."

"No, no. Sorry. I didn't mean to offend you. It would be an absolute honour to meet with Mr Regan. Please just let me know where and when, and I'll be there.

"Like I said, kid, you learn fast."

Rajesh awoke to the sound of his Bose alarm clock. For years now he had had it set to play an assortment of James Bond movie themes. This morning it was “A View to a Kill”. The classic tracks sharpened him up, made him ready from the word “go”. He would need all his wits about him when he met Regan. “Meeting you, with a view to a kill.” He hoped not.

Pushing away the crisp Dorma sheets, he sprang to his feet and walked towards the en-suite bathroom, pausing to admire his flat stomach and toned body in the full-length mirror. Standing shirtless in his pyjama bottoms, he patted his stomach proudly, all the while humming along to the background music. “Dance into the fire.”

After taking a shower, he dried himself off and padded across thick shag pile. He entered his walk-in wardrobe and turned on the strip light. Rack upon rack of designer clothes flickered to life. Dressing was a ritual Rajesh took very seriously. Much thought and consideration went into coordinating his endless Ralph Lauren outfits and his stockpile of Louis Vuitton shoes. His wardrobe was his armour, and he dressed for respect. The finishing touch was always his Daytona Rolex watch – his father had taught him long ago that a man only ever needs a Daytona on his wrist and a Range Rover on the drive, anything else was just greedy. Rajesh chuckled whenever he remembered that; the watch was fine, but his dad was so wrong about his choice of car. Speed was his buzz. He loved the thrill of a tightly wound engine screaming to be let loose on the open country lanes that surrounded his home – a modern six-bedroom detached house set in two manicured acres.

Life was good for Rajesh. Being an only son, he stood to inherit his father's successful freight forwarding company. But he was in no rush. He enjoyed his freedom and playboy lifestyle too much. His sister, Neelam, was married to an onlooker, but she spent so much time with her mother she could easily have been mistaken for living at home. Rajesh's father, Mr Thakral (as he deemed to be called), was a powerful and important man. He loved talking about his humble origins – how he had come to England in the 1960s and how he had built his vast empire with nothing more than blood, sweat, and tears. His only disappointment was that Rajesh showed little interest in the family business – except, of course, reaping the rewards. His wife, Vidya, reminded him of this at every opportunity: "Rajesh is our only son. He should be allowed to live his life before he is swamped with responsibility." Vidya was a simple woman who always saw the best in people, a traditional Indian housewife and mother who wholeheartedly believed in God's will and the power of kismat.

Rajesh knew his mother would have a mixture of freshly squeezed orange and carrot juice waiting for him in the kitchen. His favourite. She always got up early to prepare a hearty breakfast for the father-and-son duo. But today Rajesh had little time for formality. He ran past his mother in the hallway shouting, "Luv you, *Maa!*" before darting through the door.

Three days had passed since the telephone conversation at the tennis club. Rajesh was growing anxious. Regan's man should have called by now. It was also three days since he had last spoken with Tanya. Normally he would have called her within twenty-four hours of an argument, but he had other things on his mind. Why did Regan arrange for the bulldog in the Range Rover to turn up like that? Why did he want a face-to-face meeting? Rajesh had every reason to be on edge. The man was a gangster, after all, with a fearsome reputation for violence.

Joey Regan had recently made the headlines by forcibly purchasing run-down properties and transforming them into yuppie apartments. Rumour had it that people who were unwilling to sell would often meet with a tragic accident, or a mugging that involved a severe beating. Of course there was never any real evidence Regan was involved, but after a while these incidents began to stack up, and the police hauled him in several times for questioning. On each occasion he was released with an apology. Regan often boasted that prison was for "skint and thick people". In his view anyone with brains and money did not go to prison. "Look at OJ Simpson!" he would say. "Just like *everything* in the world, even justice has its price."

After his usual two-hour workout at an upmarket health spa in Gerrards Cross, Rajesh phoned Jazz and asked him to meet him back at the house. When he got there, Jazz found Rajesh in a nervous and agitated state. In order to speak freely, Rajesh led him into the Games Room – years ago his father, a keen snooker player, had converted the garage and equipped it with a snooker table, a professional dartboard, a huge flat-screen TV, and a bar complete with four leather bar stools.

As soon as they were alone, Jazz tried to deter Rajesh from having anything to do with Regan or his cohorts. He knew Rajesh was way out of his depth and, more worryingly, that the whole thing secretly excited him.

Jazz picked up a snooker ball and began rolling it across the table. "Look, Raj, I'm saying this as a friend, but what are you gonna do about this meeting? Believe me, bro, you do not wanna mess with these people."

"What's your problem? It's through your connections we made the link in the first place!"

"That was to deal with the situation outside Madhu's, not so you can go and tie a *rakhee* on Big Joe Regan!"

"I don't want to link him; he wants to link me!"

"Exactly!" Jazz needed a diversion. "Anyway, what's your piece saying?"

"Tanya's my girlfriend, not my piece. Show some respect. And she's not saying anything." Rajesh sighed and slumped down on a brown leather Chesterfield next to the bar. "To be honest, she's doing my head in. We haven't talked for a few days."

"Let me guess; you've not spoke to her since that bit of excitement with Mac?" "Yeah, more or less."

"You prick! He caused the whole scene, and now you start blanking your girl! Don't you think that's exactly what he wanted? You played right into his hands, you mark!"

Jazz was right. It suddenly dawned on Rajesh that he had allowed Mac to drive a wedge between him and Tanya. Talk about naive! He seethed with frustration but vowed never to let Mac see this. The ugly bastard would only take advantage. Instead he took his anger out on Jazz. "What's the deal? You don't even *like* Tanya!"

"It's not that I don't like her. She's from a different world to us. If you were just banging her, that would be fine. But, man, I know you; you're gonna get all Bollywood and marry her."

"So what if I do? I've known her since we were kids. Our mums were like sisters. I know her inside out. So who better to marry than that?"

"Bro, you've known *Mac* since you were a kid, too! Hell, you guys were bum chums. Why don't you just marry him?"

"Stop being an arse."

"No, seriously, man. What's the deal with you two? That prick has had it in for you since we were at college. What's his problem?"

"Tanya told me that back in the day he had a thing for her, but she dealt with it and they remained friends. When we moved out of Southall, I lost touch with him, and things just got tense from there on in. To be honest, I don't really know what the problem is, but every time we cross paths, some shit always goes down."

"You lost touch with him, but you kept in touch with Tanya?"

"Yeah, but that's different. Our mothers were friends from their childhood back in Kenya, before all the Indians got chucked out and invaded England."

"Yeah, bro. I understand that. But pussy is pussy, and every man goes that little bit further when a piece of ass is involved. It's obvious you dissed the prick as soon as your old man moved up the ranks, but you kept in touch with Tanya."

"Jazz, if you call her my piece or pussy again, I am gonna punch your lights out."

"Oh, I get it. I get it. You think you're hard now you've got gangster connections."

Rajesh hated being mocked. He looked Jazz straight in the eye. "I don't need Regan to deal with you."

Jazz saw no point in winding him up even further. "Word of advice, bro. Call your piece ... I mean *girl*-friend. We can worry about Regan later."

"Who's worried? Do I look worried?"

"Just call your girl. I gotta bail. Catch up with you later. We going on the lash tonight?"

"Depends how the conversation with Tanya goes. I'll call you."

Jazz knew that pushing Rajesh towards Tanya was the easiest way of taking his mind off Regan. As they parted, there was a silent look of acknowledgement between them; a problem was brewing, and sooner or later it would have to be sorted.

Jazz saw himself out. "Later, bro."

Rajesh got up and walked behind the bar. He needed a stiff drink before calling Tanya. Whilst pouring a vodka and Coke, he started a debate in his head. Just who the hell did Tanya think she was? How come she hadn't called for three days? Why was it always down to him to make the first move? After all, he was Rajesh Thakral – a bloody good catch! He had everything going for him, so why should he put up with her tantrums all of the time? Taking a long, hard swig of his drink, he answered his own questions. At the end of the day, who cares who makes the first move, so long as things get sorted out. For God's sake, this was his TanJa, and he would do anything for her. So what if she hadn't called. He knew she still loved him. Besides, he was far from perfect, so who else would put up with his mood swings?

Instilled with Dutch courage, Rajesh dialled Tanya's number. He felt unusually tense, not knowing what kind of a reception he would get. Tanya answered the phone after several rings but remained silent. *Women!* "Hi, baby, it's me. How's things?" He could hear her sniffle. A pang of guilt rose in his heart. Had she really spent the last three days crying? "Jaan, I know you're upset. The whole thing was my fault. Let's forget about it and move on. I've missed you so much, babe." Unable to hold back, Tanya burst into tears, sobbing down the phone. *Did someone just die?* "Baby, what's wrong? Talk to me, Jaan. What's happened?" This was out of character. Something serious must have happened. "Jaan, please. Is everyone okay? Is your mum all right? Talk to me."

Tanya gulped back her tears. "R-Rajesh ... I-I can't right now."

"Don't cut me off! What's wrong?" Suddenly his issues with Joey Regan were irrelevant. His baby was upset. She needed him. That was all that mattered. "Stay there. I'm coming over. Are you at home?"

"No, Rajesh! Don't come here. I can't handle this right now. I'll call you in a few days."

"At least tell me what the problem is. What the hell's going on?" Tanya sniffled, desperate to control her tears. "Tanya, I haven't got time for your stupid games!"

Tanya exploded. "You bastard! Do you think this is a game! This is my fucking life! Don't call me again." She hung up.

Rajesh was fuming. Instinctively, he called her back. The call went straight to voicemail. He rang again, ending the call as soon as he heard the automated voice. "Fuck!" Something was definitely wrong. He grabbed the bottle of vodka and poured a bigger shot, this time leaving out the Coke and drinking it neat. His mind was racing. Why was Tanya so upset? Trying to think rationally, he took a few deep breaths. "What now? What now?" Then it dawned on him. Months ago Tanya had called him on her sister Joti's mobile when her battery was dead. He had stored the number for just such an occasion. He scrolled through his contacts, desperately trying to recall the name he had allocated – cunningly he hadn't stored the number under a name Tanya would recognise in case she ever went through his phone. He scrolled further down. "Come on, come on!" Then he remembered. He had stored the number as "BT", which stood for Baby Tanya.

When Joti answered the phone, she sounded cold, distant. "Yeah?"

"Hi, Joti. It's Rajesh. I'm trying to get hold of Tanya. Is she with you?"

"Sorry, wrong number!"

Before Rajesh could respond, Joti hung up, leaving him staring at his mobile. What the hell was going on? He had known Joti since she was a baby. She was like his little sister. *Why the hell did she cut me off?* He sprang to his feet and started pacing the floor, his overactive imagination working overtime. Suddenly he stopped. "Screw this!" If Tanya wanted to act like a sap, it was up to her. The text alert on his phone beeped. He grinned. He knew Tanya wouldn't be upset with him for long. Impatiently he pressed Read. But the text message was from BT. *Strange,* he thought. Joti had never text or called him before. His eyes widened as he read the message: "Tanya is talking about killing herself. Please help. Cant talk."

He sprinted out of the house and jumped into his Boxter. In no time he was tearing along the country lanes, pounding the gears and thrashing the accelerator. Rajesh loved to drive fast, but this was sheer torture. He knew his baby needed him, and he would move heaven and earth to be with her.

Approaching Southall, Rajesh felt his stomach tighten. Returning so soon after the incident with Mac wasn't the wisest thing to do. Mac was an opportunist, a wounded lion just waiting to lash out. If Rajesh was spotted on the street, all hell would break loose. But none of that mattered. He just wanted to see Tanya, hold her tight, and make her feel okay.

He parked down a side street and made his way to Tanya's on foot. He knew the area well from his childhood, a place of back-to-back terraces and cobbled alleyways. Suddenly he was five years old again, playing hide-and-seek with Tanya and Mac. Nothing ever changes. We grow old, but our games stay the same.

Thinking on his feet, he texted Joti as he hurried along: "Almost there. Can you sneak me in?" He slowed his pace, allowing time for a reply. Joti responded instantly: "Mum is out. Come to the front door." Before he finished reading the text, he found himself at the broken gate of her house. He couldn't believe how run-down it looked. He loathed the fact that his Jaan lived in such a place.

Before he had chance to ring the bell, Joti opened the front door. She signalled him to be quiet and pointed up the stairs. It was years since Rajesh had been in the house. To his adult eyes, everything had shrunk. It was like stepping back in time – the same depressing wallpaper, the same threadbare carpet, the same yellowing photographs of relatives hung higgledy-piggledy on the wall. What a shithole. *Did I used to live like this?*

He made his way up the stairs and knocked once on her bedroom door. Without waiting for a reply, he entered the room. Tanya was lying face down on the bed, crying into the pillow. Tears welled up in his eyes. It pained him to see his baby crying.

He cleared the lump in his throat, knelt down next to the bed, and stroked the back of her head, taking long strands of her lustrous hair between his fingers. "Jaan, I'm here now. Everything's gonna be okay."

Tanya spun round. She was shocked to see him, but he didn't ask why. She threw her arms around his neck and squeezed him tightly. A steady stream of tears drenched Rajesh's shoulder.

He pulled her close and ran his fingers through her thick black locks. "Talk to me, baby. What's going on? Tell me what's happened. Is it that wanker Mac? If it is, I'll—"

Tanya pulled away in disgust. "Is that all you think about – Mac, Mac, Mac? Get the hell out of my house! Stay out of my life! I never want to see you again!"

Rajesh was stunned; he knew she had a temper, but this was totally out of character.

Joti came running into the room. "Didi, please don't shut him out. He can help you. Just talk to him."

"Talk to me about what?" said Rajesh. "What the fuck's going on?"

Tanya stared deep into his eyes, looking for compassion, a solution, hope – anything that would calm her fevered mind. All she saw was vengeance. "You can't help me, Rajesh. My life is ruined. Leave me alone. I'm no good to you."

He grabbed her with both hands and took her in his arms. "Jaan, whatever the problem is, we can deal with it. Our love is strong enough to take on anything."

Tanya eased herself from his embrace. Somehow she found the hope she was looking for – not in his words, but in his voice. "Raj, are sure you can handle this? Believe me, you're better off not being involved."

"Baby, I already *am* involved. Your problems are my problems. Whatever it is, let's deal with it together."

She paused, staring into space. A deep and mournful silence filled the room.

Eventually Joti broke the silence. "Didi, you guys need to talk. But please, be open with him. He needs to know."

Tanya offered her sister a half-smile in order to reassure her. Joti closed the door behind her and slumped down on the top stair. She buried her head in her knees, failing miserably to hold back the tears.

Rajesh placed his forehead against Tanya's, whispering softly, "*Ajaa.*"

Her voice turned deadly serious. “Rajesh, this will change our lives forever. There is nothing you can do.”

“No, TanJa. My life changed when we got together. I’m here for you … always.”

Tanya hesitated, realising her next two words would destroy everything they had built together. He would push her away like a diseased leper. He squeezed her hand, which gave her a final burst of courage. “I’m pregnant.”

Rajesh fell into a black hole. Blood rushed to his brain. His vision began to blur. “What! Are you sure? Have you done a test? Could this be a mistake?”

Tanya jerked her head back and stared at him with absolute venom. “There’s no mistake! But I don’t expect anything from you. I will deal with this alone. This is my kismat.”

“What do you mean, you will deal with it? Do you mean … an abortion?”

“Don’t you dare say that word! This our baby you’re talking about! I would never do anything to harm it! Never!” She jumped up off the bed. “Go, Rajesh! Just get out of here! I don’t need you! You have no part in this.”

Confused and bewildered, Rajesh rose to his feet. Tanya breathed a sigh of relief. She was glad it was out in the open. But she couldn’t look him in the eye. She felt dirty and shameful. The room fell silent once more as they both tried to read each other’s thoughts. Rajesh leaned forward to kiss her, but Tanya fell back onto the bed and buried her face in the pillow. She had never felt so alone. She missed her dad, the only man who had ever loved her unconditionally. When he died, a piece of Tanya had died with him. She thought perhaps she should join him in heaven; that would solve everything. Her thoughts turned to despair. No matter what the answer was, Tanya knew she had to find it alone.

Feeling lost and empty, Rajesh made his way out of the room. He paused for a second at the door, hoping for a reaction, hoping she would offer some kind of clue as to what he should do. But all he got was the sound of her tears. For the first time in their relationship, he had no magic remedy to stem the flow. Slowly turning the handle, he realised she really did want to be alone. He closed the bedroom door. He felt empty, as if his soul had been sucked out of him.

Joti took one look at Rajesh and knew he was leaving. All her hopes for a solution to her sister's problem were shattered. She fixed her eyes on him as he came closer; he didn't even have the guts to look her in the eye. So this was the "big success" from Gerrards Cross, was it? The man who had stolen Tanya's heart and promised her the earth? What a spineless, heartless excuse for a human being. She wanted to scream and lash out, but she didn't make a sound. Instead she watched him descend the stairs like a ghost.

Rajesh opened the front door and paused. He looked up into a cloudless blue sky, begging the heavens for a solution. Stepping out into the street, he became hypersensitive. He could hear each and every sound – the cars, the footsteps of an old lady crossing the street, even the faint scratches of a cat climbing a tree. It was if all his senses had been switched off except for his hearing, which had been magnified. He tried to focus on his thoughts. He had to work out what to do next. His mind raced through a thousand different solutions. Maybe Jazz had the answer. Jazz was an expert at bailing him out at the eleventh hour. Surely he would know what to do. Rajesh scrolled his phone memory for Jazz's number. His thumb hovered reluctantly over the Call button, but deep inside, he knew he had to speak to him.

After a few rings, his friend came on the line. "Raj. What's happening?"

"I got a situation. I need your advice, bro."

Jazz was alarmed; he had never heard Rajesh so close to tears. He figured it must have something to do with Tanya. "Are you in Southall?"

"Yeah. I'm outside Tan's house."

"You fucking prick! Are you mad!? We just about dealt with

that mah-chord Mac! Fuck knows what repercussions that's gonna cause. And you're back in Southall!"

"Jazz. Listen, bro. I'm fucked."

"What do you mean? Is Mac on the scene?"

"Screw Mac. I got a bigger problem. It's Tanya ... she's ... she's pregnant."

"Pregnant! What have I told you about riding bareback?"

"Get serious, man. What am I supposed to do?"

"Give her three hundred quid and tell her to drop it. What else can you do?"

"She's having none of it. She wants to keep the baby."

"Of course she wants to keep it, you laan! Look at who you are, what your family's worth! You're an only son. Half of all that's going to her. You sure it's even yours? I told you this bitch was trouble. She got you hooked on that ass, and now she's trapped you good and proper." Rajesh found it hard to respond. A volcano of emotion was about to erupt inside him. "Raj, listen to me. We don't really know she *is* preggers. And even if she is, so the fuck what! For all you know, the kid could be Mac's and these two are in on it together."

Rajesh couldn't take any more. He hurled the phone into the road with all his might, shattering it beyond recognition. Was this Tanya's future? Would the whole world question her innocence? Jazz had made her sound like a cheap slut who was trying to trap him for his money. "That's not Tanya," he said quietly to himself. "That's not my baby. She loves me." He looked up into the sky and smiled as if to thank God for giving him the answer.

Rajesh spun on his heels, barged through the front door, and charged up the stairs. He burst into Tanya's room. Both sisters were holding each other and crying hopelessly. Joti sprung to her feet. Rajesh brushed passed her as if she weren't there. He grabbed Tanya with both arms and lifted her to her feet. "Tanya, I'm yours. All yours. Nothing is going to change that." He put his hand on her stomach. "This baby is ours. We love each other, Jaan. We've done nothing wrong." Tanya tried to interrupt, but he placed his finger on her lips. "Shush, Tans. Let me speak. You have to know what's in my heart. You're my life. I can't live without you. This baby is gonna pull us even closer together, not push us apart."

"Rajesh, what are you saying?"

"We're not boyfriend and girlfriend. We're soul mates! We're destined to be together. It doesn't matter which direction I go in, Jaan; all roads lead to you."

She stared at him, searching his face for a familiar expression. But the truth was she hardly recognised him. Even his voice sounded strange. She had never witnessed such a blatant display of emotion. Overjoyed, she wrapped her arms around his neck, resting her head on his shoulder. "What are we going to do, Raj?"

"We're going to get married. We'll have the baby and give it the best start we can. I promise you, I'll spend the rest of my life trying to make you happy."

Tanya tightened her embrace. Her mind see-sawed from joy to despair. "How can we get married? I'm fresh out of uni, and you've got your whole life ahead of you. You want to party and travel and—"

"I still do, and I will. But I don't want any of that if you're not by my side."

"I can't ask you to make that sacrifice."

"It's not a sacrifice. It's love, taking control of our lives. Don't fight this, Jaan. It's kismat. I don't care about the details. I just know I want to be with you for the rest of my life."

Joti came forward nervously. She put her arms around her sister and smothered her in a hug. All three of them held each other tight, as if protecting the tiny spark of life growing in Tanya's womb. They were bound together by a secret – a secret that would change their lives forever.

3

Rajesh slept nervously that night, mindful of the host of problems that lay ahead. What to deal with first – announcing to his family he wanted to marry Tanya or the fact that one of east London's most credible gangsters had summoned him to a meeting? Talk about skiing along the edge of a razorblade! He stared at the bedroom ceiling and tried to put things into context.

I can't do anything about the meeting with Regan; they are calling the shots.

Tanya is pregnant; that's not going to change. So again, nothing I can do to remedy that.

That just leaves Dad. Oh shit! He'll go ballistic; I know he will. The best person to deal with Dad is Mum. How far will Dad push this? I don't really want them to know Tanya is having a baby, but without telling them, how can I marry her overnight? Maybe I should go through Neelam. Nah, she's my sister, but she only has her own interests at heart and will manipulate the situation. Mum – that's the answer! That has to be where I start with this. God, what a fuck-up!

Rajesh slid out of bed reluctantly. As he trudged across the carpet to the en suite, his body felt like lead. He looked at himself in the bathroom mirror, gazing deep into his own eyes. He knew in his heart of hearts what he had to do; he was just too gutless to do it. There was only one solution, one person who held the key to his future happiness – the legendry Mr Thakral. In his mind's eye, he could foresee his father's reaction. He pictured him erupting, finding ways to assassinate Tanya's character and threatening to disown him. But Rajesh wasn't afraid of his anger. After all, he was no longer a boy who walked in his father's shadow. He was a man – a man who was planning to marry and start a family of his own. Nevertheless, deep down he was all too aware of his father's disappointment. His lack of interest in business and his complete inability to make his mark on the world meant he was a charity case in his father's eyes. Satish Thakral's life was a true rags-to-riches story, whereas Rajesh was the product of a lavish lifestyle and pampered upbringing.

After taking a long, hot shower he considered calling his father but remembered his mobile phone was lying in pieces outside Tanya's house. On reflection, he determined that this was a face-to-face matter; his father would see a phone call as a sign of weakness.

Rajesh looked at his watch; it was 8.30 a.m. There was still a chance he could catch his father before he left for the office. Having his mother there as backup would be a bonus.

He rushed to make himself look presentable; appearing before his father looking shabby was *not* the thing to do. As he ran down the landing buckling his jeans with one hand and holdings his shoes and socks in the other, he could feel his heart pounding in his chest. Regardless of the outcome of this conversation, from this point on his life would change irrevocably.

He reached the bottom of the stairs, where he paused to tie his shoelaces. He took a deep breath and made his way across the hall. Head held high, he marched into the kitchen and stood for a second scanning the room, completely oblivious to his mother, who was standing by the sink wondering what on earth could have caused her beloved son to get out of bed so early. Vidya Thakral was a small, fragile woman with steel-grey hair she kept gathered into a bun. This morning she was wearing a light blue sari embroidered with gold flowers, its folds and curves stretching to the floor. Despite her sixty years, she still had a slim figure – decades of housework had seen to that.

Her kindly face lit when she saw him. "*Betta!* Are you okay? You look pale. I will make you some masala chai. Sit down and let's have breakfast together for once."

"Maa, where's Dad?"

"Sit down, betta. Have some carrot juice."

"Maa, listen to me." He walked over and took her by the hand. It was wet, glittering with soap suds. Jewels of drudgery. "Where's Dad? Has he left already?"

"Rajesh, what's wrong? Something has happened!"

"You know, right?" His mother nodded. "You trust me, don't you, Maa?"

His voice contained an intensity she had never heard before. She smiled at him proudly. "Your father has gone to work. He will be at the office by now. Go to him, and deal with whatever is on your mind. Remember, I am here for you … no matter what."

Rajesh leaned forward and kissed his mother on the forehead. "Thank you, Maa. I love you. I'll be back in a few hours. I'll tell you everything then, but right now I need to talk to Dad face-to-face."

"Would you like me to come with you?"

"No, thanks. This is something I need to deal with alone. Just be there for me if it all blows up in my face."

"I understand." She paused to dry her hands. "Come with me."

Vidya led him out of the kitchen and along the hallway. They entered the *mandir*, a small room she had set up as a shrine. Together they knelt down on a Persian rug opposite a small gold statue of Lakshmi, the goddess of good fortune. Emerging from the petals of a lotus flower, her four arms holding various gifts, the Hindu deity was dressed in a red robe and surrounded by four saintly elephants. Her expression was one of kindly benevolence.

Vidya closed her eyes, whispering a few words under her breath. She then turned and placed her hand on Rajesh's head.

"Betta, I pray that Lakshmi goes with you and gives you strength and confidence."

Rajesh gave her a lingering hug. He could feel his eyes begin to moisten, and he turned away sharply to prevent her from seeing his face. He left the mandir without saying a word. Vidya felt anxious but found comfort in the fact that her son was about to share his problem with his father. She had no idea what the problem was but knew that somehow it would bring father and son closer together. Hoping for a favourable outcome, Vidya lit an incense stick and bathed Lakshmi in a swirl of smoke.

Whilst driving to his father's office, Rajesh had a terrible feeling of foreboding. The surge of adrenalin that had propelled him to confront his father in the kitchen had dissipated, leaving him nervous and agitated. A voice inside his head screamed at him to slam on the brakes, turn round, and drive home. In the past he would have obeyed. Not today. Besides, it was too late. He could see company HQ looming towards him at the end of the street like some latter-day Xanadu. It was here, two decades ago, that his father had started his freight forwarding business. Back then it was nothing but a jumble of concrete sheds. Now an impressive steel-and-glass structure stood testament to his father's hard work.

Rajesh drove through the gates and manoeuvred towards his dedicated parking bay. Some time ago, in expectation of him joining the family business, his father had set up a space next to his. In all that time, Rajesh had used it precisely three times. He could see his father's Lexus and turned the wheel to pull in alongside it.

"What the fuck's going on!" He stopped short.

Like a cuckoo in the nest, a blue Ford Mondeo blocked his way. Were the staff taking the piss? Did nobody expect him to come to work? This was *his* business, *his* office, and *his* parking space. Rajesh pulled in tight behind the car. He leapt from his Porsche, slamming the door behind him. He was in such a rage over the mysterious Mondeo that he almost forgot why he had come to the office in the first place. Whoever this cocksucker was, he was going to get sacked – pronto! But before he went storming in, he had to check one thing. He walked sharply to the front of the car to confirm his name plate was still there. He considered that because of his highly emotional state, maybe he had lost his bearings and the parking space was elsewhere. His heart sank when he saw his name painted over with "MR J. B. PATEL". So it wasn't the staff who had given up on him; it was his father. He had given his parking space away to the depot manager. Rajesh's stomach churned; he had every intention of coming into the business, just not yet. But his father had thrown in the towel. This was no longer a question of a simple parking space; it was a father's perception of his son!

In a fluster of mixed emotions, Rajesh made his way into the modern three-story building. He stormed through reception, causing a ripple of surprise amongst the staff. He could almost hear them saying, "Well, well. The prodigal son returns." Keeping his eyes fixed to the floor, he paused for a second in order to gather himself. One thing was certain; the adrenalin was back. He barged past his father's secretary and headed for the teak door embossed with a brass nameplate reading "S. Thakral, Chairman".

The secretary shot out of her seat as though electrified and called out from behind him, saying, "Mr Thakral, sir! Your father's on a conference call!"

Rajesh couldn't believe it. This little six-pound-an-hour bitch had the audacity to try to stop him entering his father's office! An office that would one day be his! He spun round and shot her a cold, hard stare. The bitch knew her place all right; she sat back down and turned towards her computer screen. He stood outside his father's office and took hold of the door handle. It felt hot to the touch. This was the final door that separated him from his destiny. It took all his strength and willpower to push it open.

Suddenly he was face-to-face with the person he loved, feared, and respected most in the whole world. Sitting behind his huge desk, engrossed in a phone call, Satish Thakral cut an imposing figure. Tall, well built, with a full head of neatly trimmed hair, he wore an immaculately tailored light grey three piece suit. He was a man of supreme self-confidence, and his office reflected this; framed photos of Satish shaking hands with royalty, celebrities, and sports stars adorned the walls, along with a Queen's Award to Industry. The whole tone of the office left visitors in no doubt as to the importance of the person facing them.

Rajesh gave a nervous cough. "Dad, we need to talk."

Satish looked up. He was genuinely surprised to see his son, but his poker expression gave nothing away. He wasn't a top businessman for nothing. He spoke calmly into the receiver. "Something's come up. I'll call you back." He ended the call and stared blankly at his wastrel son. "Rajesh, can't you see I'm busy! Won't this wait until I get home?"

"Dad, I might not have the courage to face you when you get home. I need to talk to you right now."

"You'd better come in. What's on your mind? And close the door behind you."

Rajesh did as he was told. Nervously he sat down opposite his father. How to start the conversation? Before he had a chance to speak, Satish pressed the intercom and spoke abruptly to his PA, Margret, barking out, "*Ek* chai!"

Rajesh inwardly cringed. That one phrase, "One tea!" seemed to sum up his father. He had grown up hearing him say it on a daily basis. It was never "Can I please have a cup of tea?" or "Would you mind making me a drink of tea?" It was always "*Ek* chai!" Did he not know the word for "please"? Rajesh put his pet hate to one side and decided to cut to the chase. "It's about me and Tanya. I … I mean, we want to get married, and I need your blessing."

Was there no end to his son's lunacy? He fixed him with a steely gaze, his lips narrowing to a sneer. "Have you lost your mind! You want to get *married?* You can't even look after yourself! How are you going to take care of a wife?"

"Don't be like that, Dad. I know I'm a bit relaxed about things, but I know I can make this work."

"Relaxed? You're in a permanent coma! And how do you intend to support this wife of yours? How will you fulfil her needs?"

Rajesh wasn't sure if he was being questioned or mocked. "I'll get a job. Come and work with you."

Satish stared hard at his son. "Listen, boy! I have worked hard all my life to build this company. I have sacrificed more than you will ever know. I didn't do all that so you could bring home some *randee* and present her as my *baohoo!*" Rajesh jumped to his feet in protest. "Sit your backside down, boy, before I throw you out of my office!"

Sinking back into the chair in submission, Rajesh felt as if the entire conversation were slipping away. "Dad, I love her. She's the one I want to be with."

"I am not saying you cannot love her. Love as many girls as you want; just don't think you can bring them into my home."

"But, Dad, it's my home too."

"What makes it *your* home? Do you pay the mortgage? Do you pay any of the bills? Huh? It's not your *home;* it's your *house!* It's where you come back to after carousing all night and then get waited on hand-and-foot by your mother. You treat it like a hotel! Have done for years!"

"Dad, please! I need you to listen to me"

"*No,* Rajesh! You listen to me! I have never stopped you living your life or having fun. I know that boys will be boys and you need a little entertainment. That's part of growing up, but betta, you don't bring home stray animals that belong on the street and call them your family."

"That's a terrible thing to say! What planet are you on? She comes from Southall, the same area we came from before you hit the big time."

"Yes, betta, and like everyone else in Southall, I dreamed of getting out! And do you know how I did it? With hard work and determination, something you know very little about. Yet this little madam wants to do it by sleeping her way into luxury." Rajesh clenched his fists beneath the table. His father was taking him rapidly past the point of no return. "Look, Rajesh. What are her prospects of getting out of the gutter if she doesn't grab on to your coat-tails? Her family have made no progress in thirty years! They are third-generation wasters!"

"That's not true! Tanya's just qualified as a lawyer! She got a first-class degree! She's been headhunted by one of the biggest criminal law firms in London to do a year's work experience. She's one of the most intelligent people I know."

"Everyone seems intelligent stood next to you! Don't get lust and love confused, son."

"It's not about lust; it's about doing the right thing."

Satish's cocky smirk vanished. He sensed what was coming but didn't want to hear it. "What do you mean, 'the right thing'? What have you done?"

Rajesh lowered his eyes. "Tanya's carrying my baby. I'm going to be a father."

Satish sprung to his feet "Have you gone mad!? You have your whole life ahead of you! She's planned all this; can't you see? You've been trapped! It's probably not even yours! The little whore's probably not even pregnant!"

Rajesh couldn't take it any longer. He leaned over the desk threateningly. "Enough! That is enough, Mr Satish Thakral!" Satish took one step back. He was lost for words. Rajesh had never stood up to him before, or even answered him back. And calling him by his name was an insult too far. "Tanya *will* be my wife! She is the mother of my child. As for your house, Tanya and I wouldn't be seen dead living there! So, Mr Satish Thakral, I hope you're happy living in your mansion all by yourself. You will never see me or my baby … ever!"

"Oh, you think you can handle yourself, huh? And what do you intend to do for money? Little boy, the world is an expensive place when you don't have daddy's credit card in your back pocket."

"I have a degree in business and finance. I will borrow the money to start my own company, just like you did!"

"Oh! Young Mr Thakral thinks he can click his fingers and borrow the money, does he? And who do you intend to borrow it from? The banks? You don't have any collateral. The money markets? You have no experience. What about the community? No, you are an unknown. Wait, wait, you are the son of Mr Satish Thakral. That's all the credibility you need! Because the community knows that no matter what, Satish Thakral will sell his own flesh if he has to, but he will repay your debt!"

"I don't need *you* or your name! I'm my own person!"

"Well done, son. Well done. You have had a taste of a modern-day Delilah, and you are ready to start a revolution with your own father! You ungrateful cretin! Sit down!"

Rajesh felt a great sense of satisfaction. He had finally stood up to his father and saw little need to continue the argument. Instead, he gave Satish an icy stare, spun round, and stomped out of the office.

Satish boiled over. "Rajesh! ... *Rajesh!* Get back here. You're finished! You hear me? Finished! I want you out of the house before I get home!"

Elated, Rajesh quickened his pace. He had climbed his own personal Everest and had placed upon it the flag of freedom. Life would be plain sailing from here on in.

Heading out of reception, he saw an embarrassed Jainti Patel standing by his Porsche. Balding and in his mid-fifties, he was a small, insignificant man with round shoulders and a pot belly. He had worked for his father for over thirty years and was his trusted confidant.

"I am sorry, sir," Patel said. "I would not have parked here if I knew you were coming in today. Let me move my car and park yours for you."

Rajesh smiled philosophically. "Jainti Bhai, this space was

destined to be yours. You're welcome to it. Enjoy the rest of your life at S. T. Freights. I'm a free man now."

A typical bureaucrat, Patel wanted to question him further – who knew where he might end up in the company pecking order! But Rajesh was in no mood for a chat; he had the rest of his life ahead of him.

There was one loose end to tie up – his mother. *She's going to be heartbroken,* thought Rajesh. He considered that perhaps he could persuade her to come with him and be part of his new life. After all, his father had taken her for granted for years. A born grandmother, she would love his child and cherish it the way he and Neelam had been cherished when they were young. Such thoughts raced through his head as he drove home to share the news with his mother. Excited at the prospect of a new life, Rajesh could hear his father's voice ringing in his ears. Again and again he heard him calling Tanya a whore, accusing her of trying to trap him. He was a cruel son of a bitch. His heart sank. Life was like a carousel, going round and round and up and down and never stopping in the same place twice.

He headed out into the countryside, driving at a relaxed pace. He was in no rush to burden his mother with emotional issues. Relieved that the showdown with his father was out of the way, he reached into his pocket for his mobile phone. "Shit!" Realising it would take forty-eight hours to get a replacement, he decided to drive into Gerrards Cross and purchase a pay-as-you-go phone; using a call box just wasn't his style, and he desperately wanted to check in with Tanya.

The salesman in the tacky phone shop watched as Rajesh parked his gleaming Porsche in a restricted zone directly outside the window. Business had been slow all morning, so he was delighted to see him walk into the shop. Noticing his expensive watch peeking from his shirt cuff, the salesman saw the opportunity to sell him a top-of-the-range phone with a huge line rental.

"Look, man," said Rajesh, impatiently. "I normally have a

Bang and Olufsen that would blow any of these out of the water. I just need a cheap pay-as-you-go job with a battery that's charged so I can use it straight away!"

The salesman disappeared into the back and quickly reappeared with a budget Samsung. "That's twenty pounds, inclusive of a five pound top-up voucher."

"Mate, don't you have anything better than a Samsung? It's not really my kind of brand." Rajesh couldn't help mocking this prick.

"I think you'll find that Samsung is commissioned by Bang and Olufsen. So you see, sir, it *is* your kind of brand."

Rajesh's smirk morphed into a frown. "Just give me the damn phone!" He slammed a crisp twenty down onto the counter, grabbed the Samsung, and made his way back to his car.

He couldn't wait to share the news with Tanya. "Hi, *Jaan.* It's me."

"My God! Where have you been all morning? Whose number is this?"

"I'll explain later, babe. I need to fill you in on what's been happening."

"Hold on, Raj. Listen to me for a second. Your friend Jazz has called ten times looking for you. Is everything okay?"

"Jazz? How the hell did he get your number? What did he want?"

"I don't know. He sounded really panicked. He wanted to know if I knew where you were. Did you tell him about our situation? Is that why he was calling? Is he trying to talk you out of it?"

"Calm down, babe. Jazz would never do a thing like that. He's not the kind of guy who panics. Let me call him, and I will call you back."

"Rajesh?"

"Yes, *Jaan*?"

"I love you. Please be careful. Remember, you have responsibilities now."

"Okay, okay. Take it easy with the emotional pressure. I'll call you back in five."

Rajesh ended the call. Why the fuck would Jazz call Tanya? Who had given him her number? And what could be so urgent he had to involve her? Various conclusions raced through his mind as he dialled Jazz's number. Jazz answered within two rings. He must have been sat next to his phone waiting for his call.

"Jazz, it's Raj. What's going on, bro? I hear you've been looking for me."

"Where the fuck have you been? I've been calling all over London looking for you!"

"Long story. What's the national emergency?"

"Regan! That's the emergency! Fucking Regan called effing and blinding that your phone was switched off. You were told to expect his call. He reckons we've disrespected him. *We!* For fuck's sake, Raj, this has got fuck all to do with me! How come *I'm* responsible for your phone being switched off?"

"Calm down, bro. Tell me exactly what he said."

"That's it! A guy like Regan doesn't *need* to say much."

"How did you leave it with him?"

"I'm supposed to get hold of you and give you a number to call them back." "Them? You mean Regan?"

"No, you dumb fuck! Regan's not going to leave his personal number! He doesn't want a date! He wants to mess us up!"

"Why? What have we done? So what if my phone was off? You've no idea what I've been through today."

"This is no time to feel sorry for yourself. I'll text you the number. Just call it and see what they want."

"Don't text it to my number. Use the one I'm calling from."

"Why? Where's your phone?"

"Do you want me to break it down, or shall I call the gangsters that have shit you up so bad?"

Jazz didn't appreciate the sarcasm. "Fuck you, man! I'll text you the number now. Just sort this crap out!"

The text came through in a flash. He stared at the number.

He knew he had to make the call and face what was coming. But what the hell had he done to piss Regan off?

He pressed Call and waited.

"Yeah?"

"Hello. Hi, this is Raj. I believe you're looking for me."

"Prick! If the boss was looking for you, you'd be in the boot of my car right now on your way to see him."

Rajesh recognised the voice. It was the bulldog from the Range Rover. "I had a message to call you back about Mr Regan."

"Are you fresh out of school, kid? Don't be saying names on the phone."

"Sorry. Sorry, mate."

"The boss wants to see you and that sidekick of yours."

"Sidekick? You mean Jazz?"

"I don't give a fuck what his name is! Just get both of your arses to the service station at junction twenty-three on the M25 in one hour!"

"One hour? That's cutting it close, mate. I'm on the other side of town, and I don't know where Jazz is."

His voice took on a more aggressive tone. "Listen, cunt! Call me mate one more time and I'll slit your fucking throat! Hear me? Cunt! Now let me explain so you'll understand. The boss wants to see you. You're privileged to be asked, so don't be late. Being late is very bad for your health. Now I don't give a shit how you get there; just fucking get there. Is there anything in that sentence you don't understand, cunt?"

Rajesh swallowed hard. "I-I understand. Don't worry; I'll be there. Can you at least tell me what the meeting is about? ... Hello? *Hello?*" The bulldog had cut him off.

Rajesh put his head in his hands and squeezed his temples. This had to be the ultimate head fuck. He had just started World War III with his father, Tanya needed him more than ever, and his mother would probably be feeling suicidal after the phone call from Satish. To cap it all, he had to be on the other side of

London within the hour to meet a gangster at a service station in the middle of nowhere!

He glanced at his watch. 11.57 a.m. There was no time to ponder the situation. Regan was his top priority. His life depended on it. He hit the accelerator and roared off down the High Street. Rajesh knew he had no chance of collecting Jazz and being at the rendezvous on time. His only hope was to drive like Schumacher and get Jazz to meet him there. He sped towards the motorway at terrifying speed, weaving in and out of the traffic. His phone call to Jazz was short and sweet. Jazz agreed to meet but tried to talk Rajesh out of going. They both knew there was a good chance they might not come back. Even more puzzling was the fact that neither of them had the slightest clue as to why Regan had summoned them.

Rajesh felt numb. The last twenty-four hours had been like a rollercoaster on which he had experienced every possible emotion. His heart pounded in his chest as he gripped the steering wheel. But amidst the maelstrom, he still possessed an air of calm; the extreme cocktail of hope, fear, and adrenaline seemed to focus him on the situation in hand. At the end of the day, Regan was just a man; he slept, breathed, and shit just like everyone else. *Fuck it, if he wants a meeting, let's have a meeting. If there's a misunderstanding, we can sit down and clear it up. There's nothing he can do to me that I can't do to him. After all, I've just had had a showdown with Dad and come out of it intact, so how bad can this meeting be?*

His newfound courage disappeared when he saw the large blue-and-white motorway exit sign marking Junction 23, South Nims Services. His breath shortened; his legs turned to jelly. He became oblivious to the traffic whizzing past. Pressing the clutch pedal was like trying to move a huge bolder. He contemplated driving away, but it was too late; he was already in the car park. And there was the bulldog, waiting. He was leaning against his Range Rover, staring coldly at him, glancing away for a second to look down at his watch, indicating that Rajesh was late. Only fifty meters separated them. The bulldog lumbered towards him. Rajesh remained in his car; he felt a misguided sense of security and was desperate to cling to his last vestige of personal space.

He buzzed down the window. "Hi. Sorry I'm late. Got here as soon as I could. The traffic was—"

"Where's your mate?" The bulldog was in no mood for social niceties.

"Don't know. Thought he'd be here by now."

"Call him."

He dialled Jazz's number with a tense expression on his face. He stared straight ahead, avoiding eye contact with the bulldog at all costs.

The bulldog drummed his fingers on the roof of the Porsche impatiently. "Well? Where is he?"

"His phone's going straight to answerphone."

"What! What the fuck are you playing at, kid?"

"Nothing! Honest!" Rajesh franticly tried again. Still no answer. He couldn't understand why Jazz's phone was switched off. Maybe he was on his way and had hit a bad reception area.

The bulldog leaned in through the window. "Don't play games with me. The Boss wants to see both of you; now get a hold of that cocky little cunt before I ram that phone up your arse!"

Rajesh repeatedly pressed the Send button in the hope his call would finally get through. But each time he did, it went straight to answerphone. The bulldog gripped the door handle as if he were about to rip it from its hinges. That's when Rajesh noticed the odd shape of his knuckles and the scars on his wrists. They were the hands of a cage fighter. Abruptly the bulldog pulled away. Rajesh braced himself for a punch in the face, but the bulldog leaned back and pulled out his mobile. He took a few steps away from the car. Rajesh strained to hear what he was saying.

"Yeah, boss, it's me. Only one of 'em's turned up. Seems the other one's bricked it. What do you expect, boss. They're fucking Pakis. You can't trust any of 'em. They don't even stick by each other. Yeah, it's definitely him. Do you want me to wait for the other one? Apparently his phone's switched off and he's left his mate to face the crap. Yeah, yeah, some fucking friend he is! You're dead right there, boss. Well, we got the one we wanted. I'll bring him in and deal with the other one later, sweet?"

Got the one we wanted? What is that all about? Rajesh felt helpless. How could Jazz have betrayed him like that? He closed his eyes and pictured Tanya. All he could think of was holding her in his arms. He opened his eyes and saw the bulldog climbing into his Range Rover. He breathed a sigh of relief. Maybe everything was going to be all right. It was obvious Regan wanted to see them both, so maybe it was a blessing Jazz hadn't turned up. He had done his part; he had showed up at the meeting and faced the bulldog. Surely Regan would respect that? The bulldog began to reverse his car out of the parking bay. Thank God it was over. Rajesh felt the colour returning to his cheeks. He would deal with everything later, but for now he just wanted out of there.

Instead of driving out of the car park, the Range Rover pulled level with the Porsche. The bulldog leaned over and shouted through the passenger window, "Follow me!"

"W-where to?"

"Don't ask questions. We're going to see the boss."

"Sorry, I thought you needed both of us." He grabbed his mobile off the seat. "Let me try and get hold of Jazz again."

"Fuck Jazz. Was that your little game? You thought you could get out of meeting the Boss if only one of you turned up! Well fuck him. I'll deliver him to the boss in a body bag later. Now do you want to follow me, or shall I drag you out of the car and take you with me?"

"No, it's okay. I don't want any trouble. I'll follow you."

A hint of a smirk appeared on bulldog's face. "You've done good so far, kid. Keep your head screwed on and your wits about you, and you'll be riding high. Don't ever give me a reason to fall out with you. Meet with the boss, keep your head down, and all will be good. Try and be a smart arse, and I'll clip you in the blink of an eye, sweet?"

Before Rajesh could respond, the beefed-up, supercharged Vogue sped off. He hit the accelerator and raced to catch up. Despite the threats, Rajesh now felt more at ease with the situation than he had before. The bulldog's change of attitude calmed him somewhat. He was still nervous as hell and determined not to let his guard down, but their parting conversation left him feeling optimistic. Maybe he could get through this with his balls intact.

Both cars drove at high speed through the Essex countryside, racing past multi-million-pound mansions and private estates. Home to celebrities, corporate bankers and the elite of London's underworld, Essex had become a gangster's paradise; each London family displaying their success with a period mansion set in acres of land. "Look how powerful we are," they seemed to be saying. "Look at our wealth. The police can't touch us." And the Regan house was at the heart of it.

As he pulled up outside a set of huge iron gates built more for security than for decoration, Rajesh felt secretly privileged to be entering Regan's lair. After all, he was a man many people feared but not that many had actually seen.

A thug twice the size of the bulldog greeted the Range Rover. After exchanging a few words he glanced at the Porsche before turning towards a digital security panel. He keyed in the code. The overwhelming black and bronze gates swung open. The Range Rover glided through towards the house. The thug signalled for Rajesh to follow. As he entered the manicured grounds, he whispered a silent prayer.

Both cars drove up a twisting driveway before pulling up alongside an enormous fountain. The marble festivity contained the heads and torsos of four wild horses, each pointing one of the four cardinal directions, water gushing from their open mouths into three tiers of polished marble. It was more Romanesque than Essex; Rajesh couldn't decide if it was borderline tacky or an artistic masterstroke. Deep down, though, he admired Regan for having the balls to commission such an opulent piece. His eyes left the sparkling cascade and scanned the rest of the property. Manicured flowerbeds and immaculate lawns led the eye towards a border of clipped box hedges. The driveway was more like the forecourt a luxury car showroom. A silver S-Class Mercedes was parked alongside a black 7 Series BMW, a Porsche Cayenne 4x4, and a token Audi convertible. Rajesh guessed the Audi was probably there as a gesture to keep the missus happy. The exterior of the house reminded him of Stoke Poges Tennis Club; the same imposing stone staircase led up to a set of polished mahogany doors.

"This way!" said the bulldog, interrupting Rajesh's thoughts. He ushered him towards the rear of the house, which opened up onto a wooden decking area that contained a kidney-shaped open-air swimming pool. Three men were sitting at a poolside table. They all paused to look at Rajesh. He tried to guess which one was Regan. The two younger men got up and walked into the house, leaving the older man alone. He was roughly the same age as Rajesh's father, though the similarity ended there. Whereas Satish's power came from his business acumen, Regan's was derived from cold-blooded violence. He signalled to the bulldog, who in turn nudged Rajesh and indicated with his eyes, "The boss is ready for you. Don't fuck this up, kid."

Rajesh swallowed hard and made his way towards the grey-haired man, who stood up to greet him. This put Rajesh at ease. He was tall and stocky with a severe US Marine–type haircut; it was obvious he could do some damage if you got on the wrong side of him. The solid gold, diamond-encrusted Chopard on his wrist betrayed an obvious lack of subtlety – yes, he had money, but that wasn't enough; the guy wanted everyone to know it. Wearing a baby-blue shirt with a cream-coloured cravat and beige trousers, he resembled the James Bond of East End thugs.

Rajesh approached him nervously, holding out his hand. "Hello, my name is Raj." A huge, gnarled fist enveloped his soft, manicured fingers. Rajesh winced; it was like shaking hands with a scrap metal crusher.

"Manners. I like that." His accent was pure cockney. "Sit down. Do you know who I am?"

"I think so. Are you Mr Regan?"

"Son, only my bank manager calls me Mr Regan. You can call me Uncle Joe."

Rajesh sat down on a wicker chair opposite the swimming pool, the water glinting in the August sunshine. "You wanted to talk to me? Have I done something to upset you?"

"Why are you so nervous? Do you know something I don't?"

Rajesh's eyes popped. "Sorry. I don't understand the question. Are you asking me why I'm nervous sitting in your house talking to you?"

"You're obviously uncomfortable. I want to know why."

"With all due respect, Mr Regan" – Regan raised an eyebrow to show his displeasure – "Sorry, sorry, I mean Uncle Joe." He took a deep breath. "With all due respect, I don't know why I'm here. Your man over there threatened to deal with me if I didn't come. Let's face it; I've heard stories about you since I was a kid. What kid hasn't?"

Regan smiled. "And do you believe those stories?"

"I guess so. There are too many to be made up."

"So by creating an image in your mind, you've already decided I'm a man to be feared?"

Rajesh shifted in his chair. "Mr … I mean Uncle. You're Joey Regan. Look at this place. It's amazing. But you're still surrounded by … bodyguards." He had almost said "thugs" but was afraid of what the reaction would be.

"You're not what I expected. I had a vision of a cocky, ballsy fucker; the guy who stood up to Mac and his boys in his own home town and lived to tell the tale."

"I think you had a lot to do with that. Thanks, by the way."

"Yeah, but when you stepped up to Mac, you had no way of knowing I would send Teddy to help you."

Rajesh smiled. So the bulldog's name was Teddy! Maybe Regan was right; maybe people do build things up in their heads. After all, if his name was Teddy, just how vicious could he be? "Sometimes you don't have a choice, Uncle Joe. You just have to deal with what's at hand and worry about the consequences later."

Regan paused and gave an avuncular smile. He was obviously pleased with Rajesh's answer. He got up from the chair. "Walk with me. I want to show you around."

"Can I please just find out why I'm here?"

Regan's expression changed to a more serious and morbid look. He mumbled from the side of his mouth, saying, "Let's walk and talk." He turned his back and began to walk back towards the driveway. Rajesh got up and followed. "I asked Teddy to bring you and your friend. What happened to him?"

"I'm not sure. We were supposed to meet at the service station, but he didn't show. Maybe he was running late."

"Did you call him?"

"Yeah, but it kept going to voicemail. Maybe he was going through a bad reception area."

"Or maybe he just pissed his pants. I seem to have that effect on people."

"No way. I grew up with this guy. I know him inside out. He's always stuck by me."

"You've been with Teddy for forty-five minutes and me for ten. That's almost an hour. In all of that time, has this so-called mate of yours called to say he was running late? Or phoned to see how you are? Basic concept of yin and yang, son – every action has a reaction. Just like you; you were faced with a kill-or-be-killed dilemma with Mac, and you stepped up. Your friend was faced with a choice and chose to step down, leaving you holding the baby."

Rajesh's mind drifted to replay the telephone conversation with Jazz.

Regan continued. "The point is you grew some balls and came to the meeting regardless."

"I had to find out what you wanted."

"What makes you think I want anything from you?"

"Sorry, I didn't mean it like that. You've obviously called me here for a reason. I just want to know what it is."

Regan laughed. "The reason is simple, son. I enjoy meeting people with bottle. You showed bottle, and I think if it had come down to it, you would have taken Mac out, or at least gave it your best shot."

They skirted round the side of the house and walked back onto the drive. Regan took one look at Rajesh's car and smirked. "Is that your girlfriend's?"

"No, it's mine. What makes you say that?"

"It's a Boxter. A girl's Porsche!"

"Well, I like it. She's quick and gets loads of attention from the ladies."

He guffawed. "You think *that's* quick?"

Rajesh looked at the collection of luxury autos lined up in the drive. "Too right. None of those could keep up with me."

"First off, kid, don't get too cocky. A lot depends on the driver. Second, these machines ain't for fun. They're work horses." Regan turned and made his way towards three double garages attached to the side of the house. Rajesh assumed he had to follow, but his nerves made him hesitate. Regan paused and looked at him. "This way, son. I'll show you what fun is."

Rajesh jogged towards him like a lapdog summoned by his master. Regan entered a four-digit code into the keypad outside the first garage door. All three doors opened in perfect synchronicity. Behind them was a collection of some of the world's finest supercars. Rajesh was wealthy and privileged, but this was a whole different league. He didn't know which car to look at first; each was equally impressive and desirable. "Uncle J, are these all yours?"

Regan was taken aback. No one had dared abbreviate his

name before, not even his closest friends. But he quickly decided he liked it, and it made him warm to Rajesh even more. "How do you feel about your Boxter now?"

Rajesh shook his head and gave a huge grin. He knew what Regan meant all right. "Certainly puts things into perspective."

Regan walked towards a cupboard at the rear of a pillar-box red Ferrari F430. He returned with a single key and presented it to Rajesh. The key was chunky and black. He had to look twice to read the inscription; in shiny silver lettering, it proudly stated "Lamborghini".

Rajesh looked at the key and then at Regan. Puzzled and excited, he pressed for an explanation. "Are you taking me for spin?"

"Do you think I have the time to take a kid who probably has no hair on his balls for a spin? Do you think I'm lining you up for a shag or something?"

"I don't know. You've just presented me with a Lambo key. What am I supposed to think?"

Thinking's bad for you, kid. Just take the car. You'll like it. It's a dream to drive. It'll give you more of a thrill than the Aston and is easier to drive than the Ferrari or the TVR."

"I don't need to drive it to know that, Uncle Joe. It's a Lamborghini Gallardo! Probably the sexiest spots car ever. Five hundred brake horsepower with an Audi W12 engine."

"You know your cars. Why don't you take this for a few days and see how it feels. See if all the articles you've read in *Max Power* do the car any justice."

Rajesh felt patronised. "That very generous of you, but I've got my own car and really need to get back. I was told you wanted to see me urgently, so I came as soon as poss'."

"Slow down, son. I told you, I like the way you handle yourself. Come to my club in Knightsbridge on Thursday and you can swap your girlie car back then." He patted Rajesh's cheek belittlingly. "You're with the big boys now. Sit back and enjoy the ride."

Rajesh felt his soul slipping away but was overwhelmed

with the thought of driving the silver Lamborghini. He imagined pulling up outside Tanya's, not to mention the look on his father's face when he saw how well his son was doing in the space of hours of leaving home!

"What's on your mind, kid?" asked Regan.

"Well, it's not every day someone hands you the key to a Lambo and sends you on your way. It's a big responsibility."

"Not really. The worst you can do is wrap it round a lamppost because your hard-on got in the way of your driving" He shrugged philosophically. "If it happens, it happens. That's what insurance is for. You remind me of me, kid. Maybe we'll do something together in the future. Maybe not. Either way, you've got my friendship. There's no catch, kid. Just go and enjoy yourself and meet me at my club on Thursday. It's called Rouge."

"Rouge is your club?"

"Yeah. Have you been there before?"

"I tried to get in a couple of times but always got knocked back at the door."

Regan chuckled. "Don't worry, kid; those days are over. After you have hit the town with me a couple of times, all doors in London will be open to you."

Rajesh felt uncomfortable but knew that any further hesitation could offend Regan and that the flavour of the meeting could change in a heartbeat. "I'll look after the Lambo; don't worry. If you need her back before Thursday, please let me know."

"Just enjoy yourself. See how she grows on you. We'll talk later. You and Teddy have each other's number, right?"

"Yeah." He quickly remembered his telephone dilemma. "But the number he got from me was a temporary one. I'll have my phone back tomorrow." It occurred to Rajesh that his mother and sister would be trying to call him after the showdown with his father, but neither of them had his number. He was now even more anxious to leave so that he could make contact with the outside world.

Regan sensed his eagerness and was growing tired of the

bland conversation. "Call Ted tomorrow and let him have your number." He gestured towards the super sleek Lamborghini. "Now go ahead and start her up. Leave your Boxter keys with one of the boys."

In a cocktail of excitement, fear and relief, Rajesh started the engine. He could scarcely believe he was sitting in a car he had virtually masturbated over as a teenager. The thrilling roar as he edged forward helped ease the guilt about leaving his modest Porsche behind. For a few seconds it felt as though he were cheating on a loyal friend, but the feeling was short-lived as the electric gates eased open and he accelerated out of the drive. Once he'd put enough distance between himself and the Regan house, he pulled into a lay-by to annihilate Jazz over the phone. What the fuck was he playing at, setting him up like that?

Rajesh switched on the mobile – fourteen missed calls and six text messages. Most of the calls were from Jazz, but the last two were from Neelam. But Neelam didn't have this number, and Jazz knew better than to give it out – unless it had been a dire emergency. He paused for a second. Obviously Neelam had heard about the argument and was calling to side with daddy dearest. The last thing he needed at this point was a heated conversation with his sister. She was a drama queen at the best of times!

He placed the phone on the passenger seat and decided to go directly to his mother and try to salvage their relationship before Neelam put her spin on the situation. As a child, Neelam would always manipulate matters for her own ends when Rajesh was in his parent's bad books. He loved her dearly, but she could be a conniving bitch when she wanted – which was most of the time.

Using the urgency of beating Neelam to the punch, he drove the supercar as it was meant to be driven – hard and fast. As he raced home, he mapped out the conversation he would have with his mother. As long as she was fighting his corner, everything else would fall into place.

The deafening roar and intense g-forces of the Lamborghini were thrilling beyond words. Rajesh was so overwhelmed with the Italian masterpiece that the unnerving meet with Regan and the distressing family situation that lay ahead gradually slipped from his mind.

Rajesh's smile rapidly disappeared as he approached his house. He could see flashing blue lights in the drive. Thinking the worst, his mind shifted into overdrive. Regan! It had to be Regan! The whole thing had been a setup. Regan had lured him away so he could attack his family. But why? Cautiously he edged into the drive; the flashing lights were coming from an ambulance. It was parked right next to the front door. He felt a strange sense of relief. Whatever Regan had done, it couldn't have been that serious or there would have been police cars on the scene. Nevertheless, an ambulance was not a good sign, and Rajesh needed answers.

He leapt out of the Lamborghini and paced up the drive. Suddenly the ambulance drove off. Waving his arms frantically he tried to flag it down, but the driver made no attempt to acknowledge him. Sirens blaring, the ambulance screeched past and accelerated away. Rajesh turned to see his mother hopelessly crying on the steps of the house. Neelam was standing next to her, wailing uncontrollably and holding on to one of the Doric columns holding up the portico.

"What's happened?" asked Rajesh frantically. "Are you okay? Why was the ambulance here?"

His mother seemed to be lost in a trance. She could barely look at him, let alone take comfort in the fact that he had arrived. Neelam loosened her grip on the column and turned towards him. She stared with such venom Rajesh could tell something terrible had happened. Regan would pay for this!

"Neelam, what's happened? Who was in the ambulance?"

Neelam stared at him with an intense hatred. Rajesh turned towards his mother and noticed his father's Range Rover parked on the drive. He could not remember a time when his father had been home so early.

Suddenly reality slapped him in the face. He grabbed his mother with both hands. "Where's Dad? Why is his car here?"

Neelam rushed between them. Rajesh lost his grip and stumbled backwards.

His mother looked at him, her eyes filled with sorrow and heartache. "He is gone, betta. The ambulance has taken him."

"This is your fault!" screamed Neelam. "You've done this!"

Rajesh took hold of her wrists. "Neelam, I need you to tell me what happened."

"Dad came back from the office in a terrible state. He was fuming about the row he had with you. He was screaming and shouting, and then he suddenly fell to his knees, holding his chest. Are you satisfied now?"

"Did he have a heart attack?"

"No. The ambulance driver said it was a stroke. They're not sure if they've caught it in time. What if he dies, Rajesh? What are we going to do?"

"For God's sake, Neelam, get a grip! Think of Mum; she doesn't want to hear this! Let's get down to the hospital and find out what is going on."

Neelam was no longer crying. Her eyes blazed like hot coals. "You bastard! You caused this, arguing with Dad about that slag Tanya! It's because of you two that Dad had a stroke. You probably want him to die so you can live happily ever after with that bitch!"

Vidya emerged from her trance and rushed to Rajesh's defence. "Neelam! How dare you! This is no one's fault. If anything your farther is to blame. The doctor has been telling him for years to eat healthier and slow down at work."

Rajesh knew he had to step up and take control. "Mum, this is not the time for blame. Let's get to the hospital. Everything is going to be okay."

He rushed into the house and grabbed his father's car keys off the hall table. As they drove through the gates, Neelam spotted the Lamborghini parked at the entrance to the drive.

"Whose is that?"

"Erm, a friend's," Rajesh said guiltily. "I was just taking it for a spin."

Neelam looked at him with utter contempt. "I see. So while Dad was having a stroke, you've been swanning around in a sports car. Very nice."

"Just shut up for once in your life!"

Rajesh hated the sight of hospitals. As a child he had watched helplessly as his beloved grandfather fought for fight his life in Intensive Care. The memory of that event had stayed with him – that and an overwhelming sense of powerlessness that he had experienced when the old man finally slipped away.

When they arrived in Casualty, the doctor looking after Rajesh's father took them to one side and tactfully explained the critical nature of the situation. The stroke had left Satish paralysed down the left side of his body. The doctor said he might not last the night. Even if he did, chances of a full recovery were slim. The family were devastated. Rajesh asked if they could see his father and were led into a side room by a nurse. Vidya winced when she saw her husband lying unconscious with tubes sticking out of him. It was sad to see such a mighty presence in such a vulnerable state.

For two days and nights, Vidya stood vigil at his bedside. On the third day, Rajesh managed to persuade her to go home for a few hours' rest and a change of clothes. Reluctantly she agreed, but she demanded Rajesh act as his father's shadow until she returned. Satish had said very little since his stroke. At best all he could manage was a brief mumble. Even so, it was enough to fill the family with hope.

Rajesh gently brushed back a rogue strand of hair from his father's forehead. He leant over him and whispered. "Dad, I know I've been a disappointment to you, but that's all in the past. From now on I'm going to make everything okay. Just hang in there and things will return to normal; I promise. I will be the son you always wanted. You'll see, Dad; I'm going to make you proud."

Satish slowly raised his right hand and placed it on Rajesh's arm. A subtle squeeze told him he had won back his father's affection. Rajesh felt relieved to have been given a second chance. Over the next few days, father and son grew closer. Rajesh sat for hours at his bedside, reading the *Financial Times* out loud, feeding him, lifting the odd glass of water to his parched lips – in fact seeing to his every need. Despite a lack of proper communication, both of them felt a mutual affection had been rekindled. Rajesh took great pride in shaving his farther and combing his hair.

Rajesh realised that even in this helpless position his father was still a proud man and would want to maintain his dignity. When Vidya returned to the hospital, she was delighted with the reconciliation and saw Satish's condition as a blessing in disguise. She prayed long and hard for his health to improve and remained confident that her prayers would be answered.

After a week the doctors were satisfied his condition had stabilised and arranged for the remainder of his treatment to be carried out in the comfort of the family home. Rajesh was keen to follow up on the promise he had made to his father. He was determined to put right all he had done wrong. Night after night he replayed the argument in his head. Terrible things had been said on both sides, but Rajesh knew his father's stroke was down to him. Overwhelmed with guilt, he desperately wanted the pain to go away.

Satish's speech slowly improved. He began using a wheelchair to move around the house. Rajesh felt the time had come to take charge of his father's empire. He realised it was best medicine for both of them. When he told him of his plans, Satish was delighted, if a little nervous. After all, his business was his life, and behind his smile he was all too aware of the flaws in his son's character. Rajesh was intelligent, yes, but volatile and prone to act rashly – not a good mixture when it came to business. But

Satish remembered a saying his grandmother used to quote when he was a child back in India – "Better a flawed diamond than a perfect pebble" – and he contented himself with that.

From Rajesh's viewpoint, he knew the staff would resent him stepping into his father's shoes. Most of them remembered him as a teenager and had long ago typecast him as a spoilt brat. Pulling up in a Lamborghini wouldn't help. In fact, it would only inflame the resistance towards him. But what the hell. He figured that arriving at work in a supercar would boost his profile. And besides, he secretly wanted to annoy a few female staff members who had dismissed his advances in past.

Then there was Regan. Over a week had passed since their meeting. He knew the gangland boss would take a dim view of him not turning up at his nightclub to return the Lamborghini. Rajesh found it strange that the hardest men on the planet had the most fragile egos; men who didn't bat an eyelid when it came to murder and torture would suddenly throw a hissy fit if one their invitations was declined. But what could he do? Family matters came first. *Surely even the hardest of gangsters respect that,* he thought. *Still, best not to provoke him too much.* So the night before going to work, Rajesh took the bull by the horns. He texted the bulldog: "Hi Teddy. Sorry not been in touch. Dad very ill. Please tell Mr Regan I'll be coming to his nightclub 2morrow night. Car fantastic. Will return it then." Five minutes later Teddy responded: "Make sure you do!!! The Boss hates being fucked around!!" Those gangster egos – fragile as Meissen figurines.

Before going to bed, Rajesh thought about Tanya. He hadn't spoken to her in almost ten days. He'd sent messages via Jazz, telling her about the family situation, but he was consciously trying not to get too bogged down with her emotional baggage whilst he was trying to rebuild his relationship with his father. As he switched off the light, he let out a heartfelt sigh. Only God knew what tomorrow would bring.

5

Taking charge of his father's company was a daunting experience for Rajesh. From the moment he arrived, he felt like an illegal immigrant trying to find his place in society. His first big mistake was pulling up in the *Lamborghini*. The look on the faces of the staff said it all: "Here comes the spoilt little brat, come to lord it over us" – the total opposite of how he wanted to be viewed. His crass display of arrogance backfired spectacularly. From their angle it looked as though he'd purchased the car the second his father had gone into hospital. In other words, he couldn't wait to plunder the family coffers for his own ends. The company had been going for twenty-five years and had many long-standing employees. How would they feel about a cocky little shit coming in and ruling the roost? Rajesh took a deep breath, forcing all paranoid thoughts to the back of his mind. Now was not the time to show fear. The staff wanted leadership, and it was up to him to show it.

He made his way to his father's office. Rather than taking the direct route through reception, he decided to go via the distribution centre. There were two reasons for this. First, he wanted to size up the entire operation and get a sense of what he was taking on. Second, he was keen for the staff to get a good look at him. The distribution centre was a massive steel structure covering five acres. Forklift trucks darted in and out like ants, moving pallets from storage departments to the waiting articulated lorries belonging to various parcel firms. Rajesh paused for a second to admire the impressive operation. *Slick, very slick.* He smiled proudly. His father's monumental effort in building such a massive, well-run enterprise suddenly hit him. Only now did he appreciate his hard work, passion, and determination. He decided there and then to do whatever it would take to add value to his efforts.

He greeted his father's secretary with polite aplomb. "Good morning."

She smiled back nervously, wary of their last encounter. "G-good morning. How is Mr Thakral?"

"Recovering slowly. I'm taking charge." Quick and decisive. That was what was needed. "A coffee would be nice."

"Certainly, Mr Thakral."

He walked through the teak door with the brass name plate marked "Chairman"**.** As he was confronted by his father's huge, oversized desk, the memory of their showdown came flooding back. Whilst sitting at his father's bedside in hospital, he had shrugged off the reason behind the stroke. His main focus was nursing his father back to health and becoming the son he could be proud of. But now, in this solitary moment, in the very room where he had stood up to him and subsequently changed the course of his family's destiny, Rajesh faced the facts. *He* was the reason for the stroke! There was no denying it. He had reduced a proud pillar of a man to a wheelchair-bound invalid.

His attention was suddenly drawn to Jainti Patel, the depot manager, his father's most trusted employee, who had entered the room unannounced. Rajesh was grateful for the interruption; his chain of thought was beginning to choke him. Nevertheless, he resented the fact that Patel had just walked into his office without so much as a knock at the door – something he would never have done if his father had been at the reigns. So the resentment and lack of respect had already set in, had it? Right! Rajesh decided to nip it in the bud, and Patel was the ideal person to begin with. *Get him in line and the rest will soon follow*, he thought.

"Hey, J. P.! Good to see you again!" Knowing how much the simple Gujarati man would resent his name being abbreviated to J. P., Rajesh forced himself upon him without first questioning what it was that had bought him to the office in the first place. "Look. J. P., I know things have been a little crazy around here, but it's important you and I work closely together. I need you to bring me up to speed. Who owes us money? Who do we owe money to? Who are our best clients? I need you to be my eyes and ears for everything." Patel stared at him with a puzzled, slightly resentful expression. "What's up, J. P.? Look, I know that it must be a little weird, but this is all new for me, too. I'm sure if you and I put our heads together, we can steer this ship on course."

Rajesh paused in the expectation that Patel would nod in agreement, if only in obligation. Remembering their last encounter when Patel had parked his Mondeo in his dedicated parking spot, Rajesh found it obvious the guy was still carrying around a good deal of suppressed anger. "Look, Jainti Bhai." Rajesh softened his tone. "I know the last time we met things got a little heated, but it's important we move forward for the sake of the company." Rajesh despised having to pamper to the ego of an employee, but the situation warranted it, and he was well aware of how strategically important Patel was. His father had once described Patel as a "sheep dog" that kept all the sheep (depot staff) working in the right direction, and how it was important to focus on controlling the sheep dog and not the sheep.

Again Patel stared at him with an expression of disbelief. For fuck's sake! What did the cunt want? Did he expect him to grovel? Well, fuck him! Allowing his insecurities to get the better of him, Rajesh firmed his tone. "Am I getting through to you, J. P.? Are we on the same page? Huh?"

Patel felt obliged to respond. He cleared his throat and looked Rajesh straight in the eye. "I know the task at hand, and you know I will stand shoulder-to-shoulder with you to keep things running smoothly. But *Sir-ji,* I only came in to ask about your father's health. For me all other matters are secondary."

Patel's genuine concern and humility cut Rajesh down to size. He could no longer look him in the eye. Turning away to face the window, he knew his first attempt to gain respect among his employees had failed miserably.

* * *

The Rouge Club was one of the West End's most desirable after-hours haunts. Situated on an exclusive Mayfair street, it offered anonimity to Premier League footballers and pop stars keen to enjoy the burlesque environment without being pestered by the paparazzi or Joe Public. It worked on the principle that you had to be somebody to get past to the elite SAS-style doormen and therefore immune to the sight of a Play Boy Bunny or the latest addition to the *90210* cast. As excited as he was about catching a glimpse of London's finest selection of Paris Hilton wannabes, Rajesh had no particular desire to see Regan again. Privately he hoped he could hand the car keys to whoever greeted him at the door and slip away unnoticed into the night.

Cruising past Marble Arch, he was cautious not to park the Lambo in a space where it might get bumped by an intoxicated reveller leaving one of the many surrounding nightclubs in the area. Parking was always a huge issue in the capital, regardless of the time of day, but on a Friday night it seemed as though the whole of Europe was in town to party. He coasted effortlessly past the club's canopied entrance, careful not to tap the accelerator too hard and draw attention to him or the car with the unavoidable grunt from the sport exhaust. Nevertheless, the sight of the car brought envious stares from the line of people crowding the door to get in. A square-headed, square-bodied doorman the size of a refrigerator walked briskly into the street, extending his arm and gesturing him to stop. Rajesh glanced in his rear-view mirror; there were several cars on his tail waiting to pass. The confidence of the doorman was a clear display of authority, and he promptly bought the car to a halt.

An impatient driver of a black cab beeped his horn a couple of times and leaned out of the window, shouting, "Camon! Move it, mate!"

The doorman broke eye contact with Rajesh and turned slowly to face the back cab, giving the driver an intimidating stare. Rajesh looked in his mirror to witness the reaction. The driver looked down in submission whilst simultaneously pulling up his open window. A second pony-tailed refrigerator in a slick black suit and black leather gloves quickly moved a pair of traffic cones that had been strategically placed outside the entrance. The square-headed fridge stood firm in the centre of the street, oblivious to the traffic now backing up. With supreme confidence, he made swift hand signals towards the empty space cleared by the cones. Rajesh followed his cue and gently manoeuvred the car into place, taking care not to get too close to the curb and risk scraping the twenty-inch alloy wheels. Once the car was safely parked, the refrigerator made his way back towards the entrance door. He made no effort to acknowledge the line of traffic blocking the street. Rajesh had a bad feeling he was drifting deeper into "Regan Town". It was going to be a long night.

The plan to leave the keys with the doorman went out of the window. He was ushered to the front of the queue, past a throng of smartly dressed people waiting impatiently to get in. If looks could kill, Rajesh would have been stabbed in the back several times. He was escorted into the club. As he descended a flight of stairs, he heard the dull thud of dance music. A velvet curtain parted, and he was met with a strobe-lit dance floor full of cavorting couples, their faces frozen in coke-fuelled ecstasy. The club was packed, the bar in the far corner doing a roaring trade.

Before he could get his bearings, Rajesh was escorted to a private booth by two stunning brunettes. They were so alike they could have been twins. Suddenly his mind invented an erotic ménage à trois. Smiling, the twins seemed to read his thoughts. He slid neatly into a semicircle of red leather. He couldn't leave now even if he wanted to. It seemed as though gravity were working against him, keeping his ass firmly fixed to the couch. He felt comforted by the dazzling smiles of three Miss Teen America lookalikes making their way towards him. Dressed in matching figure-hugging cocktail dresses, they each carried an ice bucket of vintage Cristal with frosted champagne flutes positioned inside the bucket alongside to the bottle.

The tallest of the three, a tousled-haired blonde with pneumatic breasts, put the ice bucket down on the table and offered a cute grin. "Hello, Mr Thakral. We've been expecting you. Mr Regan will be along shortly. We're here to attend to your needs while you wait." She leaned closer to him and whispered seductively into his ear. "Do you have any needs you would like me to take care of?" She pulled away and made a soft, innocent face, conjuring up a naught-but-nice aura.

Rajesh, who had always prided himself on being swift with his responses, was lost for words. He stuttered. "I'm … I'm okay, thanks. Will, er, will Mr Regan be long? I don't really have time; I … I've got to get back to—"

He was interrupted by the sight of Regan walking through the sea of revellers. They seemed to part for him like the Red Sea before Moses. He was closely followed by Teddy the bulldog and a slick stockbroker type wearing a pinstriped suit and an outrageous canary-yellow tie. The city dandy looked totally out of place in the mafia-style milieu.

Rajesh jumped up and nervously stood to attention. "Mr Regan! Hi! Good to see you again."

Regan ignored his extended hand and slid into the booth. He wore chinos and a candy-striped shirt; the top three buttons were undone, revealing a gold St Christopher the size of a two-pound coin. *Odd the way religion and violence seem to mix.*

"I told you, kid, call me Uncle Joe. We'll get on better if you do."

Rajesh nodded and slowly took his seat, not knowing if he was supposed to sit down or stay standing at this point.

Teddy came towards him aggressively. "Camon! Do you want me to sit in yah lap?" Rajesh looked at him with a puzzled expression. "Move the fuck up, son!"

Regan raised his hand. "Teddy, Teddy. Take it easy. The kid's our guest." He smiled calmly at Rajesh. "Come closer, kid. Let's get to know each other a little better."

As Rajesh slid across, it suddenly dawned on him that he was now sandwiched between Regan and the bulldog. It was the worst place in the world to be. The bulldog signalled to the waitress to serve the champagne. His hand gesture made Rajesh jump; he was clearly on edge, and the smirk on Regan's face told him he knew it.

Leaning in slightly and placing his hand on Rajesh's wrist, Regan softened his tone. "I want you meet an associate of mine. This is Mark – Mark Shearsbe." Right on cue, the pinstripe stuck out his hand. Rajesh turned towards him. As they shook hands, Rajesh noticed his palm was hot and sweaty. Smiling politely, Mark pulled away, discreetly wiping his hand on his tailor-made jacket. "I'm glad you've have had a chance to meet. Mark is a good friend of mine. I've got a feeling the two of you are going to get on."

Rajesh shifted nervously in his seat. "Uncle Joe, thanks for the hospitality and everything; and Mark, it was lovely to meet you, but I really have to get going. Thanks for the loan of the car. I had a fantastic time." Rajesh scanned left to right for the closest exit.

"I knew you'd have a good time. Did it get you laid?"

Rajesh choked on his champagne. "Er, no, no. I just enjoyed driving it around." The thought of Tanya came rushing into his mind, and his face lapsed into sadness.

Regan picked up on it instantly. "Don't look so sad, kid. You don't strike me as the kind of person who has trouble getting pussy."

"No, no! It's nothing like that. It's just the week I've been through. My dad has taken ill, and I've been managing his company until he gets better."

Regan put his index finger on his lips and paused for a few seconds as though plotting a chess move. "There you go, kid. You've done it again!" He turned to his cronies. "Didn't I tell yah! Didn't I tell yah about this kid!" He pinched Rajesh's left cheek, which signalled he was pleased with him but left Rajesh feeling completely humiliated.

"Sorry, Uncle Joe, have I missed something?"

Regan smiled proudly. "Kid, you've proved me right once again. You've got balls. Your old man's ready to pop his clogs, and instead of falling to pieces like most spoilt pricks your age, you step up to the mark and take control of the situation! I know how to spot a winner! You were faced with a situation, and you handled it the best way you knew. I read you right."

Regan's approval elevated Rajesh. He took a swig of Cristal and eased back into his seat. "Uncle Joe, I'm really grateful for the way you've treated me, and if I can help you in any way—"

Regan almost fell off his chair. "Did you hear that, boys? The kid wants to help *me!* Listen, big shot. Sit back and enjoy. Do you know how many people would kill to be sitting where you're sitting?"

"Which is why I find all this a little confusing." Rajesh's train of thought was interrupted by a young Shilpa Shetty lookalike making her way towards the table with a pyramid of chopped strawberries neatly assembled over crushed ice in an oversized martini glass.

"Some strawberries with your champagne, gentlemen?" Avoiding eye contact, she placed the glass on the table and simultaneously turned on her heels and walked away. She was clearly uncomfortable and did a poor job of hiding it.

Regan glanced at her and then turned towards Rajesh, who was mesmerised by her catwalk-like style. Regan raised his eyebrow authoritatively. "Teddy? Who was that? I've not seen her before?"

Teddy shrugged. "Not sure, Gaff."

Mark interjected in his posh public school accent. "She's one of the recruits we just hired from a new agency."

"Fuck me! We're using an agency to get staff? There should be cues of these bitches wanting to work here. Mark, call her over and tell her to come and say hello to our friend here. He's obviously got a taste for brown pussy. Ain't that right, kid? You're partial to a bit of the old Indian takeaway, ain't yah?"

"Uncle Joe, that's not necessary. She's cute, but so what? There are fifty other equally cute women in this place."

"That's right, kid, there are. And one by one, you can fuck them all! But let's start with this one." He tipped his head towards Mark, who was now on the edge of his seat. As soon as he received the gesture, he sprinted off like Usain Bolt.

Watching Mark dash off in the same direction as Shilpa Shetty, Rajesh lowered his guard and let out a smile.

Like a hawk, Regan was on to him. "What's so funny, kid?"

"Nothing, Uncle Joe. It's just funny to see how people behave around you. Is he always that obedient?"

Regan's eyes narrowed. "Watch it, kid. Mark knows his place just like everyone else around here. Take it from me; he's a good friend. An accounting genius. You could learn a lot from him."

Rajesh sized him up as he walked towards the booth closely followed by an uncomfortable Shilpa Shetty. He was a lanky six-footer with a clumsy, awkward gait. Rajesh imagined him being bullied at school. But the class nerd had made it big and now liked to power dress to mask his insecurities.

Mark turned towards the petrified waitress. "Why don't you slide in here, darling, next to Uncle Joe?" His accent was pure public school. "Gentlemen, let me introduce you to Bav. She's only been with us for a week, so take it easy on her."

"For fuck's sake, Mark! I don't bite!" Regan patted the empty space next to him in a condescending manner." Come here, honey. Take a seat next to me. I'll make sure you're okay." With a look of disdain, Shilpa sat down but maintained a distance between herself and Regan. "That's better. Take a load off. Now, this is a good friend of mine." He paused for a second. "Kid, what's your name again?"

"Er, Rajesh ... It's Rajesh, but my friends call me Raj."

"Right, right. It's Raj. The kids name's Raj. Why don't you take him for a tour of the club? Show him all the little hiding places where people get up to no good."

Bav smiled politely, relieved to be exiting the booth. "Okay, Mr Regan, it will be my pleasure." She instantly sprang to her feet.

Rajesh couldn't help noticing her shapely figure and her thick, bouncy hair, which was teased into cute ringlets that cascaded down her back. Teddy rolled his eyes and slid across so Rajesh could exit. He was clearly unimpressed with the whole scenario.

"This way, please." She made her way elegantly towards the crowded dance floor.

Rajesh was glad to escape the confines of the booth. He quickly caught up with her. "Hey? What's the rush?"

"Sorry, sir, I didn't realise."

Rajesh had to shout over the music. Leaning in towards her, he could smell her exotic perfume. "What's all this 'sir' crap? I'm Raj. And you are?" He froze. "This is really embarrassing, but I've forgotten your name already."

"It's Bav. But don't worry about it. I wouldn't expect someone like you to remember the name of a waitress."

"Someone like *me!* Come on, what the fuck is that supposed to mean?"

"Sorry, I didn't mean to offend you. It's just ... you're clearly a big shot, or you wouldn't be sitting at his highness's table, so why would you remember my name?"

"It's not like I know these guys. Anyway, have you been working here long?"

"About a week. I absolutely hate it, but I need the money to put myself through uni. I am studying to be a pharmacist."

"That's great." He felt like he should engage her in small talk to make her feel more comfortable. "So what's Bav short for?"

"Bhavana. But most people find that to be a mouthful, so I just use Bav."

"Are you kidding? Bhavana's a lovely name! It's timeless and elegant. It really suits you." She giggled. Rajesh took it as a sign of mutual flirting. "Look, I've got to get back to those guys. Maybe you and I could have a drink sometime?"

"I don't think so. I'm at work. I'm not supposed to give out my number to customers."

"Customer? What customer? Didn't you hear Uncle Joe! I'm his friend!"

Teddy suddenly appeared. "Listen, sunshine, the Gaffa had to leave, so just relax and enjoy yourself. Anything you want, it's on the house."

"That's very kind of you, but I really have to be going."

"Bullshit. Chill out and relax." He turned to Bav. "Listen, sweetheart, you're off the clock, so make sure he has a good time."

"Sorry? What's that supposed to mean?"

"It *means* forget about waitressing tonight. Look after Mr Regan's guest and there'll be a big fat tip for you in your wage packet next week"

Bav was horrified. "Excuse me! I am a waitress, not a prostitute!"

Teddy gave her an icy stare. "Don't you raise your voice at me, little girl."

Rajesh tried to ease the tension. "Hey, guys. Relax. It's all good. I have to get going anyway."

The bulldog in Teddy resurfaced. He hated being undermined by anyone, let alone a two-bit waitress and a kid wet behind the ears. "Listen, you ungrateful little shit, you're a guest of the Gaffa. So sit back, shut the fuck up, and enjoy his hospitality! And you, you little whore, you'll do *what* I say *when* I say."

Bav's eyes started to well up, and she blurted out. "I quit!" She turned and ran towards the exit.

Rajesh was desperate to do the same, but he needed to be diplomatic. "Teddy, take it easy. We're all friends, remember? Let me go after her and bring her back. She's an asset to the club, right? You've got to know how to handle Indian girls. They're not like the white trash you usually deal with."

It was a gutsy move, but it seemed to pay off. Teddy softened his expression. "The boss was right about you. You're a ballsy little fucker." He brushed his bottom lip with his thumb as if to indicate he was mentally debating something and then smirked. "Okay, Prince Charming, go get your girl. There's a Phantom outside ready and waiting. The driver will take you anywhere you want."

"Phantom?"

"Yeah, as in Rolls Royce Phantom."

Rajesh didn't need to be asked twice. He left the club and ran up the stairs, pushing past the assembled line of hopefuls waiting to get in. Outside the air felt moist against his skin. It had just stopped raining. The pavements glistened with reflected neon – blues, indigos, reds – the colours of a city at play. He looked to his right and saw Bav stomping off down the street.

A short, fat Turkish man in a black suit and tie approached him. "Hello, sir. I have a car waiting for you." He gestured towards a silver Phantom parked in the same space he'd left the Lamborghini in almost an hour earlier.

Wow, this guy works fast, thought Rajesh. Bav had now disappeared into the London backdrop. Realising he had little chance of catching her on foot, he turned to the driver. "Can you take me down the street? I have to catch up with a girl who's just left."

"No problem, sir. Just point me in the right direction."

Rajesh climbed into back of the Phantom. He was met by the luxurious scent of leather and walnut. Every inch of the interior was fitted to the highest specification – drinks cabinet, TV. If only his father could see him now! *Poor Dad,* thought Rajesh. Still, the night was young, and you don't go staring a gift horse in the mouth. They screeched away, leaving the Rouge nightclub behind. Rajesh breathed a sigh of relief.

"There she is! Pull over, please." Rajesh didn't wait for the driver to open the door for him. Instead he jumped out to pursue Bav on foot. Halfway along Park Lane, he caught up with her. "Hey, Bav ... Bhavana! Slow down!"

She looked at him with disdain. Gone was friendly the waitress; outside the club, he was just another guy trying to get into her knickers. "What the hell do you want? Why are you following me?"

"Calm down. I just wanted to make sure you're okay, that's all."

"You're all just a bunch of arrogant pricks who think you can buy anyone with your fancy cars and gangster lifestyle. Well, I am not for sale!"

"Whoa! Whoa! Slow down. First of all, I'm not one of "them"! Come on, do I look like a gangster? And second, buying girls isn't my style. You were upset; I just wanted to check if you were okay. But if you'd rather I didn't, then I'll leave." Bav smiled. He knew he had penetrated her defences. "Look, it's late. Let me take you home. We can talk on the way. No strings attached. Promise."

She looked at him and then at the beast of a car parked next the kerb. "You want to take me home in that? It's worth more than the house I'm renting!"

Rajesh grinned at her modesty. It reminded him of Tanya. *Tanya – I wonder how she is?* "It's only a car; don't worry about it."

"That's easy for you to say. Don't you get it? We're from different worlds."

Another martyr. Rajesh began to lose interest. "Look, I'm not proposing to you or anything. I just want to make sure you get home safe. But if you prefer seeing the sights of London on a double-decker bus, then be my guest."

She could tell he was annoyed. "Sorry, I didn't mean to piss you off. It's been a crazy night; that's all. Come on; let's see what this car of yours is like."

He stopped short of telling her the identity of the car's real owner. He figured it might just rock the boat a little too much in the wrong direction.

As they made their way through the hectic London traffic, they chatted amiably. Rajesh felt strangely at ease with this virtual stranger. She told him how her father had died after years of suffering from diabetes and how her mother had brought up three children singlehandedly. She had decided to become a pharmacist after watching her father waste away, convinced that a better understanding of his illness would have made a difference to his life.

Rajesh was filled with admiration, and at the same time he was angry at the way Teddy had treated her. "Bav, I want you to do something for me. Don't look so worried; it's nothing weird. That asshole in the club was bang out of order. I want you to come back to the club with me tomorrow night and be the person you really are. I don't want them to think they can treat people like shit and get away with it. You don't come across as the kind of person who would let a jerk like that get one over on you." He was playing with her emotions, implying a touch of reverse psychology, but it was worth it just to set the record straight. And besides, he needed an excuse to see her again. It seemed premature to let the evening finish with a simple hug and a handshake.

Bav was silent for a few seconds. "I'm not sure. They don't seem like the kind of people you want to get on the wrong side of."

"Don't worry about them. You'll be with me. We won't stay long. It's about holding your head up high and sticking two fingers up to the world."

She smiled, finding his confidence overwhelming. As they approached her street, she signalled to the driver to pull over.

"Please don't drop me outside my place in this car." Rajesh looked at the depressing row of pre-war houses and understood her embarrassment. She scribbled her phone number down on a piece of paper and handed it to him. "Text me tomorrow night when you're on your way. And for God's sake, bring a more sensible car!" She leaned across and pecked him on the cheek. "Thanks for the lift."

Rajesh watched her shapely figure sashay down the path. He wasn't the only one. "Not bad is she?" he said to the driver, noticing him eyeing her up greedily.

"Oh yes, sir. Very nice. Very nice indeed."

"Okay. Take me to Gerrards Cross, please."

As the Phantom pulled smoothly away, Rajesh sank back into the parchment leather seats. He played back the evening in his mind like a silent movie. There had been plenty of highs and lows, but the night could not have finished on a higher note. Sipping the finest of champagne, being chauffeur driven home in a £300,000 car, being kissed goodnight by a lush model type – and to top it all, he had talked her into a follow-up date the very next evening. It suddenly occurred to him that he might not get into Rouge for a second time. After all, tonight he had been a guest of Regan. Would he be welcome two nights in a row? He decided not to let mere details spoil his mood. He was feeling euphoric and would worry about tomorrow when it came. He closed his eyes and salivated at the thought of the vibrant new world opening up for him – a world that had so far been out of reach, even with his relatively privileged upbringing. Like a vampire that had tasted blood for the first time, there was no turning back for Rajesh now.

6

The next morning, at nine o'clock sharp, Rajesh strolled into the office. He was in a good mood, and Patel was quick to pick up on it. A born gossip monger, Patel liked to be the hub of information at all times.

As Rajesh took his seat behind his father's desk, Patel decided to test the water. "You must have had a fun evening last night. Did you go anywhere special?"

Rajesh resented the fishing expedition. "Not really. I'm just excited about working with you, J. P."

His sarcastic tone was enough to put Patel in his place. Rajesh felt irritated by the clumsy grilling, but that didn't spoil his mood. Things were falling into place nicely. The doctors were positive about his father's recovery and he had a hot date to look forward to. He suddenly felt a twinge of guilt regarding Tanya. Apart from the odd text message, there had been no real contact between them. He knew he had to put that right – at some point, yes, but not right now, not today. Today he was focused on putting the spring back into his step, and dinner with Bav was the perfect way to start.

His father's long-standing PA, Margret, buzzed his telephone extension. "Mr Thakral, I have a Mr Shearsbe in reception to see you. He doesn't have an appointment."

Rajesh scanned his memory. The name sounded familiar "Who? I don't know any Shearsbe."

"He says he met you yesterday, and that he's here on behalf of a Mr Regan."

Suddenly the name Shearsbe slapped him in the face! It was Mark Shearsbe, the stockbroker type from Rouge. "Of course! Mark Shearsbe! Please send him in. And Margret, Mr Thakral is my father. Please call me Raj." An uncomfortable look washed over Rajesh's face. Anxious to get rid of Patel before he had the chance to interact with Shearsbe, he rushed to the door to indicate to Patel he wanted him to leave but found Shearsbe standing in the doorway. Rajesh was startled. "Oh! Come in. It's Mark, isn't it?"

"That's right. Mark Shearsbe." He walked briskly past Rajesh with a mixture of arrogance and self-confidence and sat down in the visitor's chair adjacent to the oversized throne from which Satish had reigned for many years.

Eager to learn more about the unsettling stranger, Patel lunged forward. "I am Jainti Bhai Patel, sir. Please let me present you with my card."

Rajesh was shocked at Patel's boldness. "That's not necessary, J. P. I'm sure you must have some work to be getting on with." He manoeuvred himself between them to intercept the business card, but Patel had already placed it in Shearsbe's hand.

Patel gave a brief but satisfied grin. "Okay, sir. Please let me know if you need anything. Can I get you some coffee or a soft drink?"

Rajesh flashed a venomous stare. "That will be all, Patel!" He escorted Patel to the door and slammed it shut behind him to express his contempt. He turned towards the unwelcome visitor. "I'm sorry, did we have an appointment?"

Shearsbe sat down as cool as you like, taking in the office surroundings. "Relax, Raj. I'm here on behalf of Mr Regan. He wanted me to drop off your car."

Rajesh was glad Shearsbe had returned the car; he had no

desire to go back to Regan's house. He took a deep breath and let out a sigh of relief.

Shearsbe sensed his unease. "You seem rather on edge. Don't worry; I'm only here to do you a favour. That's how it is with the Gaffa. Once you're under his wing, it's access all areas. Word of advice: don't keep questioning it or you'll drive yourself crazy. Just sit back and enjoy life. I know I do."

Rajesh smiled. Maybe he had misjudged the situation. He'd clearly misjudged Shearsbe. He could see them being good friends under different circumstances. Shearsbe was different from the usual mafia-type thugs that surrounded Regan. The guy was a pen pusher, and Rajesh was streetwise enough to handle him "Yeah, I guess you're right. But I still can't work out why Mr Regan is being so nice to me? I mean, I hardly know the bloke."

"Believe me, Raj, I've seen this scenario many times before. It's not so much that he has taken a liking to you – after all, he isn't a fag or anything – it's more a case of respect. The guy likes your style. He likes the way you handle yourself under pressure, and on some level, I guess he respects you. Now, if you're uncomfortable with that you can tell him to his face. You are coming in to the Rouge tonight? I hear you're bringing that tasty Indian waitress who told Teddy to go fuck himself. Fair play to her. Teddy can be a miserable prick sometimes, and I do like a girl who can stand up for herself."

Rajesh felt the colour drain from his cheeks. "How did you know about my plans? Have you guys been in touch with Bav? If you have a problem with me seeing her, then I won't go. I mean, I hardly know the girl, so who gives a fuck."

Shearsbe smiled enigmatically. "There you go again, jumping to conclusions. What is it with you? Are you always this suspicious, or do all white men make you jumpy?"

"No, it's nothing like that. It's just a little overwhelming that you know my plans when I've not even finalised them myself."

"I told you, you're under the Gaffa's wing now, and he looks after his own. Last night you were chauffeured back by Mr

Regan's personal driver, and he brought the boss up to speed with all of last night's shenanigans. The way I hear it, you were seriously smooth." Rajesh puffed out his chest with pride. "The boss wanted me to swing by with your motor so you wouldn't be stuck for a ride tonight. When you get to the club, just give the door staff your name and you'll be given five-star treatment. Any issue, here's my card" He pulled out a laminated card and, holding the edges with both hands, bowed slowly and held it out in front of him. Rajesh took a step back and wondered if this clown was for real. Lifting his head slowly, Shearsbe chuckled at Rajesh's reaction. "Sorry to be so dramatic. I spent a few years studying banking and finance in Japan and picked up a few of their customs." The guy certainly was a character, a likable fool, a harmless banker playing out a gangster wannabe fantasy. "You have a great setup here. I'd love to have the tour. Well? How about it?"

Rajesh raised his left eyebrow for a second but quickly dismissed any cautionary thoughts; after all, the Regan clan had all been extra hospitable towards him. "Sure. No problem. Where do you want to start?"

"How about we walk and talk and you can explain to me a little about what goes on here."

Proudly guiding his VIP visitor through the vast array of buildings, Rajesh went into detail about how the company operated. Suria Shipping was responsible for importing and exporting goods from all over the world. It was the responsibility of Suria to gain Her Majesty's customs clearance on the imported goods and collect VAT or duties payable prior to release. The imported goods could be anything from carpets to computers. The depot had a secure unit called the bonded warehouse. This was where imported alcohol and cigarettes were kept and the due diligence around customs clearance was done under much stricter conditions. The biggest advantage to Suria clients was that they could defer paying duties whilst the goods were held to be purchased in the UK or re-exported, in which case it would negate the need for VAT. Rajesh was impressed with how quickly Shearsbe was absorbing the working mechanics of this complex business; he put it down to his banking background. By the end of the comprehensive tour, the two had become more familiar with each other and agreed to catch up for a drink at Rouge later that night.

* * *

The Porsche seemed sluggish and unrefined. When shifting gears from third to fourth, Rajesh craved the buzz of the Italian thoroughbred. It seemed that for the first time in his life he had been truly spoilt. The Boxter, once his pride and joy, now seemed to him as ordinary as Patel's Ford Mondeo. Strange the way luxury corrupts. Could the same be true of Tanya? Since meeting Bav, he had barely given Tanya a second thought. No woman had ever gotten under his skin like Bav. There was something enchanting about her. But the truth was that his heart belonged to Tanya, no matter how desirable the forbidden fruit was. Tonight was about letting his hair down and having some fun, but ultimately Tanya was the love of his life. He would stay loyal to her no matter what – loyal by his own Machiavellian definition.

He debated calling Tanya to help assuage the nauseating guilt that had started to fester in the pit of his stomach. Was he really doing the right thing? Shouldn't he be spending his free time with the girl he claimed to love? On the other hand, his life had been rocked to the core, and he deserved a little excitement. He needed some "me" time. Unconsciously he began to accelerate, perhaps to shorten the journey and in turn leave little opportunity to torture himself.

True to form, he arrived at Bav's place almost twenty minutes late. He had grown accustomed to the usual feminine tantrums that went with courting Tanya. Twenty minutes late would normally equate to an hour's worth of sulking on her part. What a way to start a date!

Bav opened the passenger door, and he took in her female splendour. She wore a beige hobo skirt and a white-frilled, full-sleeved blouse. She encapsulated the contradicting styles of being effortlessly casual, radiantly elegant, and unrevealingly sexy. This girl really was different, and all at once the niggling guilt factor disappeared for Rajesh.

She smiled as she got into the car, her eyes darting from left to right as she appraised the car's interior. "Hey, this is great. A lot more sporty and fun than that tank we were in last night."

"Yeah. Uh, thanks. Listen, I'm sorry I'm a bit late. Hope it hasn't spoiled your mood?"

"Don't be silly. You're a busy guy. I didn't mind waiting for you. Besides, you're here now. Let's just enjoy the evening and get to know each other."

Rajesh was delighted with her relaxed response. How refreshing not to have to spend the first part of the evening apologising. It flattered his ego that she had understood. Obviously she regarded him as a busy, successful individual and accepted that a man with such a lifestyle would always have demands on his time. Rajesh knew instinctively that this would be an intimate evening.

Rajesh felt a rush of adrenaline upon arriving at Rouge. This time around, instead of being nervous and unconfident, not knowing what to expect, he was determined to enjoy the rock-star treatment. He parked right in front of the club, winking at the refrigerator doorman as he got out of his car, hoping to be recognised from the night before. He was relieved when his wink was reciprocated with a discreet nod. Bav was in awe of his celebrity status. She noticed how everyone in the queue craned their necks to get a view of him. They strolled into the club like A-listers at the Cannes Film Festival. Once inside, Rajesh decided to capitalise on Regan's generosity and stop questioning his motives.

The place was even more packed than the night before. Champagne flowed in every direction. They were led to the VIP area and took a seat in a private booth. Shearsbe joined them with a couple of girls that looked as if they could have starred in a German porn film. Rajesh couldn't put a foot wrong. As he simultaneously held conversations with several ladies, his confidence was through the roof. Regan arrived at the booth, followed by a cocktail waitress holding a tray of Vodka Martinis and a small antique box made of beaten silver.

Regan leant forward as if to embrace Rajesh, shouting in his ear, "Looks like the party started without me, boys! I've got some catching up to do!"

To his horror Rajesh watched as Regan slid open the antique box and placed it in the centre of the table; somehow he already knew that it contained drugs and the party was about to take whole new direction.

Bav sensed his hesitation and squeezed his hand. "It's coke," she whispered. "These guys take it all the time."

Rajesh acknowledged her attempt to comfort him with a half-smile but was unable to disguise the uneasy feeling he had towards drugs. One by one Regan, Shearsbe, and the German porn stars took a small amount of the white powder and vacuumed it away through each nostril. The focus was now on Bav and Rajesh.

"Camon, son. What you waiting for? Get some Charlie inside yah. It'll put hair on your chest." Regan slid the box towards him.

"Fuck me, Uncle Joe! You doing coke? In front of everyone? What if this place gets raided? You can't be doing drugs so openly!" A cackle of raucous laughter went around the table. Rajesh felt humiliated.

"Look around you, kid. Does it look like we have anything to worry about? We're fucking kings! We can do whatever we want!" Regan leaned in towards him and clenched his fist. "Listen, son. It's been nice hanging out with you, but if you don't like the scene, then you can piss off right now! This is no place for a fucking schoolboy."

Rajesh and Regan glared at each other. Rajesh could see the coke was taking effect, puffing up Regan's vanity, making him aggressive.

Bav took it upon herself to interrupt. "He's no schoolboy, Mr Regan. I can assure you he's all man."

Regan eased back into his chair and chuckled. Rajesh watched as Bav dipped her long fingernail into the crystalline white powder and bought a scoop of cocaine towards her nose. His jaw dropped open as she unashamedly hoovered up the drug from her fingernail. Turning towards him, she placed one hand seductively on his face, as if to reassure him that everything was okay. She slowly lifted her fingernail, offering him a scoop.

Rajesh knew his life was about to change; taking drugs was against his morals principals. Scanning the table from left to right, he saw a wall of eager faces staring at him. He turned back towards Bav and allowed his face to press deeper into her open palm. He closed his eyes as if to signal he was ready. She lifted her nail towards his left nostril, sliding her fingers through his hair, and slowly massaged his scalp. Comforted by her touch, Rajesh sensed the vibrant atmosphere of the club. With a desperate need for Regan's approval, he inhaled noisily, filling his lungs with powdered air. Keeping his eyes closed, he sunk down into the softness of the leather booth. The rush came instantly. His head began to pound. He felt almost godlike. Engulfed by a tidal wave of euphoria, he leaned his head back, an intense flash of stroboscopic light piercing his brain.

* * *

Rajesh awoke to the sight of Bav walking away from him wearing nothing but the shirt that he had worn the night before. After rubbing his eyes, he began to focus on her perfectly shaped bare ass, which was modestly showing under the tip of the shirt tail. He smiled and glanced around the room. He quickly realised he was lying in Bav's bedsit. He took a quick peek under the sheet and found he was butt naked, his painfully throbbing cock testament to a night of raw sex. It would be great if he could actually remember it. He sat up and gave the bedsit the once over – cracked ceiling, peeling wallpaper, charity shop furniture The house was a Victorian terrace converted into the most basic student accommodation. Whoever the slum landlord was needed taking out and shooting. Rajesh cringed; to think he'd spent the night in such a dump! He vowed never to repeat the experience.

Bav returned holding two glasses of orange juice. She slowed her pace as she approach the bed. Suddenly Rajesh forgot his miserable surrounds and focused on her slender body. He felt his cock stiffen.

Handing him a glass, she smiled and kissed him gently on the cheek, and then she softly pulled away. "Good morning, big boy. Did you sleep well?"

"I'm not sure I'm awake," said Rajesh, smirking. "I think I'm still dreaming."

She leaned over and kissed him again, this time on the lips – a long, lingering kiss full of erotic intensity. "Does that feel real to you?"

"Yep, that's pretty much done it. I'm wide awake now."

"Listen, I don't want to spoil the moment, but your phone's been buzzing all morning. I think someone's desperate to get hold of you." She reached out to the bedside cabinet and handed him his mobile.

Rajesh rubbed his eyes, desperate to focus his thoughts. "God, what time is it?"

"Just gone twelve thirty."

He sat bolt upright. "*What!* Twelve thirty! In the afternoon!" He glanced at his phone and saw fourteen missed calls. Most were from Tanya, a couple were from his home number, and one was from the office – probably Patel checking up on him. *The nosy bastard,* Rajesh thought. "Fuck! I've got to go!" He sprang to his feet and was suddenly conscious he was standing completely naked in front of Bav, his half-erect penis dangling freely.

She giggled at his schoolboy awkwardness. "Hey, don't worry about it. I understand. Things got a little crazy last night. We can get together later and talk. If you've got to go, that's cool."

He went to gather up his clothes that were scattered across the floor. As he stretched forward, his groin inadvertently brushed across her cheek. He took a step back, blushing with embarrassment. Bav had a slightly stunned look across her face. Coquettishly, she glanced towards his partially raised shaft which seemed to have found a new lease of life. Slowly, expertly, she knelt down in front of him, keeping her eyes fixed on his. With a swish of her hair, she gently took hold of his throbbing manhood. Closing her eyes, she opened her mouth and slipped in the tip of his fully erect tool, sucking its full extent with long, wet, exaggerated movements. She thrust her head back and forth, speeding up her motion and rocking back and forth. The sounds she made were deliciously obscene. Without pausing or slowing her pace, she reached out and took hold of his hands, placing them tightly on her scalp. Rajesh interlocked his fingers and pulled her head firmly towards him, simultaneously thrusting his hips back and forth to match the tempo of her greedy mouth – a lovely, wet mouth dripping with saliva. He quickened his thrusts and could feel his rock-hard shaft ready to explode. His grip tightened. He gave one final push and emptied his come into her mouth. Immediately he relaxed, unlocking his fingers.

Bav licked away the last remains of his salty eruption. She swallowed, exaggerating the sound. "Mmm, that was nice." She then turned away and took a large swig of orange juice.

As she stood up, she could see Rajesh was lost for words. She smiled matter-of-factly. "I'm going to take a shower. I know you'll come looking for me real soon. I'm sure that the radar in your pants will drag you here. Call me later, and then you can take care of me in the same way."

He was so overwhelmed that all he could manage was "What the fuck happened last night?"

"Shush, babe. Let's talk later. Right now you've got to get back to your world and deal with those missed calls."

Fuck! He'd completely forgotten about the calls! Fine example he was setting to the office. It was now almost 1.15 p.m. Half the day was over! Before he could think of anything clever to say, Bav made her way to the bathroom and locked the door behind her. He took that as a cue to exit. After scrambling around to gather the remains of his clothes, he dressed in a mad dash. He paused for a second when he heard the bathroom door unlock and figured she wanted to wish him a more formal goodbye, but instead she simply tossed his shirt out of the half-opened door and slammed it shut again.

He grabbed his shirt and rushed out of the door, shouting, "Bye!"

Outside the house, the midday sun hit him right between the eyes. He buttoned up his shirt as he ran to his car; he then got in and reached into his pocket for his mobile. He needed to phone Tanya, and fast. *No, no,* he thought. *Better to drive back the office first, grab a cup of coffee, get my head straight, and then give her a call. Women and hangovers don't mix.*

As soon as he arrived, Patel fell on him like a vulture. A host of problems needed his attention: a shipment of mobile phones had arrived from China without the proper paperwork, two of the company's articulated lorries had been targeted by illegal immigrants and were being held in Calais by French immigration officials, a delegation from HMRC were on the premises carrying out a security check on the bonded warehouse, and if that wasn't enough, an irate customer was prowling around in reception, demanding to know where his consignment of cigarettes had got to.

Rajesh's head was in a spin. There was a lot more to running a company than simply sitting behind a desk looking important. As Patel reeled off the list of problems, he couldn't help noticing

Rajesh's unkempt appearance: his crumpled suit, the stale odour of booze and perfume, the love bite on his neck, his haunted, bloodshot eyes. *So he's been out on the tiles again, has he?* thought Patel. *Very nice, I must say, while his poor father lies crippled at home.* Each time Patel put a question to him, he was met with a blank stare.

"Please, Sir-ji, we must sort these things out."

"Um?" answered Rajesh, staring at the floor.

"What should I deal with first?"

Rajesh's mobile rang. He looked at the screen: "Tanya". *Shit!*

"Sir-ji?"

It was all too much for Rajesh. He had a splitting headache, and it was getting worse by the second. He snapped. "Oh, *you* sort it out, J. P.! That's what I pay you for!" He grabbed Patel by the arm and marched him to the door. "Now if you don't mind, I'd like a little privacy. And tell Margaret to send in some coffee – hot and black!"

He closed the door collapsed onto a chair. A million thoughts churned inside his head. His phone rang again: "Tanya".

"Hi, TanJa. How are you, babe?"

"Rajesh, where have you been? I've been trying to get hold of you."

The sound of her voice cut through his hangover like a scythe. My God, this woman was carrying his child! She deserved better. And besides, it wouldn't be too long until her pregnancy began to show. He needed to act fast. Suddenly he blurted out, "Listen, Tanya … let's get married."

Both families agreed that the sooner the wedding took place, the better. It was decided a civil ceremony would best suit the hurried nature of the occasion. Not that Tanya's family had any say in the matter; it was Satish Thakral, dethroned and helpless in his wheelchair – though still the driving force of the family – who reluctantly gave his blessing. Privately he was far from happy his only son was marrying a gold-digger, but what could he do? The young make mistakes and the old end up paying for them.

Sitting in his wheelchair whilst staring out over the garden, Satish seethed with indignation that his family had been unable to arrange a traditional Hindu wedding. But that's what happens when little gold-diggers from Southall trick their way into a family. As for Tanya, she could hardly complain. After all, her family were poor and unable to provide a dowry, let alone contribute to the cost. And besides, after the wedding she would be living in the Thakral household in Gerrards Cross. She had met Satish on a couple of occasions in the past – a Thakral family barbecue, a Boxing Day party – and had found him both aloof and arrogant. She decided not to rock the boat.

The happy day would take place in four weeks' time, in the middle of September. Rajesh's mother threw herself into the preparations. There was so much to do – invitations to send out, caterers to be hired, a venue to be booked – the list was endless. Secretly Vidya was thrilled; not only was her beloved son finally settling down, but her days were also filled with tasks that were a lot more exciting than doing housework. She felt alive again, in touch with the outside world. The only cloud on the horizon was Rajesh. He seemed ill at ease and bored with the whole process.

One morning, a week into the planning, Vidya was serving him breakfast. She suddenly noticed how tired he looked – dark circles around his eyes, a faint pallor to his skin, a slight trembling of his hands. She put it down to his newfound responsibility of running the family business. Her heart went out to him. He'd hardly been home during the past week. Poor boy – all those late nights at the office were beginning to take their toll.

She poured his favourite morning tipple – a mixture of freshly squeezed orange and carrot juice. Putting her hand on his shoulder, she said, "You are working too hard, Rajesh. Don't think I haven't noticed. Slow down."

Her gentle voice broke into his thoughts. He'd been mulling over a number of apartments he was due to visit that morning. Determined never to stay at Bav's scruffy bedsit in Holloway again, he had decided to purchase their very own love nest – somewhere classy and discreet where he could fuck the living daylights out of her.

Rajesh looked up at Vidya and smiled. "Don't worry, Maa. I can handle it."

It was the first time she had seen him smile in weeks. She gave his shoulder an affectionate squeeze. "Good. Now what do you think about this?" She handed him a glossy brochure with a front cover that featured a stately home. "Galton Hall. It's not far from here. It would make a perfect location for your wedding."

Not the wedding again! He gave the brochure a cursory glance. "Looks nice, yeah."

"Should I book it?"

"Whatever you think."

"It is not what I think, Rajesh. You will have to show Tanya. Both of you need to decide. When are you seeing her next?"

"Er, I'm meeting her for lunch today."

"Good. Then take the brochure along and show her. Also, could you ask her—"

His mobile rang. He glanced at the screen: "Regan". He jumped up from the table. "Sorry, Maa, gotta go. Business." So as not to hurt her feelings, he downed the glass of juice in one go and gave her a kiss. "Oh, by the way, I won't be home tonight."

"I hardly ever see you these days."

"Busy, busy. Have to meet a client in central London for dinner. I'll grab a hotel. See you tomorrow." He walked briskly to the door.

"Rajesh?"

He turned to see his mother holding out the stately home brochure. "Sorry, Maa. Don't know where my head is these days."

As he took the brochure, she held on to his hand and stared into his eyes. "Be gentle with her."

"Who?"

His answer took Vidya by surprise and set the alarm bells ringing. "Who? Tanya, of course."

Rajesh felt himself blush crimson. "Oh! Yeah! Course I will, Maa. Love you." Once outside the house, he was quick to answer his mobile. "Uncle Joe! What can I do for you?"

A chirpy cockney accent filled his ear. "It's what I can do for you, son. Yeah. I'm 'avin a bit of a bash at the house a week on Saturday. Wondered if you'd like to come over?"

"Sounds great. I'd love to."

"Nice one. By the by, Mark Shearsbe's on his way over to see you. He'll fillyou in on the details. You out with Bav again tonight?"

Was the man a mind reader? "Yeah, think so."

"Lavvly. Give her one for me."

"Will do, Uncle Joe."

"And feel free to pop into the club."

Rajesh ended the call and hurriedly scrolled to Mark

Shearsbe's number. He had a couple of apartments to see, and the last thing he wanted was Shearsbe hanging about at the office Patel would only try and ingratiate himself whilst giving him the third degree. As he pressed Dial and ran towards his Boxter, he noticed his father staring at him through the window. This pleased Rajesh to no end. With the phone welded to his ear, it looked as though he were rushed off his feet for the betterment of S. T. Freights. He gave his father a quick wave and jumped into his Porsche.

"Hi, Mark. It's Rajesh. I believe you're coming over to see me?"

"Morning, Rajesh. Yeah."

"Is there any chance you can make it around eleven thirty? I've got a few things I need to sort out first."

"Not a problem. See you then."

One problem sorted, one more to sort out – Tanya. He set the phone to Hands Free and accelerated out of the drive. It was a beautiful morning. A fine mist rolled across the fields, pierced here and there by shafts of sunlight. Rajesh slammed the Boxter into third as he sped along the country lanes, narrowly avoiding a tractor that suddenly emerged from a farm gate. *Bloody yokels!* "Morning, TanJa," he said seconds later. "How's my favourite girl?"

The softness of her voice told him his charm offensive had hit the mark. "I'm not feeling too good. This morning sickness is getting me down. God knows how long it will last."

Rajesh grabbed the opportunity to avoid lunch. "Aww. Sorry to hear that, babes. Listen, if you'd rather not meet up later, I—"

"No, no. We have so much to discuss – the wedding and everything. Besides, I *want* to see you … I miss you."

She sounded upset. Those hormones must be kicking in. His sister had warned him about this. According to Neelam, a woman's body during the early stages of pregnancy was volcano of emotion, with tears and tantrums only moments away. "Be gentle with her," his mother had said. And *he* had been thinking about *Bav!* He was becoming obsessed. "Hey, don't cry, Tans. Of course we'll meet. We'll have a nice lunch and talk about whatever you want."

"Thanks for being so understanding. I love you."

"Love you too, babes. Later."

The first of three apartments he was meant to view that morning was located north of the river, in Pimlico. It was a one-bedroom apartment on the fifth floor of a modern development. Light and spacious, it had a balcony and gated parking. What Rajesh liked about it most was the mirrored wardrobes in the bedroom. Whilst the estate agent gave him the blurb, he imagined lying on the bed, fucking Bav and marvelling at their reflection. Live porn. He agreed to buy the apartment there and then. He had a good feeling about the place. Bav would be delighted.

The paperwork took longer than expected. He was desperate to get into the office before eleven thirty, before Shearsbe arrived. He was late. *Why am I always late?* he wondered.

He made his way out of the city. The traffic was light. Pulling into the car park at S. T. Freights, he glanced at his watch: 11.22 p.m. *Made it!*

As he strolled into the outer office, he noticed his PA Margaret hard at work. "Get us a coffee, will you, Marg." He had shortened her name purposely, determined to be different from his autocratic father.

Margaret seemed to like the new regime. She smiled and said, "Of course, Rajesh."

"Cheers. Oh, and when Mark Shearsbe arrives, send him straight in, would you."

"He's already here."

Rajesh stopped dead in his tracks. "Say again?"

Margaret stared at him over her thick-rimmed spectacles. "Mr Shearsbe. He arrived, ooh, about half an hour ago. Don't worry; Mr Patel is looking after him." Margaret must have noticed the look of thunder on Rajesh's face. "Is everything all right?"

Rajesh ignored her and hurried towards his office. No, everything was not all right! *What is Shearsbe playing at? I told him to be here at eleven thirty! And now Patel's poking his nose in!* As he grabbed the door handle, he heard the sound of two men laughing. Rajesh burst into his office to find Shearsbe and Patel sharing a joke.

The instant Patel clapped eyes on Rajesh, he gathered up a tea tray. "Good morning, Sir-ji. I was just leaving."

"Good," said Rajesh abruptly.

Mark Shearsbe got to his feet. "Your man here's been telling me about his grandmother. Apparently she lives with him. Can't stop farting, by all accounts. Why you Asians don't stash your grannies in old people's homes like we do I'll never know." He shook Rajesh's hand. "Good to see you, Raj. Sorry I'm early. I was in the area and thought, 'What the hell.'"

Once Patel had left the office, Rajesh calmed down. "That's all right. I see you've had tea."

"Yes, yes. Your man sorted me out. Not a bad number two. Very helpful."

"A bit nosey for his own good sometimes, but he does know the business back to front," said Rajesh, sitting down behind the desk. "What can I do for you, Mark?"

"I wondered if you fancied some lunch. I'm meeting a few guys from the city at Sketch. Have you ever eaten there?"

"No, no. I hear it's fantastic. And very expensive."

"Two hundred pounds for a main course; just a tad. Glad I'm not paying. The boss has an account there and told me to help myself."

Rajesh smiled. He couldn't help but admire Shearsbe's couldn't-care-less attitude. Whereas *he* was wracked with guilt every time Regan did him a favour, Shearsbe simply lapped it up, taking advantage of everything that came his way. *Why can't I be more like that?* "I'm very tempted, Mark."

"What's stopping you?"

The Devil was on his shoulder, willing him to accept. "No, I can't. I'm having lunch with my fiancée." *Damn! Shouldn't have said that!*

Shearsbe's nerdy features lit up. "What? You're getting *married!* To *Bav*?"

"No, no! God no!" Rajesh hesitated. "It's a long story." *What the hell, Mark's a nice guy.* "I've been seeing this girl for years. We're childhood sweethearts. To cut a long story short, she got pregnant and I'm doing the decent thing."

A cynical grin spread across Mark's face. "You Asians and your family honour. Dear me! I'd have given the girl five hundred quid and told her to get rid of it. Does Bav know about this?"

"Not yet."

"Shit, Raj! You've got everything going for yourself at the moment – you're well in with Regan, you've got yourself a shit-hot girlfriend in Bav, you've just taken over the family business – what do you want to get married for? The world's your oyster!"

Shearsbe was right, and Rajesh knew it. He felt like a fool; a sucker. He stared hard at the desk, lost for words. Eventually he looked up and shrugged. "I guess I'm trapped."

Shearsbe saw how hurt he was. He decided not to push it. "Listen, mate, if there's anything I can do to help, just ask. I mean it; you're a nice guy."

Rajesh was touched. "Thanks, Mark. Appreciate that." He paused. "There is something ... Don't let on to Bav. I'll tell her when I'm ready."

"No problem. When are you getting married?"

"In three weeks."

"Three weeks! Talk about a shotgun wedding!"

* * *

The Boxter's engine growled angrily, mirroring Rajesh's mood. Anchored to the tarmac along Uxbridge Road, he was waiting for a gaggle of school kids to vacate the zebra crossing. As he drove over to Southall, he kept replaying the conversation with

Shearsbe. "Shit, Raj! You've got everything going for yourself at the moment; what do you want to get married for? The world's your oyster!" He cringed as he recalled how he'd let his guard down: "I guess I'm trapped." He slammed the steering wheel in frustration, scolding himself. "Never do that again! Never show anyone your true feelings. What a fucking idiot!" A fat black kid stopped halfway across the zebra crossing to admire the Porsche, just like Rajesh used to do at his age. Normally Rajesh would have given him a friendly wink. Not today. He blasted the horn. "Fuck are you looking at! Shift your arse!"

Shocked, the black kid scurried away. Rajesh shook his head and drove off. Two minutes later he pulled up outside Tanya's house half an hour late. He beeped his horn as usual, letting her know he'd arrived. Tanya opened the front door and came rushing down the path. She was smiling. That was unusual.

She opened the passenger door and leaned in. "Mum's at home. Do you want to come in and say hello?"

I see, thought Rajesh. *A few weeks ago I was persona non grata: "Idiot! The big deal is, good little Indian girls shouldn't be dating naughty little Indian boys, however rich they are." Now all of a sudden I'm flavour of the month!* "No, thanks," said Rajesh. "We're late already."

Tanya was hurt but didn't show it. She got in and flung her arms around him. "It's lovely to see you. I've missed you so much."

Rajesh gave her a quick peck on the cheek and started the engine. "I thought we'd go to Madhu's."

"After what happened last time? Say Mac sees your car?"

"I don't give a shit." The way he felt at that moment, he would have welcomed a confrontation with Mac. Who knows, maybe Mac and his troops would give him a good beating and put him in hospital. That would stop the wedding.

Inside Madhu's, Rajesh found it hard to concentrate.

Tanya told him about how delighted her colleagues at the law firm were about her forthcoming wedding. "Of course they're all sorry I'm giving up my career – especially my mentor, Neil Acherson, who's been really nice to me – but—" She noticed Rajesh was fiddling with his napkin and had a faraway look in his eye. Tanya shook her head. "You're not interested, are you?"

"Hmm?"

"The fact that I'm giving up my career! You're not even interested in the wedding!"

Rajesh snapped out of his lethargy. "Of course I am, babes." Hurriedly he fished into his pocket and brought out the Galton Hall brochure. Good old Maa! He unfolded it and laid it on the table in front of her. "See! I've been looking at venues all morning; that's why I was late. This is the best one so far."

Tanya was pleasantly surprised. She flicked through the brochure. The place was perfect – beautifully appointed Georgian staterooms, superbly manicured grounds. Idyllic. She slid her hand guiltily across the table and interlocked his fingers with hers. "It's stunning, Rajesh."

"Thought you'd like it. Took a look at the place this morning. It's five-star. I'll book it if you like. Plus, and here's the big surprise, I've decided to book the Hilton on Park Lane for the reception."

She leaned across that table and kissed him on the lips. "You think of everything."

Not quite. He'd yet to contact Bav to arrange tonight's shenanigans. He couldn't wait to tell her about the apartment. He smiled as he imagined the ultra-special blow job she would give him.

"What?" asked Tanya.

"Sorry?"

"You're smiling?"

"Oh, I was just thinking how lucky I am."

* * *

Rajesh exploded in her mouth, the entire length of his cock tingling. Bav stuck out her cupped tongue to show him the puddle of warm semen. Like a cat lapping cream, she closed her mouth and greedily swallowed, accentuating the sound for erotic effect. Rajesh stared mesmerised at her undulating throat, imagining his salty come slipping down like melted wax. Through curtained hair he could see her big brown eyes dilating with pleasure. *Dirty bitch.*

"I can't wait to move in," said Bav, on her knees wiping her mouth with a tissue. "No more hotels."

Rajesh was so overcome with pleasure he had to sit down on the bed. "Yeah, we'll be able to lie in all morning without being disturbed."

They were staying in a boutique hotel just off the King's Road. It was 7.30 p.m. They began to get dressed. They had a table booked for eight at the Ivy. Bav had suggested eating there. "It's full of all the right people. You never know who you're going to meet." She also had another suggestion. Watching Rajesh pull on his pink Ralph Lauren shirt and silvery grey trousers, she said, "I'd love to take you clothes shopping."

Rajesh narrowed his eyes, his pride clearly dented. "Nothing wrong with the way I dress!"

She was quick to smooth things over. "I'm not saying there is, baby." She paused whilst slipping on her bra, the sound of lace caressing her flawless brown skin. "I mean, you look really sexy and everything, but—"

"But what?"

"Well, you're mixing with a whole new level of people now. Look at Mark Shearsbe. Look how he dresses – Savile Row suits; dark, serious colours. I can't stand the guy, but he really does look the business. Most of the big shots in Rouge dress like that. Serious clothes for serious people." She noticed him looking crestfallen. "All I'm saying is, baby, I don't want people treating you like some playboy. There's a lot more to you than that."

Rajesh digested her words. He turned and looked at himself in the full-length mirror. *Hmm. "Serious clothes for serious people."*

He did look as though he'd just stepped off a yacht in the south of France.

As they walked into the Ivy, Bav's words hit home. Rajesh glanced at the men dotted around the restaurant; they were power-dressed in mute colours – Armani, Hugo Boss. Suddenly he felt ill at ease, as though it were his first day at school. The same thing happened when he entered Rouge later that evening. He'd never taken much notice of what the men were wearing before; he was too busy ogling the scantily clad bimbos and semi-naked hostesses. But now he saw for himself the refined couture, the bespoke suits and tailored accessories.

Standing at the bar, he said to Bav, "How about you and I go shopping tomorrow?"

Bav understood immediately. She took hold of his hand and gave it a squeeze.

A blonde hostess came over. "Excuse me, Mr Thakral. Mr Regan insists you join him at his table."

Rajesh looked over towards the VIP section and saw Regan waving at him though a sea of faces. Though he wanted to spend time with Bav, he knew he couldn't refuse. As they approached Regan's booth, he got up and bustled forward, taking Rajesh by the arm.

"You sit down, Bav. I just need a quick word with his nibs here."

Bav slipped into the booth. Regan took Rajesh through an exit curtain and down a long corridor. At the end was a green leather door.

"Thought you'd like to see my office," said Regan. He opened the door onto a windowless room dominated by an antique desk, a semi-circular bar, and a huge flat-screen TV. "The inner sanctum." The walls were decorated with flock wallpaper replete with black-and-white photographs of boxing legends – Ali, DiMaggio, Frazer. "Drink?"

Rajesh contrasted the cheap gold frames with the expensive desk. He also noticed that not one note of the pounding, thumping music inside the club permeated the room. For some reason the advertising slogan for the film *Alien* sprang to mind: "In space no one can hear you scream."

"Er, vodka and tonic, please, Uncle Joe."

"Bollocks! We're celebrating!"

"Celebrating?"

Delving into a glass cabinet that held pictures of Regan with B-list celebrities and boxing has-beens, he produced a bottle of premium, single-malt forty-year-old Macallan. He unscrewed the top and smirked. "You're a dark horse, you, kid."

Rajesh suddenly felt ill at ease. Surely Regan hadn't found out about him buying the apartment in Pimlico already! "Sorry, Uncle Joe, I—"

"Shearsbe told me you're getting married."

"Oh, yes! Yeah!"

"Why didn't you let on?"

"It's only just been arranged."

"Shotgun wedding. Yeah, I heard. Sure you know what you're doing?"

"I'm stepping up to the plate."

"Nice to hear it, son. That's what I like about you; you're different from most of the toerags these days. Takes character, owning up to your responsibilities. Nice girl, is she?"

"The best." He paused, his conscience gnawing at him like a ravenous wolf. "Sound like a hypocrite, don't I, carrying on with Bav?"

Regan popped open the cork and filled two champagne flutes. "Not at all, not at all. Had tons of mistresses down the years myself; nothing wrong with that. Men of power have always had 'em. Perks of the job. Well, you need to let off steam, don't you? It's only right." He handed Rajesh a fizzing glass and sat behind his desk. "Cheers. Sit down; I'm gonna give you some advice." Rajesh took a seat opposite Regan on a brown leather sofa. He felt a presidential-style address coming on, though what he heard would scarcely have been broadcast from the White House. "You see, Rajesh, Joe Public out there hasn't got a fucking clue; they live dull, miserable lives – paying their taxes on time, always sticking to the rules. Stupid bunch of cunts. But we're not like that, you and I. We take what we want, when we want. Hard work? Fuck that; that's for other people. So don't go worrying yourself about being a hypocrite, 'cos you're not. Remember, morals are for morons. It's survival of the fittest, son, and the fittest need their pleasures."

It could have been the rush of champagne, but Rajesh suddenly felt his conscience fade into the background to be replaced by an overwhelming self-confidence. "Thanks, Uncle Joe. I needed that." He was so carried away with the moment that he added, "And you will come to the wedding, won't you?"

"That's very kind of you, son. It'll be my pleasure. Before all that, there's my party to enjoy. Eh! I've just had a thought! We'll double it up as your stag do!"

"Fantastic! Can I bring Bav?"

"Bring who the fuck you want. There'll be loads of women there." Regan got up and slipped on his jacket. "Right, I'm off up the West End. Bit of business to take care of. You go and enjoy yourself."

As he made his way back into the club, Rajesh was met by an excited Shearsbe. He pointed to three smartly dressed middle-aged businessmen sitting in a private booth sipping chilled white wine. "See those guys over there? They're partners in a Swiss telecom business – mobile phones, that sort of thing. They're looking for a distribution company in the UK, so I told them about S. T. Freights. Do you want to meet them?"

"Yeah! Great!"

"Very impressive, Sir-ji. Your father will be so pleased."

"D'you think so, J. P.?"

"Oh yes. Sole distribution? Very impressive."

"It's not a done deal yet. They still have to check the place out first."

"Then you have nothing to worry about. Our facilities are the finest in the UK."

Rajesh was sitting at his desk, Patel hovering over his left shoulder. They were looking at a glossy marketing brochure for Élan Électronique that Rajesh had acquired previous night.

"If you don't mind me asking, Sir-ji, how did such a prestigious company come to your attention?"

"You've heard of them, then?"

"Oh yes."

"By networking in all the best places. It might look as though I don't do much around here, but while you're tucked up at home with your family, I'm out working, damned hard. Gone are the days of sitting in the office like Dad. You have to get out there and make things happen."

"Very impressive."

Patel was beginning to get on Rajesh's nerves with his repeating himself. But Rajesh would need his expertise when the Swiss clients paid him a visit, so he offered him a carrot. "Let me be straight with you, J. P. I'm looking to take this company forward. I want us to expand globally. Dad didn't have the guts to do it, but I'm in charge now. What I'm trying to say is, I'd like to take you along for the ride."

Patel's podgy face broke into a simpering smile, his head rocking from side to side like a metronome. "Oh, Sir-ji. You don't know how happy that makes me feel. When you first took over from your esteemed father, I was certain you would give me the sack. Thank you, Sir-ji. Thank you."

Rajesh hated grovelling of any kind. "All right, J. P., enough of that. Back to work. The Swiss guys should be arriving at two. I'll give you a shout when they get here."

At precisely two o'clock, Margaret buzzed the intercom. "The gentlemen from Élan Électronique are here to see you."

Rajesh looked at his watch and grinned. Typical Swiss, their timing, as ever, was perfect. *Must be in their genes.* "Thanks, Marg. Show them in, would you." He suddenly felt nervous. It was, after all, his first major deal. If he could pull it off, then maybe the desk he was sitting behind wouldn't feel so big. The door opened and he got to his feet. *"Bonjour Monsieurs."* Shearsbe had advised him to speak a few words of the lingo. Apparently they appreciate the gesture. "Come in, come in. Find us okay?"

The oldest of the three, Christophe Autueil – a slim, distinguished man with dark, wavy hair flecked with grey – thrust out his hand. "Why yes. It was not a problem." He spoke perfect English with just a hint of a French accent, the kind women swoon over. "I must say, Mr Thakral—"

"Rajesh, please."

"I must say, Rajesh, from the little we have seen of your company, it looks extremely impressive." He paused and quickly scanned the office. "You met my business partners last night – Roger and Daniel."

"Of course. Nice to see you again." Rajesh shook hands with the two younger men. All three were dressed in immaculate dark-blue suits – Roger's with just a hint of pinstripe. Bav was spot on. "Would you like a coffee or anything?"

"Oh no, thank you. We have a plane to catch at six thirty. We would very much appreciate a tour of your facilities."

"Yeah, yeah. No problem. Time is money, after all. Just a sec." He picked up the phone and called Patel's office. "Jainti Bhai, meet me outside the main office right now, would you. The guys from Élan Électronique are here."

"Very good, *Sir-ji."*

Rajesh led them out into the car park. It was a blustery day; the clouds were scudding across the sky. Luckily the Swiss had come at a busy time; trucks were roaring in and out of the main gate.

Straight away Christophe began to fire questions at him. "What sort of volume do you run at?"

Rajesh had no idea what he was talking about. "Volume? We're full most of the time."

Christophe smirked. "Er, no. I mean, percentage-wise, what is the balance between goods imported and goods exported, not forgetting those awaiting clearance in the bonded warehouse?"

Rajesh was out of his depth; if only he'd taken more notice when Patel was explaining about the business. And where the fuck was he? The bastard was always there when he wasn't needed! "Er ..." All three faces stared at Rajesh anxiously.

"The, er ... the volume ... er ... let me see." Suddenly Patel came rushing out of the building. *Thank fuck for that!* "My assistant here has all the latest figures. I'm only aware of last month's, which are probably of no use to you at all."

Rajesh introduced Patel, and they began their tour of the complex. On their way over to the bonded warehouse, which the Swiss were anxious to see, Rajesh pulled Patel to one side. "Where the fuck were you!? Don't ever leave me waiting with clients like that again!"

"Sorry, Sir-ji, I was—"

"I don't want to hear it! Just come when I call next time!"

"Yes, Sir-ji."

The bonded warehouse was a two-story steel structure

featuring a state-of-the-art security system approved by HM Revenue and Customs. As soon as they entered its massive reinforced doors, Rajesh could tell his Swiss clients were impressed. Stacked against the walls from floor to ceiling were steel pallets packed with goods of all descriptions, from alcohol to cigarettes to electrical equipment. Between the pallets, forklift trucks buzzed around loading and unloading.

The Swiss formed a huddle and spoke to one another in French. Unfortunately for Rajesh his grasp of the language only stretched to saying hello and ordering a beer. Nevertheless, he could tell the men looked pleased.

"If I could just ask a question," said Christophe, after a minute or so perusing the building.

Rajesh nodded. "Anything. Anything you like. Shoot."

"Do you provide BTI facilities for your customers?"

Rajesh froze. "BTI? BTI? Er, let me think. Do you mean British—"

Patel was quick to interject. "We have always provided binding tariff information. That is one of the things which set S. T. Freights apart from our competitors."

"Certainly is!" said Rajesh, nodding furiously. "It's what sets us apart. Definitely."

"Excellent, excellent," said an enthused Christophe. He paused and glanced at his two colleagues, who in turn smiled and gave him a nod. "Well, Rajesh, I think we can safely say your facilities are just what we are looking for. I congratulate you."

"Great. If you'd like to come to my office, we can sort out the paperwork."

Rajesh led them out of the bonded warehouse and back towards the main office. Buoyed by his first major deal, he nevertheless still felt irked that Patel had twice saved his blushes. He saw a chance to regain his authority – two forklift truck drivers were standing around idly chatting. He shouted so loudly Christophe and his colleagues almost jumped out of their skin. "What the *fuck* are you two playing at! Eh? Get back to work, you lazy bastards!" Satisfied, Rajesh winked at Christophe. "I like to show them who's boss."

After the contract was signed – for the importing and storage of seventy thousand mobile phones prior to distribution – Rajesh toasted the deal with champagne. When the Swiss had left to catch their plane, he raised his glass to Patel. "Well done, Jainti. Listen, in future, I want you to show any new clients around. Got that?"

"Very good, Sir-ji."

Rajesh couldn't wait to ring his father and tell him the good news. Lounging back in Satish's chair, feet on the desk, he was cockiness personified. "Hi, Dad. Just pulled off a major deal – a *major* deal. I said I'd make you proud, and I will."

Satish was delighted. Touchingly he slurred his congratulations down the phone. Rajesh felt ten feet tall. It was the first time in years his father had spoken to him with such warmth. He rang Bav immediately. "Hiya, sexy. I've had a brilliant day. Fancy a bottle of bubbly before going shopping?"

He met Bav in Hush, an exclusive cocktail bar on Brook Street, Mayfair. Bav suggested meeting there because the owner was Roger Moore's son and she knew how much Rajesh liked anything associated with James Bond. After downing a bottle of Krug, they made their way around Knightsbridge's most exclusive shops. They started off in Emporio Armani, where under Bav's expert eye, Rajesh bought three suits from the Collezioni range – one dark blue, one black, one a deep indigo with a faint pinstripe – each made from 100 per cent wool and costing a tad under fifteen hundred pounds. The jackets were single breasted with a two-button fastening, two slash pockets, and a high-class silk lining.

"Oh yes," said Bav as he tried on the last of the suits. "They look great on you."

Admiring himself in the mirror, Rajesh had to agree. Gone was the playboy stepping off the yacht. Now a man of power and influence stared back. And the mute colours really did suit him, making him appear more thoughtful and, thrillingly, more intimidating. He could now swan in to any of London's most fashionable establishments and feel at ease.

They visited several more shops, buying shirts, trousers, cashmere sweaters, ties, brogues – a whole new wardrobe for twelve and a half grand. *Worth every penny,* thought Rajesh. After loading up the Porsche, he gave Bav a quick peck on the cheek.

"What's that for?" she asked.

He gestured to the bags of shopping. "For helping me with my new look."

A cheeky grin lit up her beautiful face. "I've not finished yet."

"What do you mean?"

She glanced at his dark, wavy hair that infringed upon his collar in wavelike tufts. "Do you trust me?"

"Yeah, course I do."

"Come on then."

She led him a short distance along Knightsbridge and turned left into Trevor Street. Halfway down they stopped outside Bennett's, a trendy men's hair salon.

"You want me to have my hair cut?" asked Rajesh nervously.

Bav grabbed his arm. "It's the finishing touch. Trust me."

It took a lot of trust for Rajesh to sit quietly in the barber's chair whilst his locks were shorn and sculptured by Dale, a stick-thin homosexual who flirted with him outrageously. He watched impassively as the sides of his head were shaved Beckham-like, the back given the same treatment.

"All the guys are wearing it this way," said Dale. "You look a million dollars."

"Oh wow!" said Bav, standing behind him as Dale removed the white sheet and dusted his neck with a soft brush. "You look like a young Al Pacino."

"He *does!*" squealed Dale.

Rajesh was astonished. A hard edge had been added to his handsome boyish features. The effect was both charming and menacing, like some evil dandy. He was delighted. Coupled with his new wardrobe, he felt like a butterfly emerging from a cocoon. A feeling more powerful than any cocaine high swept over him. He was ready to take on the world.

An hour later Rajesh was sitting opposite Bav in La Gavroche. They had just ordered starters and were enjoying their first sip from a bottle of

Rajesh decided to come clean. "I need to tell you something, Bav. There's no easy way of saying this. I'm getting married." He saw her flinch. "Believe me, if there was a way out, I'd take it."

"When?"

"Three weeks."

He waited for the explosion of female scorn. None came. Instead she looked up at him calmly and said, "Do you want to finish with me?"

"Of course not, baby!" He was amazed at her reaction; if it had been Tanya she would have slapped his face and drenched him in Margaux. "You and I are good together. No way I'm giving you up."

She grabbed his hand. "Do you mean it?"

"Every word."

Tears welled up in her eyes. "Let's not bother eating. Let's go to a hotel."

He called the waiter over and settled the bill. On their way out, his mobile rang. He looked at the screen: "Home". His heart sank. "I'm gonna have to answer this." He dived into the Gents. "Hello?"

It was his mother. She sounded anxious. "Sorry to bother you at work, Rajesh, but you need to come home. It's your father; he's not feeling well. He's making some awful noises."

Rajesh shook his head in frustration and was about to say "Why don't you call the doctor?" when his mother burst out crying. "Okay, Mum. Keep calm. I'm on my way."

He dashed out of the Gents and slipped Bav a fifty-pound note. "Sorry, babes, you'll have to get a cab home. My dad's had a relapse."

As he pulled into the drive, Rajesh saw the family GP exit the front door and walk towards his car. He screeched to a halt beside him. "Hi, doc. What's happened? Is my dad okay?"

Doctor Campbell, a rotund Scotsman in his early sixties with chalk-white hair and bushy side whiskers, leant into the car, a concerned looked etched across his bloodshot face. "Aye, just aboot. The poor man had a seizure, but he's pulled round noo."

"Is it serious? What caused it?"

"Stress, son. Stress. He'll be fine so long as he doesn't get any shocks. Plenty of peace and quiet is all he needs."

Rajesh breathed a sigh of relief. "Thanks, Doctor Campbell."

"Nae problem, son. Nae problem. He's a fine man, your father. Take care of him, won't yea?"

"I will."

Rajesh got out of his car. He noticed his sister's car was parked on the drive. Before opening the front door, he glanced at his watch; plenty of time to drive back into central London and meet up with Bav. He imagined slipping off her bra and sucking those gorgeous coffee-coloured nipples. No, he was home now. He had to do his duty. When he opened the door, he saw Neelam walking up the stairs carrying a glass of water.

She turned to see who it was. "Oh my God! Look at your hair! I hardly recognise you!"

"Never mind about that," he said. "How's Dad?"

"A lot better now … Oh my God! Mum will have a fit when she sees you!"

He rushed past her on the stairs. "Grow up."

Slowly opening the door to the master bedroom, he saw his mother leaning over the bed, wiping his father's forehead with a cloth. Satish was propped up on two pillows, his face partially covered by an oxygen mask. His laboured breathing was a sign all was not well.

Rajesh moved towards the bed. "Hi, Maa. How's Dad?"

When his mother saw him, her initial smile was replaced by a look of shock. "Oh, betta … your beautiful hair." The look of anger on her son's face told her not to pursue the matter. She took hold of his hand. "I am so glad you are home. Bless you for rushing back."

"What happened? Dad sounded fine when I rang him earlier."

"He was. He was so pleased when you told him about the new contract. Then, later on, when we were discussing Tanya moving in, he …" Oh dear. She had let the cat out of the bag. She tried desperately to backtrack. "It wasn't just that … He-he has a lot of things on his mind. He feels so frustrated, sitting all day in his wheelchair. Oh, betta, I have no idea what caused it."

Rajesh knew what had caused it, but his sympathy at that moment lay with his mother. Poor woman. All her life she had played the peacemaker, getting flak from both sides, forever in the line of fire. He felt so sorry for her. "Shush, *Maa*. It's just one of those things. At least he's still with us."

"Yes," said Vidya, her eyes moist with tears. "Thanks be to God."

Suddenly there was movement on the bed. Satish had opened his eyes and was gesturing at Rajesh.

Vidya got to her feet. "I'll leave you two alone. Can I get you anything, Satish?"

"Ek chai!"

Rajesh winced at his father's abruptness. Vidya smiled and left the room.

Rajesh sat on the bed, holding his father's hand. "How are you, Dad?"

"Better for seeing you." His whispered voice through the oxygen mask sounded harsh, alien-like. Slowly, using his other hand, he pulled the mask from his face. "That's better … Doctor

Campbell insists I wear it … He is a good man, but he reeks of whisky … You would think he would know better, being a doctor."

Rajesh grinned. His father was still his old judgemental self. "Yes, I smelt it on his breath when I spoke to him just now."

Satish looked at him warmly. "I'm … I'm so proud of what you did today. You have to understand, betta, the business … the business means everything. It would kill me if anything happened to it."

Rajesh felt his father's grip tighten. "I know, Dad. I know."

"Please … please take care of it for me."

"I will, Dad. Don't worry."

9

Regan's party couldn't come soon enough for Rajesh. For over a week he had played the dutiful son, setting off for work early, getting back in good time to sit with his father, and praying with his mother in the mandir. He even had the odd civilised chat with Neelam. Consequently he saw nothing of Bav, who purposely kept a low profile. It was her way, she said, of giving him space, though in reality she knew her forced absence would only inflame his passion. She promised him a "night to remember" when they next met, which would be at Regan's party in three days' time. To tease him further she sent him some sexy photos of herself on his iPhone – coquettishly dressed in brand-new lingerie, breasts thrust forward, legs wide apart, her tongue peeking from her lips. "This is all yours," she was saying. "You can have me every night once we're in our new apartment."

It did the trick. Within seconds of seeing the photos, Rajesh rang the estate agents to find out when he could pick up the keys. They told him it would take just a couple of weeks. He couldn't wait. Then there was Tanya. Luckily, because she was so busy with her own personal arrangements for the wedding – buying a dress, sorting out the bridesmaids – they hadn't seen one another since their lunch at Madhu's. Only once did she ask to meet him. The law firm she worked for was throwing her a leaving party. None of the girls in chambers had seen Rajesh, so she was keen to show him off. The firm – Standish and Grove – was situated on Chancery Lane, close to Lincoln's Inn. When he turned up dressed in a dark pinstripe suit with his hair slicked back, Tanya hardly recognised him. She had to admit, though, that his new image really suited him. She basked in the reaction of her female colleagues, who were breathless in their praise.

One thing that did concern Tanya was his behaviour – instead of the usual flirtatious, fun-loving Rajesh, she now witnessed a more subdued, condescending side of his nature, one she hadn't seen before. Nothing seemed to please him; the white wine was too warm, the canapés too boring. In fact "boring" was a word she heard a lot from him that afternoon. Midway through the party, she introduced him to Neil Acherson, QC, her mentor and head of chambers. Rajesh took an instant dislike to him. He hated intellectuals – especially tall, good-looking ones. Neil was in his fifties and had breezed through Oxford and gone on to become one of the country's youngest criminal barristers. His supreme inner confidence, his modesty, his impeccable manners – everything about the man frightened Rajesh to the core. He was living proof that there was more to being a success than simply looking the part.

"Well, you're a very lucky man," said Neil, in his refined, cut-glass-class accent. "Tanya's a lovely girl; we're all dreadfully sorry to see her go." He looked at Tanya. "I don't suppose you'll change your mind?"

"No," said Rajesh rudely. "No wife of mine needs to work."

* * *

As a respite from family commitments, Rajesh spent his lunchtimes in the company of Mark Shearsbe. The two had become close friends since the Swiss deal; the phones had been delivered, and S. T. Freights were creaming in a nice profit. Rajesh admired Mark's business brain, especially when it came to the import–export business. Mark had an amazing list of contacts, and he was generous enough to share them. The day before Regan's party, Rajesh decided it was time he took advantage of

Shearsbe's talents. They were dining in Nobu, courtesy of Regan, when he came up with the suggestion.

"Listen, Mark. I want to put a proposition to you."

Shearsbe dabbed his mouth delicately with a napkin. "Sure, go ahead."

"Well, you can say no if you like; I know how busy you are and everything, but I'd like to offer you a consultancy role within S. T. Freights. Nothing major, just pop into the office a couple of times a week. You've been really helpful, and I want to make it worth your while. Believe me, Mark, you'd be doing me a favour. I've run it past Patel, and he thinks it's a great idea; in fact, it *was* his idea. So what do you say?"

Shearsbe thought for a moment. "Well, I'm flattered. Really flattered. Yes, I don't see why not."

Rajesh was thrilled. "Fantastic, Mark! Welcome to S. T. Freights. Waiter! Bring us a bottle of Remy Martin Louis XIII cognac."

The waiter duly obliged. With all the pomp and ceremony befitting a drink costing £120 a glass, he brought over the heart-shaped bottle made of baccarat crystal. It sat on a silken cushion inside a red leather box with a gold hinge.

Shearsbe was impressed. "You're pushing the boat out."

"Why not," said Rajesh. "You only live once."

* * *

"Don't put the fucking thing there, you silly cunt! The guests need to use the garden!"

It was the afternoon of the party, and Regan was standing in his spacious conservatory, giving a local DJ a dressing-down for blocking access to the French windows with his turntables.

"Sorry, Mr Regan. I'll move it right away."

"Yeah, you do that … Pillock."

He left the conservatory and went into the kitchen to supervise the catering staff. Over a dozen people were busy unloading boxes and preparing food for the night's festivities. He ran his eye over the operation. *Very efficient. Mind you, I'm paying 'em enough.*

Regan needed the night to go well and was unusually tense. After years of feuding he had finally made peace with a rival firm. The party was being thrown to welcome them back into the fold – let bygones be bygones, with no hard feelings. The Clayton family were Scots Irish who ran their West London manor with an iron fist, controlling drugs, gambling, and prostitution. Theirs was a fraction of the size of Regan's operation; nevertheless, over recent years they had become a thorn in his side. Regan could have wiped them out as easily as crushing a fly, but he didn't. An expert strategist, he decided a gang war would only drag in the police and make life difficult for everyone. As Don Corleone famously said in *The Godfather: Part II,* "Keep your friends close, but your enemies closer."

There was one more thing to check on before he could enjoy a long, pre-party soak in the Jacuzzi. He strolled out into the garden and phoned Rouge. "Danny? It's the boss. Just checkin' the girls are sorted for tonight? Lavvly. And listen, I only want the best. No dogs, understand? Very important. And make sure the Charlie's top notch ... I don't know, at least a kilo."

Rajesh put on his dark blue Armani suit, maroon-coloured shirt and lead-grey tie. The tie had a tiny geometric pattern and was a present from Bav. After spraying a liberal amount of Tom Ford aftershave – Tuscan leather – he slipped on a pair of black brogues. One final look in the mirror told him all he needed to know: slick and sophisticated, with a hint of the night. Exiting his walk-in wardrobe, he cringed as he passed row upon row of brightly coloured shirts hung on the rail. He flicked off the strip light as though extinguishing a bad memory. He grabbed his mobile off the dressing table and texted Bav: "C u in half an hour. Can't wait! **XX.**" As he was about to drop the mobile into his inside pocket, he thought he'd better text Tanya, just to keep her sweet: "Missing you.x."

Before leaving, he went to his father's bedroom to say goodnight. Upon opening the door, he found Satish propped up in bed asleep. This once proud lion of a man, whose merest footstep used to strike fear into him, was now a ghost of his former self. The sight reminded Rajesh of a visit he'd made to India when he was young. One day his uncle took him into the forest, where they came across a former maharaja's palace, crumbling and covered in vines. Even at that young age he was struck by the poignancy of such magnificent grandeur gone to wrack and ruin. Rajesh closed the door upon his father and shuddered. Desperate to escape the confines of the house, he rushed outside and jumped into his Porsche. He needed bright lights and excitement. Life was for living after all. He inserted a CD: *How you Like Me Now?* by The Heavy. Turning up the volume, he stabbed the accelerator and set off towards central London.

He pulled up outside Bav's seedy bedsit. A flash of curtain upstairs told him she was on her way down. But nothing could have prepared him for the sight that met his eyes. Emerging from the tattered front door was a vision of erotic beauty. She had somehow managed to pour herself into a gold mini dress. It had a deep-plunging neckline, sexy ruched bodice, and delicately laced-up sides. Absolutely nothing was left to the imagination. Her partially bare breasts seemed to float freely whilst the sparkling hemline swung lightly over her long, glistening, freshly waxed honey-coloured legs. Rajesh's jaw fell open. When she climbed into the car and said "Hi, baby!" and pecked him on the cheek, his senses were overpowered with the distilled essence of body oil, perfume, and hair lacquer; whilst mixed in, hardly noticeable, he detected her musky, fundamental core. As his hands caressed her bare back, he felt his cock stiffen. He wanted to flip the passenger seat down and fuck her there and then.

Managing to resist the urge, he drove out of London and headed into the Essex countryside.

"You look beautiful," said Rajesh. "Every guy at the party will want you."

"Well they can't have me. I'm yours."

Bav glanced out of the car window. With each passing mile, the houses increased in size. She couldn't believe the opulence, the overwhelming sense of wealth. As they flashed past one stunning, cream-coloured mansion, she caught a glimpse of a woman climbing into a black Bentley. She had served wealthy people in Rouge, watched as they snorted coke and cavorted on the dance floor; so this was how they lived, was it? "What's Mr Regan's house like?"

"Wait and see."

Bav didn't have long to wait. The car turned into a narrow lane, skirted a leylandii hedge, and came to a halt in front of a pair of massive, gold-tipped wrought-iron gates. They were manned by two of Regan's burly, shaven-headed henchmen dressed in black suits. Cool as you like, Rajesh gave them a wave, and they opened the gates. Like the entrance to some medieval castle, the driveway was lined with flaming torches. Bav felt her stomach churn with excitement. "Oh, wow."

Rajesh smiled. "Wait till you see the house. It's amazing. I'm gonna have a place like this one day." Bav put her hand on his inner thigh and stroked the outline of his cock. They rounded the final bend. "Check this out." The driveway suddenly opened up, and there was the house, floodlit and surrounded by luxury cars. "Now that's what I'm talking about."

"Oh my God!" exclaimed Bav. "Look at all the cars! And look at that fountain! It's like something out of Ancient Rome!"

Caesar himself was standing at the front door, greeting a crowd of guests. When he saw Rajesh getting out of the car, he crunched across the gravel to meet him. Arms outstretched, he wrapped him in a bear hug. "Raj! Great to see ya, son!"

"Hi, Uncle Joe. Thanks for inviting me."

"Pleasure, son, pleasure. Fuck me, who's this?"

"Bav."

Regan drank in her cascading curls and voluptuous body tinselled in gold. "What, Bav? The girl from the club? Really? Fuck me, darlin', I hardly recognised you. You look stunnin', sweetheart, stunnin'."

"Thanks, Mr Regan."

"Right, you two." He linked them both and marched them towards the house. "Let's go inside and have some fun. That's an order."

Walking into the hall was like walking onto the set of TOWIE. Groups of meat-headed men in Hugo Boss and Paul Smith stood around drinking champagne with their glitzy girlfriends. Spray-tanned to perfection, they were dressed in a kaleidoscope of outfits – long white Grecian gowns, polka-dot dresses, micro skirts revealing a slice of ass – each girl brazen with big hair, fake boobs, and false nails. They teetered across the floor on skyscraper heels, carrying their sex like nitroglycerine. Loud, raucous laughter and high-pitched squeals filled the air. Rajesh noticed Teddy the bulldog, coked up to the eyeballs, standing in the corner with his rowdy friends. Teddy caught sight of him and raised his glass. Rajesh was thrilled. He knew that once Teddy accepted you, you were well in.

"The bar's through there," said Regan, pointing to the conservatory. "Help yourselves. There's enough Charlie to sink the Titanic, so don't hold back."

As Bav moved towards the door, Regan tugged Rajesh's sleeve. "There's someone I want you to meet." Right on cue, a Jordan lookalike sashayed over. She was blonde, about twenty years old, wearing a sparkly silver mini skirt and low cut T-shirt, the outline of her nipples pushing through. "This is Karen. Karen, meet Rajesh."

Karen giggled. "Hi, Rajesh. Mad 'er, innit."

"Hi, Karen."

Regan sent her away with a brusque "Go and get us a drink, Kas'. I wanna talk to Rajesh." He watched her sexy arse disappear into the crowd of guests. "Listen, son, she's yours for the night.

Sex-mad, she is. Do anythin'. Take her upstairs and fuck her brains out if you like."

"That's very kind of you, Uncle Joe. I really appreciate it, but if you don't mind, I'm happy with Bav tonight."

He raised an eyebrow curiously, noticing in a split second that Rajesh's new confidence and attire were probably down to Bav. "Oh ... please yourself. Come and see me later. I've got something for you."

Rajesh walked into the conservatory. He was met by a wall of sound. The disco was in full swing, a mirror ball showering the dance floor with coins of light. He caught up with Bav at the bar. "Sorry about that. Regan wanted a word."

"That's okay. You're a busy guy."

Bav was so understanding. He kissed her on the cheek and grabbed one of the many glasses of bubbly lined up along the bar like soldiers on parade. "Let's go somewhere quiet. I can't hear myself think."

They left the madness of the conservatory and found solace in the lounge. The enormous room had a domed ceiling and was furnished with white leather sofas, pink marble coffee tables, and an array of gilded mirrors set above antique bureaus inlaid with ivory. Dotted here and there were small bronze art nouveau statues of naked women juxtaposed with busts of Roman emperors. Like his office at Rouge, it was a mixture of ancient and modern. Clearly Regan didn't know which century he preferred. *Balls, let's have it all!* Rajesh thought it bad taste. Bav, on the other hand, revelled in the opulence. She loved the way her feet sank into the deep shag pile carpet, so different from the bare linoleum back in Holloway. What Rajesh did like was the symbolic nature of the room. Here was someone who exuded power, not taste, and he wanted people to know it.

It was quieter in here; just a few couples were sitting around having drinks. One of them was Mark Shearsbe and a busty female in her early twenties. He was on his knees, about to snort a line of coke off the marble coffee table, when he saw Rajesh. "Raj! Mate! Come and join us!"

"Do we have to?" whispered Bav. "I can't stand him."

"Mark's a great guy. Come on; it'll be fun."

They made their way over and sat down. Rajesh eyed Shearsbe's date for the night. She was small, blonde, and bubbly. Cannon fodder for rich boys.

Mark did the introductions. "This is Donna. Donna, this is Raj and Bav."

"Hiya."

"Coke, anyone?"

"No thanks, Mark." said Rajesh. "I'm okay with champagne."

"Bav?"

"Ooh! Don't mind if I do."

"Ladies first."

Bav and Donna knelt down either end of the long line of coke. They each hoovered up a large portion, their pretty faces meeting in the middle. As they did so, Donna winked at Bav. It was a come-on if ever there was one.

Bav smiled and sank back onto the sofa, rubbing her top gum with her forefinger.

"Sure you won't have some, Raj?" asked Shearsbe, chopping up a fresh line with his gold Amex. "Things are going to get pretty wild."

He wasn't wrong. Boozed up and drug fuelled, soon most of the couples in the room began to lose their inhibitions. French kissing turned to fumbling and heavy petting, and within the hour the party descended into a full-blown orgy. Rajesh watched goggled-eyed as a petite brunette in the far corner gave her muscular black boyfriend a blow job. The guy was heavily tattooed and had a diamond in his tooth. He lay there like some fabulous sultan, his legs spread apart and his right hand resting on her head, bobbing it gently up and down as though bouncing a basketball. The lights were dimmed. Moans. Grunts. The unmistakeable slapping sound of fucking.

Bav stared at Rajesh. Without taking her eyes off him, she put her hand on his groin. Leaning in close, she smiled coyly, flicking her tongue in his ear. "Someone's got a hard cock. Fuck me."

Shearsbe, who was sitting opposite, fondling Donna's enormous breasts, must have heard, because he looked over and winked at Rajesh. Rajesh smiled back. He was desperate to fuck Bav. But not here. Not in front of everyone. He was a show-off, but not that much of a show-off. He needed privacy to really enjoy himself. He remembered Regan inviting him to use one of the bedrooms to fuck that Jordan lookalike, Karen. He stood up and gave a nervous cough, "Excuse us." He took Bav by the hand and led her out of the room.

Holding hands, they crossed the hall and climbed the sweeping staircase, stepping gingerly over semi-naked couples overwhelmed with passion. Like exhausted salmon, they had failed to make it to the spawning grounds of the bedrooms. After opening several doors along the landing, Rajesh eventually found a vacant room. It had a big four-poster bed, its plump duvet scattered with cushions.

Bav fell to her knees and began to loosen his belt frantically. "You want me, don't you? Say you want me." She was wild, her hair covering her face like a banshee.

"I want you. Fuck yeah, I want you."

She undid his trousers and let them fall to the floor. "What are you going to do to me?"

"I'm gonna fuck you inside out. Cover every inch of you in come."

Slowly, she inched his Armani shorts down. She then took his stiff cock in her hand and began to wank it slowly, rippling and unrippiling his foreskin. "You're very hard, aren't you? Fuck me, you're rock hard." Kneeling closer, she let slip the straps of her dress to reveal her voluptuous naked breasts. Cupping them in both hands, she smothered them over his cock, wanking it back and forth, her erect nipples like pincers. "Mmm, that's nice, baby." She tongued the tip of his cock maddeningly before enveloping it in her soft, wet mouth. Bav realised that a week from today, precisely, Rajesh would be on his wedding night. No way would that bitch be able to match this. His groans of pleasure cemented the fact. Something extra special was needed to weld him to her, to keep him coming back for more in the weeks and months ahead.

As if to answer her prayers, the door inched open and Donna poked her head in. "Hiya. Mind if I join you?"

Shocked, Rajesh looked down at Bav, who was frozen in mid-suck. It was too much to ask, wasn't it? He'd always dreamt of having a threesome. Surely Bav wouldn't agree. Surely. Expecting her to politely decline, he was amazed when she carried on sucking him and said, "Mmm. Why not."

Oh my God! His Christmases had come all at once!

Donna strolled in and began to undress. "Mark sent me. He said he wants you to enjoy your last week of freedom." She removed her bra and knickers, casting them onto the floor. Her body was amazing: petite, curvaceous, her huge breasts standing proud like fleshy mountains, a tuft of blonde hair surrounding her wet, moist mound. She stood next to Bav, seductively caressing the top of her head. "Let me help you with that."

Bav got to her feet. Rajesh gazed up at their perfect naked bodies – porcelain and honey. They were facing one another, their breasts millimetres apart. Donna reached out and stroked Bav's hair. "You're beautiful. Let's give this guy a night to remember."

Please, Bav, thought Rajesh, *please don't freak out.* Talk about positive thinking! To his gobsmacking amazement, Bav grinned cutely and kissed Donna on the lips. Donna put her hands on Bav's breasts, kneading them roughly, caressing her nipples with both thumbs. She then sucked each one until they stood erect. Rajesh had never felt so turned on in his life. Donna knelt down in front of him. She swished her hair back and forth, looked at his cock, and winked. "Now, what have we got here?"

His cock was so hard it felt as though it were made of steel. She took him in her mouth, rolling her tongue around the end of his shaft. He gasped as though diving into cold water.

Bav walked behind him and folded her arms around his chest. He could feel her nipples against his back, her soft pubic down shimmering against the cheeks of his arse. She whispered seductively, asking, "Is that nice, baby?"

His mouth was dry, but he managed to answer. "Fucking gorgeous, yeah."

"Good. I really want you to enjoy yourself."

He was enjoying himself all right! Keeping one eye on Donna, he watched as Bav got onto the bed and spread her legs.

Donna noticed too. She took one long, lingering suck and slowly released his cock with a soft pop, a strand of saliva connecting them like a bridge across a gorge. She looked over at Bav, who was fingering herself. "Mmm, time for some brown sugar." She got up, took Rajesh's hand, and led him over to the bed. "Wait there for a second."

Rajesh obeyed. He could do little else. He was a zombie, a mindless android controlled by two other beings. If they'd have asked to him to stand on one leg and bark like a dog, he would have done it.

Donna slid onto the bed. First she caressed Bav's thighs, peppering them with kisses. She slowly worked her way up until she reached her destination; she then pushed her face between Bav's legs. Now it was Bav's turn to gasp. Like sampling an exotic delicacy, Donna began tonguing Bav's wet c, licking up and down and side to side. Bav closed her eyes and moaned. Donna stuck her peach-like arse up in the air. She slapped it hard and looked round at Rajesh as though issuing a challenge. "What are you waiting for?" A red mark appeared, like a bullseye.

Surely this was a dream. Rajesh didn't wait to find out. He climbed onto the bed, took his cock in his hand, and entered Donna from the back. Her warm, moist juice enveloped his shaft like liquid velvet as he thrust deeper and deeper inside her. She sighed as he began pounding away, slowly at first, then harder and more aggressively, his groin throbbing against her gorgeous firm white arse. She placed both hands on the bed sheet to steady herself. He noticed her freshly lacquered nails, purple with gold stars, obviously the latest must-have in the nail salons of Essex.

"Oh yeah! Fuck me, yeah!"

"Fuck her, baby!" shouted Bav in encouragement.

From his position above, he could see the sweep of Donna's back, whilst beneath her, writhing around on the bed, Bav was massaging her own breasts as Donna feasted on her pussy. All three were in ecstasy, a sort of erotic trance. He pounded harder and harder until Donna let out an orgasmic scream. Bav soon followed, yelping and arching her back. Mesmerised, Rajesh carried on fucking, his thighs battering into her. Donna slid her hand under him and cupped his balls, rolling them in her palm like dice. Unable to hold out any longer, he closed his eyes and came, a rush of crimson light flooding his brain. He slammed into her one final time, shuddered, and then collapsed triumphantly onto the bed.

"Oh wow!" said Rajesh, panting. "That was amazing."

Donna gave him a kiss. "My pleasure, sweetheart."

Both women lay on either side of him, covered in sweat. Like a decadent rock star surrounded by groupies, Rajesh slid his right arm across Bav's shoulder and cuddled her. She had her eyes closed, panting. Wanting to share in the moment, Donna snuggled up to him, resting her head on his shoulders and wrapping herself in his left arm. Bav opened her eyes and saw Rajesh stroking Donna's back. Fired with jealousy, she reached over and tugged his left arm free; she then wrapped both his arms firmly around her. Sensing a territorial threat, Donna lay there staring at the wall. She could hear Bav whispering and giggling in his ear. Losing patience Donna finally got up off the bed. She grabbed her clothes and began to get dressed, keeping her eyes on Rajesh, hoping he would invite her back into bed.

Bav glanced at Donna and read her mind. Smothering Rajesh in kisses, she pulled his head towards her and buried his face in her breasts. Realising she was beaten, Donna left the room angrily, slamming the bedroom door.

Rajesh sat up. “What's wrong with Donna?”

Bav shook her head contemptuously. “God knows ... Silly cow.”

He collapsed back onto the bed, his mind reeling with sexual imagery. “Did that just happen?”

She snuggled up to him and giggled naughtily. “I think so.”

He stared at the ceiling, his manhood somehow compromised. “I didn't know you liked women.”

“I don't. I did it for you.”

He propped himself up on one elbow and stared at her lovingly. “Really? You did that for me?”

“Well, when Donna walked in and I saw your face, I knew that's what you wanted. I'll always give you what you want.”

Rajesh enveloped her in a hug. “Oh, baby, nobody's ever said that to me before.”

After getting dressed they went downstairs to rejoin the party. Most of the guests were in the dining room, helping themselves to food; their sexual exploits had made them ravenous. Regan had surpassed himself by offering his guests a gourmet buffet laid out on several tables. The high-class caterers served up a variety of cuisines, from Italian to French to Japanese. Rajesh was about to help himself to a plate of sushi when he felt a tug on shoulder. It was Regan, glass of scotch in hand, beaming from ear to ear. He had just left a meeting with the head of the Clayton family. The meeting had gone well, and he was in a good mood. He'd managed to persuade Frank Clayton not to expand his territory further west. It was a masterstroke of diplomacy – a threat wrapped up in an offer: behave yourself and you'll get a bigger slice of the action.

“Enjoying the party, Rajesh?”

Yes, Uncle Joe. Fantastic.”

"Lavvly." He tipped back his scotch. "Come with me, I'm about to make it even better."

They pushed their way through a throng of partygoers and walked outside. It was a warm, still night; billions of stars glittered above their heads like mica.

Regan led him across the drive towards one of the double garages. "Just think, this time next week you'll be a married man."

"Don't remind me," said Rajesh, his head still full of images of his recent ménage à trois. That Bav, she certainly knew how to please a man.

Regan keyed in the code. The garage door swung upwards. A host of strip lights flickered on automatically. Rajesh took in the rows of supercars gleaming in the artificial light. He shook his head at the sheer wonderment of it all. In the centre of the garage was a mystery – one of the cars was covered in a white dust sheet. Rajesh tried to guess the make by the shape, but he couldn't. It was low and fierce looking, like a slumbering tiger.

Regan smiled. He walked over to the mystery car and patted the roof. "Got this delivered today. Brand spanking new. Call it a wedding present from me to you."

"What?"

Regan took hold of the dust sheet. Like a slick magician – *hey presto!* – he tugged it clear to reveal a pristine, pillar-box red Ferrari 458 Italia, its sleek lines and sculptured body an awesome example of cutting-edge design.

Rajesh's jaw fell open. "Do you mean ..."

Regan threw him the keys. "It's yours, son. Enjoy."

"Oh my ... On my *God!*" He walked over to the car as though in a trance, running his hands over the bodywork. The upward sweep above the rear wheels was so reminiscent of Donna's arse it almost gave him a hard-on. "Really, Uncle Joe? It's mine? No joke?"

"It's yours! Fuck me, how many more times!" Rajesh threw

his arms around him. "Steady on, son, don't want people getting the wrong idea."

Rajesh let go and they both burst out laughing. It was too much. He'd just fulfilled a three-in-a-bed fantasy and now this. Life couldn't get any better. A few weeks ago he might have questioned such an act of generosity. Not now. Shearsbe had taught him to take whatever came his way and not feel guilty about it. He jumped into the car and started the engine; the aggressive, throaty roar of the 4,498cc V8 filled the garage. He buzzed down the window, beaming at Regan. "Fucking unbelievable!" He stared at the space-age dashboard and imagined cruising around London, the epitome of twenty-first century excess.

Tanya adjusted the veil of her wedding dress and gazed at her refection in the full-length mirror. Made from silk organza, it was a strapless fishtail gown with a soft, pleated bodice and heavily embellished diamante-beaded belt. Although Rajesh had told her to spend whatever she liked – the designer boutique she had purchased it from was one of the most expensive in Chelsea – Tanya had gone for the simplest, most refined dress. She hated anything showy or over-the-top. Despite that, it still cost £3,850.

"Can we come in yet?" asked her sister Joti, waiting impatiently with her mother outside the bedroom door.

"Just a minute!" She took a deep breath and looked at herself once more. It was an odd moment, there, in the silence of her bedroom. She had the feeling she was looking at a stranger. This person was about to leave her childhood home, get married, and move in with a new family in Gerrards Cross. She placed her hand on her stomach; luckily any sign of the pregnancy was hidden beneath the carefully crafted silk couture. Tanya turned sideways and checked her profile, just to make sure. "Okay. You can come in now."

Her sister and her mother entered the room reverently. Both were dressed in long traditional saris – Joti's a peach colour with gold trimming, her mother's an emerald green with silver brocade.

Joti took one look and her big sister and gasped. "Oh Tanya! You look beautiful!"

Tanya turned to face her mother. "Well, *Maataji,* what do you think?"

Hard work and constant worry had aged Tanya's mother. Fifty-five going on seventy, Kaylash was small and thin with a shrunken, heavily lined face the colour of tea-stained parchment. She shook her head in amazement, tears spilling down her rutted cheeks. "Oh darling, I wish your father was alive to see you now."

"I'm sure he's looking down on us, Maa," said Joti.

A male voice sounded from downstairs. "The car is here!"

There was no turning back now. Tanya peeped through the curtains to see a vintage Rolls Royce bedecked with pink ribbons ease to a halt outside the house. "Look at the car! Look what Rajesh has sent for me!" She sighed with relief, convinced he would send a bad-taste stretch limo. Behind the Rolls was a luxury coach containing Tanya's relatives.

When her mother had left the room, Joti took Tanya's hand. "Don't get mad, but I've got to ask: you're sure you want to go through with this? You can still change your mind, you know."

"I love him, Joti."

"That's all that matters. Now let's go."

Tanya picked her way carefully down the stairs with Joti following close behind, holding the train. Waiting for her in the hall was Uncle Sunil, her deceased father's older brother, a large portly man in his sixties dressed in a morning suit. Sunil had come to England with her father back in the seventies. When her father died, Sunil had taken over his fatherly duties, which included walking Tanya down the aisle.

When he saw her, his chubby face broke into a smile. "Oh my. What a ray of sunshine." He opened the front door and took her by the arm. "Your carriage awaits."

They walked outside. Tanya was suddenly overwhelmed by a wave of sadness; she realised she was leaving her childhood home for the last time. Of course she could visit as often as she liked, but she could no longer call it home. Despite living in a rundown area, she still held a grudging affection for the place. All the neighbours were out in the street to get a good look, some of them surrounding the car. There were gasps of admiration for the blushing bride. The chauffer opened the passenger door. Sunil and Tanya pushed their way through the crowd and got in.

Sunil smoothed down the creases of her dress. "All set?"

Tanya nodded.

* * *

"How you feeling, bro?"

Rajesh stared through the tinted limousine window, the English countryside rushing past. He felt his life slowly unravelling. "Don't ask."

Jazz knew what to do. He leaned forward and took a bottle of vodka from the limo's mini bar. "Drink?"

"No thanks."

"Come on, it'll do you good."

"Go on, then."

Rajesh unscrewed the top and tipped a generous helping of vodka into his mouth. He let out a long sigh. It was two thirty, and he was on his way to Galton Hall. The main reception was to be held at the Hilton Hotel on Park Lane later that evening. Only close family from both sides – about 130 people – had been invited to the actual ceremony. Both Rajesh and Jazz were dressed in morning suits – light grey waistcoats, a white carnation in each lapel. *More like a mourning suit,* Rajesh had thought whilst getting dressed earlier in the day. He glanced behind him at the fleet of limousines carrying his relatives. Determined to arrive Oscar style, he'd hired fifteen stretch limos. Like a presidential motorcade they purred one behind the other along the country lanes.

"Thanks for asking me to be your best man. I'm honoured, bro. I've not seen you for weeks; thought you might have chosen someone else."

"Come off it, Jazz. You were always going to be my best man." That was a lie; Rajesh had given serious thought to asking Mark Shearsbe. In the end he decided against it; too many nosey parkers at the wedding asking who the white guy was no one had seen before.

"At least the weather's fine," said Jazz, after a long, uncomfortable pause – one of many that morning. "Might have been pissing it down."

"There is that." So, their lifelong friendship had come to this – discussing the weather. The reason for all those silences was obvious: Tanya. Jazz hated her and would rather talk about anything than mention her name.

"How's life at S. T. Freights?"

Now it was Rajesh's turn to clam up. He was light years ahead of his old friend now – new business, new friends – so there was no point in giving him the low-down. Jazz belonged to the past, like those colourful shirts he used to wear. "Oh, you know. Good days and bad days." His mobile beeped. He fished it out of his pocket and looked at the screen. It was from Bav: "Thinkin of you.xx."

"Who was that?"

"No one you know." Bit rude, that. He was an old mate after all. "Just someone from work wishing me good luck."

Jazz was about to say, "You're gonna need it, bro," but thought better of it.

The limousines swept through a picturesque village. The locals were dumbstruck by the sight of so many luxury cars; obviously a rock star or A-lister was getting married at the hall. After half a mile the cars slowed down and turned right through an enormous stone arch. After clattering over a cattle grid, they headed down a long driveway bordered by mature oaks. Between the trees, a large herd of deer stood spread out across the rolling parkland. As they crested the brow of a hill, they got their first view of the house, a palatial Georgian mansion built of Portland stone.

"Check it out!" exclaimed Jazz.

Rajesh stared at him like a man possessed. "Have you got the ring? Have you got the ring?"

"For fuck's sake, bro!" He delved into his top pocket and brought out a small red leather box chased with gold lettering that read "Cartier". "Look! That's the tenth time you've asked!"

He opened it to reveal a large diamond set in gold and surrounded by sapphires – Tanya's birthstone. A nice touch, that. She had yet to see the ring, and Rajesh was sure she'd be bowled over. So she should be; it had cost a small fortune.

Up to this point Satish – travelling in the second limo with his wife, daughter, and son-in-law, Ajit (a useless drip of a dentist in his early forties) – was sitting quietly in the back, not saying much. But when the car pulled up outside the hall and he caught sight of Tanya's family – the Rasis – waiting to greet them, he almost had another seizure. Appalled at their cheap clothes and excitable manner, he shook his head and said, "Look at the state of them! Scum of the earth!" He couldn't believe his son was marrying into such a family.

Ajit, keen to keep in with the old man – after all, he might pop off anytime and leave something nice in his will – tutted loudly, agreeing. "Riff-raff!"

They all headed inside, Satish manoeuvring himself along in his brand-new electric wheelchair. The reception hall was light and airy with a marble chequerboard floor and rich stucco plasterwork featuring swags and medallions. Portraits of the Galton family hung from the walls. Satish stared at this glorious dynasty, the finely honed cheekbones and haughty demeanour, imagining that one day his own family might reach such dizzying social heights. Not much chance of that, judging by the poor quality of the Rai gene pool.

It wasn't the friendliest of starts. Instead of greeting one another in the traditional Indian manner – both families mixing happily together whilst acknowledging the fact that the bride's family are about to hand over their daughter – the Thakrals and

Rais eyed one another suspiciously; the former looking down their noses at their soon-to-be poor relations, the latter frightened out of their wits by such an ostentatious arrival and salubrious surroundings. Staring down at them from the frescoed ceiling was a drunken Bacchus lounging on a bed of vines, a sardonic grin on his face as if to suggest the utter folly of human existence.

It was Rajesh's mother who made the first move. She walked over to Tanya's mother and said, "How is the bride? Is she looking forward to getting married?"

Kaylash, unused to mixing in such well-heeled circles, stuttered. "Y-yes, Mrs Thakral. She is up—"

"Please, Kaylash, I have I told you many times, call me Vidya."

"Yes, Vidya. She is upstairs waiting for the call."

Luckily the awkward atmosphere was broken by the opening of a pair of panelled doors and the registrar announcing, "Would you like to come this way."

Both families trooped into the drawing room. Rows of chairs had been set up on either side of a makeshift aisle – Thakrals on one side, Rais on the other. At the far end of the room was an arbour festooned with roses. Rajesh and Jazz walked to the front whilst the guests took their seats. A string quartet struck up. All the guests craned their necks to get a view of the bride. Rajesh and Jazz stood to attention. As the first strains of the "Bridal Chorus" rang out, Rajesh glanced behind him. His heart skipped a beat. Walking towards him was a vision in white; his Tanya, the girl he had fallen in love with all those years ago. He remembered the first time he saw her; she was running down the corridor at primary school. A teacher shouted at her to slow down, but she stuck her tongue out and ran off laughing. She was wilful and independent even then.

Tanya arrived at his side holding a bouquet of white lilies. Uncle Sunil nodded and stood to her left. Rajesh peered through the veil at her lovely elfin face. She smiled at him adoringly, her brown eyes sparkling beneath the embroidered lace.

He leant towards her and said, "You look gorgeous."

She lowered her head modestly. He loved her for that – the fact that she didn't realise how beautiful she was.

The registrar smiled benevolently and led them through their vows. In the deathly quiet room, Rajesh made a terrible mistake. When asked to repeat, "I, Rajeh Thakral, take thee, Tanya Rai, to be my lawfully wedded wife," for some reason he came out with "I, Rajesh Thakral, take thee, Tanya Rai, to be my lawfully wedded knife."

Knife? A sharp intake of breath was heard amongst the guests. Tanya looked askance at Rajesh. The registrar's eyes popped. Only Jazz found it amusing, his stern features betraying the hint of a smile.

Rajesh wanted the ground to open up. He felt the eyes of the room drill into the back of his head. "Wife," he added quickly. "Wife."

The faux pas was soon forgotten when Rajesh took the ring from Jazz and slipped it onto Tanya's finger. She was taken aback by the sheer size of the stone, as well as the beautiful way its multifaceted surface glinted in the afternoon sunlight streaming in through the sash windows. Uncle Sunil's jaw dropped open as he imagined how much the thing had cost, whilst Kaylash couldn't get over the size of the rock. Neelam was filled with jealousy, staring at her own pinprick of a diamond and inwardly cursing her useless husband and his one-horse dental practice. Even Satish tied himself up in knots as he tried to work out the value of the bauble. His only solace was the fact that S. T. Freights must be doing well in order for his son to have been so foolhardy.

Smiling, the registrar announced the couple were now man and wife. As Rajesh lifted Tanya's veil and gave her a kiss, the room filled with spontaneous applause. Rajesh looked round to see his mother dabbing her cheeks with a handkerchief. Satish, on the other hand, stared blankly at the floor.

After toasting the happy couple with champagne brought into

the room on sliver trays, everyone made their way outside. The Rais, climbing aboard their luxury coach for the journey back into London, were far from happy with the situation. They had starved themselves all morning in expectation of a feast, only to be told it was now taking place miles away.

When Rajesh and Tanya got into the vintage Rolls, she threw her arms around him. "I'm so happy, Rajesh. The ceremony was beautiful. You look so handsome in your suit. I can't believe we're married."

Neither could Rajesh. For some reason the euphoria of the service had evaporated, leaving behind in him an empty feeling. The person holding his hand was now his wife – Mrs Thakral. She was pregnant with his child. A few months ago he wouldn't have thought it possible. He couldn't get over the sensation that an invisible ball and chain had been attached to him during the ceremony. He began to panic. It was as if he were standing on a sinking ship and all the lifeboats had departed. He suddenly felt claustrophobic.

He reached into the walnut mini bar, his eyes flashing, a manic smile on his face. "Let's have a drink ... to celebrate. Whisky? Vodka?"

Tanya snuggled up to him. "Nothing for me, thanks. I don't want to spoil the moment." Resting her head on his shoulder, she sighed gently, "My husband."

When the coach carrying the Rais drove along Park Lane and pulled up outside the Hilton, there were was a collective gasp of astonishment. Staring up at the iconic glass skyscraper, they all agreed that Tanya had done well for herself marrying into the Thakrals. They couldn't wait to get inside and start stuffing their faces. Speaking of the Thakrals, they had already arrived and were waiting in a large group outside reception. Filing off the coach, the Rais were met by the concierge, who led them over to their in-laws. Tradition dictated that men and women split into two groups before entering the venue.

"Ladies and gentlemen, ladies and gentlemen, could I have

your attention, please!" asked the concierge. A hush descended. "Thank you." He pointed to two separate lifts. "Now, in order to make your way up to the grand ballroom, would the men take the right lift and the ladies the left."

The grand ballroom! Kaylesh was convinced she was dreaming. An unseemly scrum developed as the attendees made their way towards the lifts; the Thakrals elbowing the Rais out of the way. The men began to enter in single file, Satish in his wheelchair first in the queue. The ladies weren't so lucky. Eager for their lift to descend, they had crammed themselves up against the door. When it arrived and the doors finally opened, they were confronted by a large group of Japanese tourists with luggage who spilled out, barging their way through the sari-wearing guests.

"Careful, please!" pleaded the concierge.

It was an hour before everyone had gathered in a spacious room just off the grand ballroom for cocktails and canapés. The number of guests had swelled to 550 – distant relations, friends, and work colleagues of both families. Such a high-class event was the perfect excuse to show off; some of the more wealthy guests arrived in flashy sports cars and limousines. Dressed in the latest designer outfits, they strutted around like peacocks. It was East meets West as Versace, Dolce and Gabanna, and Vivien Westwood rubbed shoulders with exquisite crystal-adorned saris replete with threaded gold patterns highlighted by necklaces of diamonds and rubies.

Amidst the dazzling maelstrom the Rais fell on the canapés like wolves, stuffing down mini chicken kebabs in yoghurt and lemon marinade, smoked spicy aubergine petit puris, asparagus tips in tamarind parcels, grilled tiger prawns in lime and garlic, skewers of cardamom-flavoured lamb kebabs, and lime trout on ajowan puri. The choice was as mindboggling as the food was was delicious. Kaylash and Uncle Sunil didn't know what to stuff in next. One canapé had hardly been swallowed before the next one was snatched off the tray and shoved in. Satish watched their antics from across the room, shaking his head in disgust. To think he was now related to this lot!

Meanwhile the new Mr and Mrs Thakral were settling into the honeymoon suite on the twentieth floor. They would join the rest of the guests just before the start of the wedding banquet.

"Look at the view!" said Tanya, staring out of the window across Hyde Park. "I can see Buckingham Palace!"

Rajesh was in the en suite dressing room. He had just showered and was changing into his sherwani, a traditional coat-like garment made of pure silk. Rajesh had chosen a creamy gold sherwani with a maharaja *angrakha*-style pattern decorated with intricate designs and a heavily embroidered collar, front panel, and cuffs, along with matching gold trousers. A pair of silk slippers completed the outfit. "Yeah," he said after getting dressed. "I tried to get us a room there, but they were full up." He heard her laugh. He took a swig of scotch, sat down on the chair, and began to text Bav: "Just been made an honest man. Can't wait to be dishonest with you.xx." He switched his phone off and joined his wife in the bedroom.

As he opened the door, Tanya was putting the finishing touches to her *lengha choli, a* traditional Indian bridal outfit. Placing her embroidered veil on the top of her head, she turned to face Rajesh. She was wrapped in butter-coloured silk decorated with vertical flora and heavily embellished using Swarovski crystals. Adorning her head was a silver *maangtika,* pearl earrings, and a gold nose ring, or *nath,* hooked up to her hair. Both her wrists and forearms were festooned with bangles. Around her neck she wore a fan-shaped necklace made of gold filigree dripping in yellow crystals specially designed to match both their outfits.

The sight of her took his breath away. "Look at you," he said eventually.

"Look at you," she answered, smiling.

Rajesh picked up his ebony swagger stick and they stood next to one another, admiring themselves in the mirror. Staring back at them was a sight that reminded Rajesh of some old photos he'd seen from the days of the Raj – a maharaja and maharani standing outside one of their many palaces, dressed in their finery, about to attend some colonial function; he the master of all he surveyed, she the dutiful and ever attentive wife. Suddenly the phone rang, breaking the spell.

Rajesh picked it up. "Hello? ... Okay. Okay." He put the receiver down and looked at Tanya. "They're ready for us."

Downstairs the master of ceremonies had finally got everyone's attention. "Ladies and gentlemen, if you'd like to take your seats in the grand ballroom."

A set of double doors was opened and the guests made their way inside. The sight that greeted them took their breath away. The room was a flickering fairyland of candlelit tables and glittering chandeliers, each table an oasis of crisp white linen bristling with silver. In the centre of every table was a crystal stand holding an array of plates, bowls, and glasses. The magnificent display was set off by a huge vase of purple orchids. The Rais had never seen anything like it, except of course in a Bollywood movie. At the far end of the room, looking out over the dance floor, stood the top table. After consulting the table planner, the attendees took their seats. Kaylash, Uncle Sunil, and Joti made their way to the top table along with Satish, Vidya, Neelam, Ajit, and Jazz.

When all the guests had quietened down, the master of ceremonies took to the floor. "Please be upstanding for the bride and groom."

Everyone got to their feet. The grand ballroom darkened, and a spotlight picked out Rajesh and Tanya framed in the doorway. To the strains of Shania Twain's "Looks like we made it", they entered holding hands. Clapping and cheering broke out as they walked amongst the guests towards the top table. Tanya could see her aunts and uncles beaming with pride. Rajesh looked every inch the proud husband, though one or two guests did notice he'd had quite a lot to drink.

Husband and wife took their seats. The master of ceremonies said, "Please be seated. Dinner is served."

The Rais were delighted, nodding and gesticulating at one another. At last, the main event! The Hilton swung into action. An army of waiters entered the room carrying trays of food. Wine waiters hovered and poured. Each table had its own dedicated waiter who oversaw the spectacular array of dishes. There was *Jhinga Kalimirch* (tiger prawns tossed with shallots, tomatoes, ground spices, and crushed peppercorns), *Tali Macchi* (pan-fried fillet of sea bass with fine beans and raw mango on a sauce of tomato with mustard, curry leaves, and coconut), lobster masala (diced lobster tail tossed with browned shallots, tomatoes, and spices, finished with crushed pink and black peppercorns) *Hyderabadi* shank (slow-cooked lamb shank with turmeric, yoghurt, browned garlic, and freshly ground spices), and *Gosht Dum Biryani* (boneless lamb with basmati rice, browned onions, herbs, rose water, ground spices, and saffron sealed with a pastry lid). Each dish was served with mountains of rice, *nams,* chapattis, and a host of chutneys, pickles, and dips. The Rais thought they had died and gone to heaven, such was the aroma of the food. But before anyone could tuck in, a very important ceremony had to take place; as dictated by tradition, the bride and groom had to place a morsel of food into each other's mouths, signifying they would share all their worldly goods from that moment on.

All eyes were on the top table. Rajesh and Tanya each picked up a small amount of food. As they were about to place it in each other's mouths, Rajesh's attention was suddenly drawn to the door. He saw the burly figure of Regan enter the room. To the shock of everyone present, Rajesh suddenly got up and rushed over to where Regan was standing, leaving Tanya open mouthed. She tired her best to hide it, but she was clearly upset. Vidya couldn't believe her son's behaviour, whilst Joti shook her head angrily. To save the family from being dishonoured any further, Satish picked up his food and began to eat, signalling to everyone to do the same.

Rajesh shook Regan warmly by the hand. "Uncle Joe! Thanks for coming. I'm really honoured."

"My pleasure, son. Wouldn't have missed it for the world."

"Is Mark coming? I did invite him."

"Yeah, later." Impressed, he looked around the room. "Fuck me. You Asians certainly know how to throw a party. Proper fucking bling!"

"Thanks." Rajesh clicked his fingers at a waiter who happened to be walking past. "You! Get Mr Regan a table, and make sure he has anything he wants."

"Certainly, sir."

"If you don't mind, Uncle Joe, I'll have to be getting back to my wife."

Regan burst out laughing. "Blimey, son! You've only been married five minutes and you're under the thumb already!"

Humiliated, Rajesh forced a smile. "Something like that. See you later."

"No worries, kid. You go and enjoy yourself. Eh, and you'd better hurry up; you're wife's looking over, and she's none too pleased ... My ears are burning."

Tanya was leaning across, talking to Jazz. "Who is that man Rajesh is with? I don't like the look of him."

Jazz could see Rajesh walking back towards the top table. Jealous of his relationship with the capitol's premier-league gangster, his answer was short and sweet. "He's bad news, Tanya. Bad news."

Rajesh sat back down next to Tanya. He picked up his glass and downed the contents in one. "Sorry about that. Just had to see to a very important guest."

"Really!" Tanya said, fuming. "He's obviously more important than me!"

Still smarting from the sarcastic under-the-thumb jibe, Rajesh's blood boiled. He was about to say, "Yes! As a matter of fact, he is!" but he realised that would only throw fuel onto the fire. Instead he looked at her and said, "Don't ever question what I do ever again! You've got what you wanted; we're married, aren't we?"

Husband and wife ate their meal in silence, barely looking at one another. Jazz realised his lifelong friend had changed beyond recognition.

After the speeches came the dancing. A fourteen-piece band had set up – brass section, keyboards, guitars, backing singers – and was ready to play. The first dance was reserved for the newlyweds. Not wanting to ruin yet another tradition, Rajesh took Tanya by the hand and led her onto the dance floor, a frozen smile on his face. Picked out by a spotlight, they walked to the centre of the floor and took hold. Right on cue, one of the most romantic songs ever written came drifting out of the sound system: "Maula mere maula". Its slow, sumptuous melody filled the Grand Ballroom. The music seemed to pacify Rajesh. Leading his wife around the floor, he smiled warmly. She, too, was lost in the moment, pulling him close and whispering, "Don't let's argue, Rajesh. I love you too much."

By now Shearsbe had arrived and was sitting with Regan. After dancing with Tanya, Rajesh joined them at their table and ordered a bottle of champagne. The booze began to flow spectacularly. Pretty soon all three were slumped in their chairs, pissed out of their brains.

"I-I remember my wedding day," Regan said, slurring his speech. "Yeah … we had it in an East End pub called the Blind Beggar. Famous, it was … The … the Krays used to drink there. Those were the days … Gone now. Bastards pulled it down."

"When are you going to get married, Mark?" asked Rajesh, his eyes glazed and heavy-lidded.

"Me? Never. I love the single life too much."

"No woman would 'ave you, you mean," Regan said, laughing. He stumbled to his feet. "I wanna meet her."

"Who?" asked Rajesh.

"The new Mrs Rajesh. I … wanna meet her."

Rajesh looked round and saw Tanya dancing with one of her

young nieces. He signalled to her to come over. When she arrived at the table, Rajesh rose unsteadily to his feet and held her hand. "Tanya, this ... this is Mr Regan ... but you can call him Uncle Joe. He's one of the nicest men in the world." Introduction over, Rajesh crashed back down onto his chair.

Tanya took an instant dislike to this huge bear of a man grinning at her as though she were a Las Vegas showgirl. There was something cruel about his eyes, something menacing.

"Hello," she said politely.

Turning on the charm, he got up and took hold of her hand. "You're stunnin', darlin'. Absolutely stunnin'. A proper little Indian princess. You've done well for yourself there, Rajesh."

"Not bad is she?"

Tanya felt like the prize exhibit at a medieval slave auction. She had never seen Rajesh so drunk; she tried to lure him away. "Rajesh, your mother would like to speak to you."

Keen to show Regan he wasn't the least bit under-the-thumb, he waved her away abruptly. "Later. I'm busy."

Tanya saw a gleam of satisfaction light up in Regan's eyes. She bent down and kissed Rajesh on the cheek. "Okay, darling. Don't be long." It took all her willpower to look at Regan and smile. "It was nice to meet you, Mr Regan."

He gave her a cheeky wink. "The pleasure was all mine, darlin', I assure you."

She turned and walked away, seeking friendlier faces. She noticed her ex-colleagues from chambers laughing and joking on a table nearby. At least someone was having a good time. Neil Acherson saw her coming and stood up to give her his seat. Having only ever seen her in Western dress, they all remarked as to how beautiful she looked. As she sat down, Neil congratulated her on the wedding. Pulling up a chair he said, "The door's still open if you want to come back to work."

Meanwhile the dance floor was packed with gyrating couples. Some of the richer guests, fuelled by alcohol and rich food, were trying to outdo each other by seeing who could give the largest amount of cash to the band. One drunken businessman after another stumbled forward and, with a theatrical gesture, tossed a handful of notes onto the stage. This was met with cheers from his family and friends, only to see him outdone a few moments later by another wealthy entrepreneur. All were either related or had some form of business connection to the Thakrals. Watching this excess from the sidelines were the Rais. Acutely aware of their own stricken finances, all they could do was look on enviously whilst fiddling with their napkins.

Later in the evening the master of ceremonies informed everyone that a sumptuous buffet was about to be served in the next room. The Rais' ears pricked up – now this was something they could get involved in – and they headed there en masse. A charming sight awaited them – Vidya, keen to please her more elderly Indian guests who were homesick for the old country, had hired a catering company that specialised in Indian street food. Colourful stalls had been set up offering a variety of old favourites such as *Aloo Vada* (individual potatoes coated in gram flour batter, deep fried and served with a variety of chutneys, such as green chutney, date-and-tamarind chutney, or plain old tomato ketchup), *Moong Dal Chilla* (spiced lentil crepes smeared with extra-spicy garlic chutney, chopped green chillies, and roasted onions), *Papadi Chaat* (crispy Indian crackers layered with potatoes, chutneys, *chaat masala* and yogurt), and *Aloo Chaat* (cubed potatoes fried in hot oil, served with pickles and garnished with chopped red onions and coriander leaves). A sitar and tabla player added to the authentic atmosphere by playing a host of evening ragas.

By 4 a.m., those guests not staying at the hotel, including Regan and Shearsbe, had long since departed. After being thanked by Kaylash and Uncle Sunil, Vidya and Neelam saw the Rai clan, boozed up and stuffed to the gunwales, onto their coach for the journey back to Southall. Kaylash couldn't thank her new sister-in-law enough, saying it was the best wedding she'd ever been to and she couldn't wait until they all got together again.

Arm in arm, Rajesh and Tanya got out of the lift on the twentieth floor and made their way down the corridor.

Giggling and unsteady on his feet, Rajesh stumbled along, slurring. "Now *that's* what I call a *wedding!*"

Tanya opened the door of the honeymoon suite and guided Rajesh over to the bed.

He crashed down and said, playfully. "Undress me, wife. I'm going to make passionate love to you."

"Promises, promises."

She helped him off with his clothes before disappearing into the bathroom. It had been a long day, but she was full of nervous energy. Determined to make this a special moment she undressed and took a quick shower. After rubbing expensive French body oil all over skin she put on a sexy black negligee. One final look in the mirror and she was ready.

She opened the bathroom door and, for dramatic effect, switched off the light. "Here I am, darling." She padded across the floor and slid into bed. Rajesh had his back to her. She cuddled up to him, kissed his neck, and blew into his ear. "Make love to me." She expected him to turn over and ravish her, but instead he just lay there, dead to the world, snoring his head off. It was all too much. She had put up with insult after insult – his rudeness during the important food ceremony, his failure to mix and show respect to her family and former work colleagues, his drunkenness, his preference for the company of that pig of a man Regan – and now this. She turned over, curled up into a ball, and burst out crying.

"How is married life suiting you, sir-ji?" asked Patel, placing a bundle of papers on the desk.

Rajesh shook his head. "I've only been married six weeks; what do you expect me to say!" If he were honest, he would have said it hadn't been the best of starts. Tanya was finding it difficult to adjust to her new life as a member of the Thakral household, dominated as it was by Satish, who hadn't made her at all welcome. Despite being a semi invalid, he could still throw his weight around. Vidya was trying her best to help her to settle in, but it wasn't easy. A couple of times Rajesh had come home from work to find his wife lying on the bed in tears. He put it down to the rollercoaster of hormones surging through her body. She was now three months pregnant, and it showed. Her bump was getting bigger by the day. Another bone of contention was the fact that they hadn't gone on honeymoon. He was far too busy, he said, to swan off to the Maldives whilst S. T. Freights needed all his attention. He promised to take her somewhere nice after the baby was born. Tanya reluctantly agreed.

"Early days, I suppose," said Patel. "Yes, I am very sorry I didn't come to the wedding."

That's because I didn't invite you, thought Rajesh. "I brought you a piece of wedding cake, what more do you want!" he said sarcastically.

"And very nice it was too, sir-ji. Mr Shearsbe tells me it was a lavish ceremony."

"You're supposed to be working with him, not discussing my wedding!"

"Oh no, you misunderstand. It just came up in general conversation." He cleared his throat. "I must congratulate you, sir-ji."

"What for?"

"For employing Mr Shearsbe. He is very knowledgeable about the import–export business. Your father would never have brought in an outsider. You are to be commended."

"It's called having your finger on the pulse, J. P. Watch and learn. Watch and learn."

Shearsbe had been with the company now for just over a month. On the two days per week he came to work at S. T. Freights, it was Patel's job to liaise with him. Rajesh had installed Shearsbe in an office next door to his own and a few doors down from Patel's. They seemed to be getting on okay, judging by the amount of time Patel spent in there. And the effect was miraculous. Patel had ditched his worn-out suits and now came to work in smarter, trendier ones. Rajesh was delighted with the transformation; it could only benefit the company to have such a well-dressed employee showing clients around. Rajesh congratulated himself on bringing Shearsbe on board as business was starting to pick up. They both had the same vision – to expand S. T. Freights into a global enterprise. Shearsbe brought with him a huge list of contacts. One of them was an Italian company based in Milan called Spirito. According to Shearsbe, the company had connections not only in China but also in the bourgeoning and lucrative South America market. Rajesh was keen to set up a meeting with Spirito and had been banging on at Shearsbe to make it happen. Later that day he got his answer.

It was lunchtime and they were driving through central London in Rajesh's brand new Ferrari 458 Italia. Shearsbe was waxing lyrical about the car, saying how talented he thought the Italians were at design. "Speaking of Italy, I've managed to arrange a meeting for you with Spirito in Milan."

"When?"

"In two days."

"Two days! And you're only just telling me!"

"I only found out about it this morning. I thought you'd be pleased."

Rajesh didn't want to admit it, but as a married man, he was no longer a free agent, able to do whatever he pleased. He now had to take his wife into consideration. *Why the fuck did I get married!* he thought. "Sorry, Mark. Of course I'm pleased. That's brilliant news, thanks. Do you want to come with me?"

"Can't, I'm afraid. Got other fish to fry." He brushed a speck of dust from his pinstriped trousers. "Why don't you take your wife along? She'd love it."

"You must be joking. I see enough of her at home." He suddenly had an idea. It was over a week since Bav had moved into their new apartment in Pimlico. Because of family commitments, Rajesh hadn't found time to visit her. She was mad as hell and needed placating. *Perfect!*

Over lunch in Sketch, Shearsbe filled Rajesh in on Spirito. "The CEO's an amazing guy called Roberto Rosica. He's stinking rich and loves the good things in life."

"Sounds like my kind of guy."

"Oh, he is. A real bon viveur, or whatever the equivalent is in Italian. Having said that, he's very choosey who he does business with. If he likes what he hears, he'll send his representatives over to check S. T. Freights out. I'm telling you, Raj, the guy's a serious global player. If you can do a deal with him, then the sky's the limit."

"I'll do my best."

"Let me give you a tip; he's got a huge ego, so flatter him. You never know, you might get an invite to his villa on Lake Como."

After a long lunch washed down with the most expensive claret, Shearsbe paid the bill. "My treat. You get it next time." He then headed off to another meeting.

Rajesh sat back and sipped his Grand Marnier, excited at

the prospect of skimming Bond-like across Lake Como in a speedboat. As far as he was concerned, it was a done deal. He texted Bav: "Hi, baby. Wear something sexy. I'm comin over later." He couldn't wait to see the look on her face when he invited her to Milan.

* * *

"Milan! Rajesh, that's fantastic! Oh my God, I can't wait to go shopping!"

"Wait till you see some of the shops down Monte Napoleone. They're out of this world."

She bounced around the room like a child on Christmas morning. "Milan! Milan! Oh, wow!" She kissed him and gave him a hug. "What time do we fly?"

"Nine thirty. We'll get there just in time for lunch. I rang Easyjet this morning and booked the tickets." Bav's face suddenly clouded. "What's wrong? Don't you like flying?"

"Of course I like flying."

"Well, what is it then? Is the flight too early?"

"Nothing like that, no. I'm ... I'm just disappointed you booked with Easyjet, that's all." She stroked his arm soothingly. "Rajesh, a guy in your position shouldn't be travelling on a budget airline."

"I shouldn't?"

"No. You should be flying first class. British Airways, Air France. It's more expensive, but it's worth it. They treat you like royalty – first-class lounge, the best food, not mixing with the scum in cattle class. You're a successful businessman. You're above all that."

Two scenarios popped into his mind. In scenario one he was queuing up with a group of loudmouth scumbags on their way to Milan for a piss up; in scenario two he was relaxing in the hushed confines of the first-class lounge with celebrities, sports stars, and millionaires, sipping champagne whilst waiting for the flight to be called. No contest.

"You're right, Bav. What the fuck was I thinking of. I'm above all that now." He grabbed his phone, rang British Airways, and booked two first-class tickets. "That's what I'm talking about."

Bav's face broke into a devilish grin. Exhilarated, she threw her hair back and, one by one, began to pop the buttons on his shirt. As she did so, he looked around the room. She'd spent a lot of money on the apartment by the look of it – expensive brown leather sofa and matching armchair, ultra-modern mint-green glass dining table, plasma screen TV, Bang and Olufsen Hi Fi. *She's obviously maxed out the credit card I gave her. I wonder how much she's spen—*

Bav must have noticed him adding up the cost of her purchases. Expertly she slid her hand down between his legs, cupping his balls.

Never mind. She's worth every penny. Suddenly his phone rang. "Who the fuck's this?" He glanced at the screen: "Home." "Shit, I'll have to answer it. Hi, Maa ... What? You're joking. Okay, okay, calm down. I'll be home in forty-five minutes." He ended the call. "I don't *fucking* believe this! Tanya's had a huge row with my dad and locked herself in the bedroom. The joys of married life! I'll have to go, Bav. Sorry."

"That's okay. Don't worry."

He was amazed at her patience and understanding. "Thanks. I'll make it up to you in Milan."

Fuming, Rajesh jumped into his Ferrari and screeched out of the underground car park.

When he got home, he marched straight up to his bedroom. He hammered on the door. "Tanya, it's me. Open up."

After a few seconds, he heard the key turn in the lock. The door opened slowly. Tanya stood there in floods of tears. She threw her arms around him but felt his body cold and unresponsive.

"What's going on, Tans? I've had to rush back from an important business meeting."

She clasped her hands to her face and sobbed. "I'm sorry, Rajesh ... Your Father, he ... he treats me like a servant."

"I hope you've not been upsetting him, the condition he's in?"

She looked at him and screamed. "What about *me!*"

He backed off. "Okay, Tanya, calm down. Just tell me what happened."

"I … I went into his bedroom to bring him the newspaper. I gave it to him and plumped his pillows. He … he looked at me like I was dirt. I asked him if he wanted anything else, and he said, '*Ek chai!*' just like that. Not 'Please would you bring me a cup of tea'. Just '*Ek chai!*' I asked him who he thought he was talking to."

"You didn't say that, did you?"

"Yes! I'm not having anyone treating me like that. I'm supposed to be his daughter, not some skivvy!"

"What did he say?"

"He said I should watch my mouth, and … and …" – her bottom lip trembled. – "and that the only reason I'm part of the family is because I'm pregnant." She burst out crying again.

Rajesh sat her down on the bed and gave her a cuddle. "Hey, now, come on. He didn't mean it. It's just his way."

"I don't care! I'm not having it! You'll have to speak to him."

Rajesh had enough on his plate without acting as referee between two forceful personalities. It was his worst nightmare – an unstoppable force against an unmovable object. There was no way his father would listen to him. He decided to play for time. "Okay, Tanya. I'll wait for things to calm down and have a word with him when I get back from Milan."

She looked at him open mouthed, her eyes smudged with tears. "Milan? What are you talking about?"

Shit! "Oh, yeah, sorry. I forgot to mention, I'm going to Milan on Friday."

"This Friday?"

"Yeah. It was short notice. I was only told today. Big investment opportun—"

She shook her head. "Please, not this Friday."

"What do you mean?"

"Don't tell me you've forgotten?"

"Forgotten what?"

"You said you'd come to the hospital with me. It's our baby's scan! You promised. You've missed the last two. Rajesh, you promised."

He was caught in the headlights. "I—"

"*You promised!*"

"Don't shout; my parents'll hear you."

"I don't give a shit! Some husband you are! You're out all day and most of the night! I hardly ever see you, and now you tell me you're off to Italy and can't make our baby's scan!"

Pushed into a corner, he came out fighting. "And why do you think I'm out all day? Eh? I'm trying to build a future for you and the baby." He stood up and started pacing the floor like a demented lecturer. "I'm not out there enjoying myself, you know! I work hard! Damned hard! And this is the thanks I get – dragged back from an important meeting because of a few cross words between you and Dad."

"A few cross *words?* Rajesh, he *insulted* me!"

"*And I said I'd sort it out, right!*"

"*Now who's shouting?*"

"*Don't be so fucking facetious!*" He knew he had to calm down, and fast, otherwise the TV would be through the window. He took a deep breath. "Look, I don't want to go to Milan. I have to. It's a once-in-a-lifetime opportunity. If I pull it off, it'll be worth a fortune to the company."

Money, money, money. He was obsessed with it. Tanya had heard enough. She got up off the bed and pushed him towards the door. "Get out."

"Tanya? What are you doing?"

"You think more of S. T. Freights than you do of me! Get out! You're not sleeping in here tonight!"

He pushed her away and opened the door. "Right! Fuck you! I'll sleep in the spare room then!"

"Good!"

"Good!" He walked onto the landing and slammed the bedroom door.

* * *

The Airbus 320 dipped its wings. Thirty thousand feet below, like an ocean frozen in mid-tempest, Rajesh could see the Swiss Alps stretching into the far distance, their peaks, like white horses, capped with snow, mountain upon mountain. He nudged Bav and pointed to a tiny Alpine village nestled on the valley floor. She nodded, her gold bangle earrings tinkling beneath her liquorice-black hair.

The intercom crackled. "Ladies and gentlemen, we are about to begin our approach into Malpensa Airport. The temperature in Milan is a balmy seventy-six degrees. Local time is ten thirty. Thank you."

Bav squeezed Rajesh's arm excitedly. Mindful she was visiting the style capitol of the world, she had chosen to wear a Stella McCartney equestrian tweed jacket and black tuxedo trousers. Like a flower emerging from winter, day by day she was blossoming into a sophisticated woman. And she had taken to flying first class, breezing onto the plane as if she owned it, even snapping her fingers at the steward when there was a delay in serving the complimentary champagne. Rajesh loved it, revelling in his mistress's newfound confidence. The prickly cocktail waitress from Rouge was now the height of cool urban chic.

They took a taxi from the airport and drove into the centre of Milan. Bav stared fascinated at the busy cityscape of neoclassical buildings intersected by quaint, old-fashioned trolley cars. She caught glimpses of well-dressed couples entering cafés and cutting-edge boutiques with names she had never heard of.

After turning off Via Manzoni, the taxi pulled into a fifteenth-century cloistered courtyard that was now home to the Four

Seasons, a five-star hotel in the epicentre of the fashion district. They were escorted into reception by an immaculately dressed concierge. Bav had stayed with Rajesh in some nice hotels in Chelsea, but nothing like this. The interior was a combination of modern Italian design and historic architectural detail – Kalusto sofas and side tables sat beneath richly decorated Renaissance-era hand-painted ceilings. Rajesh had booked the Visconti Suite, a sumptuous set of rooms on the third floor overlooking the inner courtyard. There was a king-size bed, a whirlpool bath, and a working marble fireplace. Bav was stunned; she had only ever seen such opulence reflected in the pages of glossy magazines. And now here she was, starring in one! Even the air was luxurious, smelling of expensive furnishings, discreetly scented bed sheets, freshly cut flowers, and the finest perfumed toiletries. So different from the acrid lavender Air Wick she once used to mask the chip shop stink that seeped into her bedsit in Holloway.

The meeting with the head of Spirito, Roberto Rosica, was due to take place later that afternoon. Although Rajesh could have made it back to London in a day, he was determined to enjoy a long weekend, so he had booked the suite for three nights, telling Tanya he had other meetings to attend. Not that there had been any verbal communication between them; he had simply left a note on her dressing table whilst she slept.

It was time for some fun. Rajesh clapped his hands. “Right! Let’s go for lunch!”

Having visited Milan before, Rajesh knew exactly where to take Bav on her first excursion – Galleria Vittorio Emanuele II, an exclusive shopping arcade a few streets away. They strolled past La Scala, the sun beating down on tourists and locals sitting on stone benches opposite a statute of Leonardo. Entering through an archway at the rear, Bav had the sensation of walking into a palace. The marble-floored interior was lined with designer shops and restaurants. At its centre was a huge octagonal glass dome featuring mosaics depicting the four continents. The couple strolled through the arcade at their leisure, Bav pointing at the many designer handbags and accessories filling the Prada shop window. Rajesh made a mental note of one bag in particular that caught her attention – a cream-coloured Saffiano calf-leather handbag with gold-plated fittings, a snip at €1,290 – before guiding Bav into a canopied restaurant. When presented with the wine list, he had a mini crisis; he knew nothing about Italian wine, and there were so many to choose from. So he ordered the most expensive one on the menu – a bottle of Trebbiano Valentini, a classic white wine from the Abruzzo region. The waiter nodded his head in approval. Preening, Rajesh winked at Bav. The wine complimented perfectly their *filetto di salmone con salas verdi agri agrumi e fagiolini* – grilled fillet of salmon with a citrus salsa verde and buttered fine beans.

"I could get used to this," said Bav, conscious of being stared at by each passing Milanese male.

"Good. I want you to."

Puffed up with self-importance, she looked around and almost had to pinch herself. Lunch in Milan. Wow. But deep down she knew she was worth it, that this was the life she was destined to live. Rajesh, too, felt supercharged with excitement. He cast his mind back to a few months ago, when the highlight of his day was lunch at Stoke Poges Tennis Club with Jazz. The mere thought made him cringe. He'd come a long way since then and was determined to go further. Now he had tasted the high life, there was no going back.

After lunch they took a stroll around Piazza del Duomo, a massive rectangular square dominated by Milan Cathedral. Shaped like a medieval crown and built entirely of white marble, the gothic facade stood out dazzling against the blue sky.

Rajesh pointed up through a forest of marble pinnacles covering the cathedral roof to a gold statue of the Madonna glinting in the sun. "I wonder how much that's worth?"

Bav was too busy studying what the Milanese women were wearing to be bothered about boring old architecture. Noticing a beautifully crafted Hermès handbag on the arm of a passing *signorina,* she puffed out both cheeks and said, "A fortune, probably."

They meandered through the streets, stopping off in various cafés. Rajesh could tell Bav was itching to go shopping. He decided to withhold the pleasure; plenty of time for all that tomorrow. He had an important meeting to attend to.

At three thirty they went back to the hotel so that Rajesh could pick up his briefcase. Inside was information about S. T. Freights and a glossy brochure Shearsbe had persuaded him to have printed to promote the company. Rajesh also had Patel's mobile number handy in case Roberto Rosica asked any difficult questions. He would nip to the loo and ring Patel, who was on standby.

"Hopefully this won't take too long," said Rajesh after checking his briefcase. "Order whatever you want from room service."

Bav had disappeared into the en suite to run the whirlpool bath. "Baby?"

"Hmm?"

"In here a minute."

He opened the bathroom door to find a naked Bav sprawled Cleopatra-like in the churning marble pool, the steamy atmosphere glossing her hair and shoulders. She smiled coquettishly. "Hurry back."

He had seen some beautiful things that day – cars, clothes, cathedrals – but nothing compared to this. His felt an electrifying twinge in his shaft. He wanted to dive in and ravage. He looked at his watch – 3.45. No time. "Stay right there."

Shearsbe had given him the address of Spirito's head office, so he took a cab to the business district a few kilometres away. On his way over, his mobile rang. Expecting it to be Tanya, he glanced at the screen and was surprised to see a Milanese number.

Who the hell knows me in Milan? "Hello?"

A gregarious Italian voice boomed out. "*Ciao, Signore* Thakral! *Come sti?*"

"Sorry, who is this?"

"Roberto Rosica. We have an appointment, yes? Signore Shearsbe gave me your number. I hope you don't mind me calling you?"

"Not at all! How are you, Mr Rosica?"

"*Bene, bene.*"

"I'm just on my way over to see you."

"Wonderful. I have an idea. Why don't we meet in the Hilton for drinks? I think we will be more comfortable there, no?"

"Fine by me."

"The hotel is just opposite our head office. Meet me in the cocktail bar. When you get there, make yourself known to the waiter. He will show you to my table."

"Fantastic, Mr Rosica. See you in five minutes."

Rajesh was glad they were meeting somewhere relaxed; there was less chance that he would be asked awkward questions there. As he walked into the Hilton, his mind was catapulted back two months ago to his wedding day. He thought about Tanya sitting alone in their bedroom in Gerrards Cross, too proud to go downstairs and make peace with Satish; and Satish, the epitome of intransigence, too stubborn to offer her an olive branch. What a mess.

Possessing the uncanny knack of putting dark thoughts to the back of his mind – life was for living after all – Rajesh strolled in to the cocktail bar with the air of someone used to negotiating huge business deals. He felt at home amidst these surroundings of pleasure, with their hushed ambience and discreet chit-chat. They had become, in fact, his office. He spoke to a waiter who led him over to a table in the corner. As he approached, a distinguished man in his early sixties got to his feet, an engaging smile lighting up his handsome, weather-beaten face.

"Ciao, Signore Thakral!" He offered his hand. "Roberto Rosica; delighted to meet you."

Rajesh shook it warmly. "Great to be here. Thanks for seeing me."

"Not at all. Not at all." Slim and impeccably dressed in a bespoke charcoal-black suit, white shirt, and pencil-thin grey tie, he had the look of a faded matinee idol.

"Please, Signore Thakral, take a seat."

"Rajesh, please."

"As you wish." They both sat down at a table overlooking Centrale, Milan's main railway station, its imposing fascist facade thronging with commuters. "Are you enjoying yourself in Milan? How long are you here for?"

"Three days. And yes, it's amazing."

"*Bene, bene.*" Signore Rosica removed a chilled bottle of white wine from an ice bucket and filled two empty glasses. "I would like you to try this. It is from my vineyard."

"Really! You own your own vineyard?" Shearsbe was right; the guy was a real bon viveur!

He smiled proudly. "*Si.* I have a small winery of a few hundred hectares near my house in Como. Tell me, what do you think?"

These were the types of questions Rajesh's preferred to answer; not difficult ones like "Do you provide BTI facilities for your customers?" Yes, this was a more up his street. Rajesh sipped the wine thoughtfully. Remembering Shearsbe's advice to "flatter the guy", he massaged his ego expertly. "Oh! Mr Rosica! It's absolutely delicious! There's a lovely citrus flavour to it. It's one of the nicest wines I've ever had."

Signore Rosica nodded enthusiastically. "*Si! Si!* The slopes of my vineyard are close to a lemon grove. Somehow the flavour has, how you say … transmuted."

"Transmuted. Definitely."

"Ah, I see we are on the same wavelength. And now I would like to talk about your company."

Rajesh opened his briefcase, took out the glossy brochure, and handed it to Signore Rosica. For the next ten minutes he studied it carefully, nodding and murmuring to himself in Italian. Rajesh stared out of the window whilst sipping his wine, which he honestly found to taste mildly acidic.

Eventually Signore Rosica looked up. "I'm very impressed with your facilities, Rajesh. Very impressed. What I need is a company that is true to its word. If they say they will deliver by a certain date, then I need them to deliver – unlike the company we are dealing with at the moment, who are constantly letting me down."

Rajesh sat back confidently, spreading both arms across the back of the sofa. "Rest assured, Mr Rosica. S. T. Freights aren't like that. We put the customer first at all times. And we don't bullshit. If we say we're going to do it, we do it."

"Excellent, excellent."

Rajesh took another sip of wine. No, it wasn't very nice at all. Medicinal, in fact! "Mmm, delicious. What is it your company deals in, exactly?"

"Microprocessing chips for mobile phones. We are one of the world's biggest suppliers. But we don't advertise ourselves. Our main customers are in South America, where, as you know, they prefer to be discreet."

South America! Rajesh saw the world opening up to him. "Absolutely! No point in showing off. Discretion's our byword."

"I like what I hear." He sat back and loosened his tie. "Perhaps we could do business together?"

"I'm sure we can."

You come highly recommended by Signore Shearsbe. He is a well-respected man in this industry."

"That's good to know."

"I would like to offer your company a year's contract. If it works out, we will roll the contract over. Is that acceptable?"

"Absolutely!"

"Very well, I will send my representatives over to England to check on your facilities. If everything is in order, I will have my lawyers draw up a contract."

Rajesh saw a vast fortune pouring into the company accounts. He wanted to leap up and punch the air. Instead he gave a cool, confident grin. "Fantastic. You won't regret it."

"And now I would like to cement our relationship." He gestured to the waiter, and they were promptly served a silver platter of beluga caviar and bottle of Bollinger Grande 1969

They drank one another's health. After a few sips, Signore Rosica's phone rang. He answered the call and got to his feet. "I'm very sorry, but I have a car waiting to take me to the airport."

Rajesh was surprised by his abruptness. "No problem. Going anywhere nice?"

"Switzerland."

"Have a good flight. I hope everything's okay?"

"Fine, fine. It was a pleasure meeting you. Next time you are in Milan, you must come to my house in Como." He turned to leave. "Oh, by the way, where are you staying?"

"The Four Seasons."

"Then may I recommend the restaurant there: Il Teatro. The food" – he kissed the tips of his fingers – *"Bellissimo!"*

Rajesh got up and shook Signore Rosica's hand. "Thanks. I might just do that. I'll definitely take you up on visiting your house in Como."

* * *

"The guy's loaded, Bav! Absolutely loaded! I had him eating out of my hand! He's got a house on Lake Como! He's invited me to stay next time I'm over! He's even got his own vineyard! I drank some of his wine! How cool's that!" Rajesh was pacing up and down the Visconti Suite, his mind exploding with possibilities. "That's how you do business! You don't fuck about like my dad; you get in there and charm the bastards." Fuelled by champagne and adrenalin, he swept back his hair, oddly referring to himself in the third person. "Rajesh Thakral! Businessman of the year! Fucking *yes!"*

With immense satisfaction Bav watched him strut and preen, delighted she had transformed the naive playboy from Gerrards Cross into a sophisticated wheeler-dealer.

Rajesh delved into his briefcase. "I got you this." He brought out a box stamped with the Prada logo.

"For me?" Bav took it from him and opened it up. Inside was the Saffiano calf leather handbag she had commented on in the Galleria. She threw her arms around him. "Oh Rajesh! It's lovely! Just what I wanted!"

Later that night they took Signore Rosica's advice and dined at Il Teatro. The food, as promised, was "*Bellissimo*". When Rajesh summoned the waiter to pay the bill, he had a pleasant surprise. The head waiter shook his head. "There is no need. It has all been taken care of. A Signore Rosica has settled everything." Rajesh was overwhelmed by the gesture, but at the same time he felt undermined by Rosica's worldly sophistication.

Rajesh and Bav spent the next two days sightseeing and shopping. Like a couple of newlyweds, they wandered the streets and boulevards hand in hand, kissing in cafes and smooching in shop doorways. He was so intoxicated with Bav that on a trip down the exclusive Monte Napoleone he gave her free reign to buy whatever she desired. Like a Vandal sacking ancient Rome, she licked her lips and plundered each passing emporium – Dolce and Gabanna, Armani, Valentino, Chanel, Prada. She was ruthless in her pursuit of booty, buying dresses, skirts, scarves, blouses, jackets, underwear, belts, shoes – so much, in fact, that she couldn't carry it all at back to the hotel, despite its convenient location in the next street. Instead, like some latter-day Liz Taylor, she ordered each shop to deliver her purchases to "The Four Seasons – the Visconti Suite." It tripped off her tongue as lightly as salmon mousse.

During their long weekend, Rajesh spent of thousands of Euros on her. But he didn't care. It was worth it just to see the look on her face whenever a trinket caught her eye – the Bambi-like stare as she held out some dress or other, showing him the exorbitant price tag, followed by the wide-eyed look of innocence that said, "Please can I have it, baby? *Pleeeeease*"; and, when he nodded, the shriek of joy as she clutched it to her breast and kissed him on the lips. And then later, back at the hotel, practising the dark arts of her sexuality, she discovered that, as is the case with most men, there was a kinky side to his nature. Their lovemaking took on a harder, more aggressive edge. He was swept away by her obscene openness, her willingness to do anything, her ability to anticipate his every erotic desire, no matter how demeaning. In such moments he realised he should never have got married. Jazz was right; Tanya had trapped him.

12

Stepping off the flight from Milan that drizzly November evening, Rajesh felt his heart sink. Winter was on its way; the clouds over Heathrow were dark and foreboding. On the one hand he was elated about the situation with Spirito, but his domestic situation spoiled the triumph. Whilst waiting for his suitcase to appear off the carousel, he contemplated accepting Shearsbe's invitation to a "booze up" in Rouge to celebrate the deal, which, according to Shearsbe, was as good as sealed, and then spend the night with Bav. But he knew he couldn't. His pregnant wife was anticipating his arrival.

He dropped Bav off at her apartment in Pimlico, watching for a moment as she stood in the illuminated foyer with her many designer shopping bags before being swallowed by the lift. Even driving his beloved Ferrari had lost its zing, especially when the gates of his house in Gerrards Cross loomed up in the headlights. He sighed. Time to face up to his responsibilities.

All day Tanya had looked forward to her husband coming home. She was shocked to find his note on her dressing table on Friday morning but decided not to make a big deal out of it; after all, he was working hard for her and the baby. Despite the terrible atmosphere pervading the house all weekend, she had tried her best to be cheerful, even popping into the conservatory to see if Satish wanted anything. All she got from him was a cold and unequivocal "No!"

Vidya's heart went out to her; she knew what a strong

character her daughter-in-law was and how much of an effort it must have been for her to try to break the ice with her Satish. On Saturday afternoon, when Neelam and Ajit came over, Vidya invited Tanya to go shopping. They drove into Gerrards Cross and had a coffee together. Tanya hardly uttered a word. She was distant, her thoughts swirling like the bubbles in her cappuccino. In an effort to cheer her up, Vidya took her to a designer boutique and offered to buy her a new dress. She said thanks, but she wasn't interested. As they walking along the High Street, Vidya put her arm around Tanya's waist and said, "You must be strong. I know how difficult it is to move in with a new family. Things will get better; I promise." Tanya burst into tears, thanking her mother-in-law for her kindness and understanding.

Determined to create a cosy atmosphere for Rajesh when he came home, Vidya had prepared a nice family dinner. She and Tanya were in the kitchen, putting the finishing touches to the meal when they heard the front door open and close. Tanya's stomach somersaulted.

Vidya noticed how tense she looked and gave her a reassuring smile. "In here, betta."

Rajesh walked into the kitchen, masking his frustration behind a huff of tiredness.

Tanya looked at him plaintively. She ran forward and gave him a hug, caressing the back of his neck. "I've missed you."

Rajesh felt the swell of her stomach press against him, a forceful reminder of his obligations. He eased her away. "That smells nice, Maa."

"Tanya and I have been preparing it all day. How was Milan?"

"Yes," said Tanya. "Did you manage to see *The Last Supper*?"

"What?"

Tanya smiled playfully at his ignorance. "Honestly, Rajesh! The fresco by Leonardo Da Vinci! It's what Milan's famous for!"

"Too busy doing deals for any of that." Besides, he had seen other treasures, like Bav's voluptuous breasts glazed in baby oil, arching above him in mid-thrust, her coffee-coloured nipples longing to be sucked. "I need to take a shower."

Tanya followed him upstairs. Alone in their bedroom, she sat on the bed and watched him undress. "Well?"

"Well, what?"

"How did it go? Did you manage to get the contract?"

"Oh, that? Yeah. Can't wait to tell Dad; he'll be really pleased." He couldn't think what else to say. He had known Tanya all his life, and yet here he was, tongue-tied. He knew why. It was guilt, pure and simple. Then he remembered what Regan had said about powerful men down the ages having mistresses: "Morals are for morons." Bolstered, he suddenly found his voice. "How are things between you two anyway?"

Tanya shook her head. "Not good … I'm *really* trying, Rajesh, but he's very difficult."

He let out a frustrated sigh.

"What's that supposed to mean?"

"I thought you might have sorted things out while I was away."

"What, in three days? It's going to take longer than that. He is so bitter towards me."

"You're gonna have to try harder, Tanya; that's all."

"Why is it down to me? Why don't you have a word with him?"

Rajesh exploded. "Fuck me! I've only just walked through the door! I've got enough problems at work without this! Just be patient; he'll come round."

Normally Tanya would have stood her ground, giving him a mouthful. Instead she watched him disappear into the bathroom and close the door. What the hell was wrong with her? Why didn't she stand up for herself? Like an overloaded junction box, she realised her body was flooded with differing signals – the Tanya of old yelling at her to speak her mind; the new pregnant Tanya, overflowing with hormones and harbouring new life, desperate to keep the peace. So this was what motherhood was all about, was it? Compromise – an ability she had lacked since childhood. She punched the bed in frustration. Eventually she calmed down. Hearing the shower splashing against the glass screen, she had an idea.

Rajesh was soaping himself when the shower door opened and, like a genie, a naked Tanya suddenly materialised amidst the steamy vapour. Slowly she put her arms around him, hugging him tight. The water poured off him disconcertingly – he was melting. "Make love to me?" His body felt rigid, unresponsive. Upset, she raised her head and looked into his eyes questioningly.

Rajesh froze. He felt himself being X-rayed. She was staring right into his soul, into the very depths of the Visconti Suite. Terrified his guilty expression would give him away, he looked down at her bourgeoning stomach, her cute belly button already distended. "It's not safe, Tanya. I don't want to hurt our child."

She kissed his neck passionately. "You won't. The gynaecologist at the hospital said it's safe to make love right up until I give birth."

Birth, gynaecologist, hospital – he could almost smell the anaesthetic. Unlike Bav's provocative preamble to sex that gave him an instant hard-on, these sexless words put him right off. Still, he didn't want to hurt Tanya's feelings. He was a bastard, but not a complete bastard. "I'd rather not take the chance, TanJa."

She stared at him in despair. "Is that it? We're not going to make love until after the baby's born?" Silence. Desperate for some kind of physical connection with her husband – anything – she sank to her knees and kissed his stomach, lowering her head though the needles of water towards his flaccid manhood. She tried coaxing it into life.

But Rajesh had had the life sucked out of it in Milan; it was tired and sore and needed a rest. Besides, it was Bav's domain. He lifted her up. "It's okay, Tans. I'm just tired, that's all." He slid open the shower door and stepped out. "What's for dinner? I'm starving."

Tanya stood motionless, a stream of water mingling with her tears. She dried herself off and walked back into the bedroom.

Rajesh was sitting on the bed smirking. Suddenly he produced a box from behind his back. "This is for you." It was wrapped in gold paper and expertly tied with a yellow bow. "From Milan. Go on, open it."

Tanya took hold of the box. She tore off the gift wrapping to reveal the Prada logo. Inside was a Saffiano calf-leather handbag identical to the one he had given Bav.

"Well, what do you think?"

Tanya forced a smile. "It's lovely, Rajesh. Thanks."

"Cost a grand, that."

"Did it?"

"Yeah. What's the matter; don't you like it?"

"Course I do."

"You don't look it."

"I *do!*"

"Cost a grand."

"You've just told me that." She noticed him looking downcast, so she grabbed his hand and patted it reassuringly. "It's lovely, Rajesh. Really. I love it."

Ego intact, he jumped to his feet. "Let's eat."

"Let me dry my hair. I'll be down in a minute."

When he'd left the room, she picked up the thousand-pound handbag and threw it against the wall.

During dinner Rajesh told his father all about the deal he'd managed to pull off in Milan. He couldn't praise himself highly enough, boasting how his new way of doing things was making the company rich. "I'm telling you, Dad, the days of sitting behind your desk waiting for deals to fall into your lap are long gone. Long gone. You have to go out there and make things happen."

Sitting at the table in his wheelchair, Satish nodded politely. He was thrilled the company was doing so well, but he didn't like being told his methods were old-fashioned. He felt helpless. Watching the company expand and not being part of it was hell. If he could only get out of the damned wheelchair! It didn't help when Vidya noticed a dribble of curry running down his chin and wiped it clean with her napkin. "Don't *do* that, woman! Wait until I ask!"

Tanya shot Rajesh a "see what I mean" look. The atmosphere around the table was terrible, not at all what Rajesh expected on his triumphant return. Where were the compliments, the "I'm so proud of you"? It was like a funeral! He thought about Shearsbe celebrating the Spirito deal in Rouge, gorging himself on girls and champagne. If he were single he'd be right there with him, sharing in the feast, not stuck in this domestic nightmare. To liven things up, he produced his overnight bag from under the table. He unzipped it and handed out two small gift-wrapped boxes, one each for his mother and father. Instead of beaming smiles, he was met with blank stares.

"What's this?" asked Vidya.

"Present from Milan."

"But it's not my birthday."

They still didn't get it! "I know it's not, Maa. I've just pulled off a mega deal. I wanted you to share in my success."

"Oh! Right!"

As Vidya began to unwrap her present, Tanya noticed that Satish was struggling with his; with hardly any strength in his fingers, he was picking at the ribbon helplessly.

"I'll do that for you," said Tanya, reaching across the table.

If she thought her kind gesture would be appreciated, she was wrong. Satish simply tutted and said, "If you must!"

Rajesh watched eagerly as his mother and father opened their boxes and stared dumbstruck at the contents – a platinum-and-diamond bracelet for Vidya, a gold Rolex studded with rubies for Satish. Tanya looked at each extravagant present and felt sick to her stomach.

"Oh my … It's lovely!" exclaimed Vidya. "So expensive!"

"Don't worry about that, Maa," said Rajesh smugly. "The money's rolling in." Satish gazed at the twinkling timepiece. As far as he was concerned, his son was just showing off. More than that, he was rubbing his nose in his own mediocrity. "Look what I can afford", he was saying. "Maa's always wanted a diamond bracelet, now I've got her one. See, I told you I'd be successful." For years Satish had urged Rajesh to get off his backside and make something of himself. Now that he had, he made Satish feel like a second-class citizen. It was Rajesh, not he, lording it over the dinner table. How he longed for the days when he would tear into his lazy son. His pride dented, he went on the attack. "It's a very nice watch, Rajesh. I hope the money's come out of your pocket, not the company's."

Rajesh was stunned. It was as though his father had thrown the Rolex back in his face. The ungrateful old sod! Still he wouldn't give him the credit he deserved. Desperate to control his temper, he gripped the tablecloth and said, calmly, "No, Dad. *I* paid for it, with my *own* money."

"Good," said Satish.

Vidya watched these knife-edge exchanges, convinced a full-blown argument was only moments away. Mindful of his father's precarious state of health, Rajesh stayed silent.

The evening was a disaster. Rajesh got up from the table. "I think I'll have an early night."

Tanya stood up. "Me too."

They left the kitchen and went upstairs. Outside their bedroom Rajesh said, "I'm gonna sleep in the spare room. Early start in the morning. Don't want to disturb you." He gave her a quick peck on the cheek.

Numb, Tanya could only watch as he trudged into the room next door. Rajesh got undressed and climbed into bed. Before switching off the light, he lay there deep in thought. He couldn't believe the way his family had treated him. He thought about his friends at Rouge; the smiles and back-slaps he would have received when he walked through the door. He contrasted Bav's reaction on getting her present to Tanya's. But what really got under his skin was his father's arrogant snub. It was obvious; the old man was jealous. Switching off the light, he vowed to get his own back – he would turn S. T. Freights into the biggest import–export company in Europe. No, scratch that – the world!

* * *

The next morning, Vidya was in the kitchen as usual, preparing Rajesh's orange-and-carrot juice. She gazed out across the back garden and noticed a light dusting of snow had begun to fall. Suddenly she heard the front door close. Peering out of a side window, she saw Rajesh hurriedly climb into his Ferrari and accelerate out of the drive. He had never, ever missed breakfast, let alone left the house without saying goodbye. She looked at the diamond bracelet glittering on her wrist; she had worn it that morning for her son's sake. Vidya took it off and shook her head in dismay. What was the point of riches without love?

In the weeks leading up to Christmas, the Thakral household saw less and less of Rajesh. When he did make an appearance, it was usually late and he was tired and grumpy. His absence had a strange effect upon the family. Little by little their shared sadness seemed to create an unspoken bond between them. There were knowing glances around the dinner table when Rajesh failed to come home, often without letting the family know. Satish would motion towards the empty place setting, shake his head, and tut loudly. "In all the years *I* was in charge of the company, I always made it home in the evening."

Tanya, who had once been so busy with her law career, found the day-to-day routine stultifying. To allay the boredom she would help Vidya with the housework, scan magazines, and go for long solitary walks along the country lanes. She missed the hustle and bustle of London, the human contact. The highlight of her day was when Kate, the district nurse, came over to see to Satish. Kate was the same age as Tanya, and newly married. They would grab a quick coffee together in the kitchen, and Kate would chat about her husband, Steve, a bricklayer, and the struggle they had each month to pay the mortgage. Tanya listened enviously as Kate sang Steve's praises – the night she came home from work to find he'd cooked her a meal, the occasional red rose left on the pillow, their shared dreams of moving to a bigger house. "Of course," said Kate, glancing at the luxury kitchen, "We couldn't afford anything like this! You're *so* lucky, d'you know that." Tanya would smile wirily and think, *If you only knew.* Watching Kate gulp down her coffee before heading off to see another patient crystallised how miserable and unfulfilling her life had become. She found herself spending more and more time in the mandir, lighting incense sticks and praying to Shiva and Lakshmi.

One morning, a week before Christmas, a huge storm covered Buckinghamshire in a blanket of snow. From her bedroom window, Tanya looked out across a frozen landscape of cotton-wool fields and snowed-in cottages, wisps of smoke drifting for their chimneys. In the distance she could see the spire of St. Michael's church pointing up into the bright blue sky like an icy finger. She got dressed and was about to go downstairs when a knock sounded on her bedroom door.

"Come in." To her surprise, Vidya entered, shivering in her dressing gown. She looked pale and had trouble breathing. "Is everything all right?"

Vidya shook her head, holding on to the door for support. "No. I feel terrible. I think I'm coming down with flu."

"Go back to bed. I'll bring you a cup of tea."

"Are you sure?"

"Of course!"

Tanya took her arm and led her along the landing towards her bedroom.

"I better go in the spare room," said Vidya, stopping halfway down. "I don't want to give my germs to Satish."

Tanya made her comfortable and then went downstairs into

the kitchen. The phone rang, and Tanya anwered. It was Kate, the district nurse, her usual bubbly voice full of concern.

"I'm really sorry, Tanya, but I can't make it over today. We're snowed in at the clinic. None of us can get out. Do you think you'll be able to cope with Satish?"

Tanya was mortified. "Er … I'll try."

"You'll be fine. Just give him a wash and take him to the loo. I'll try my best to come over tomorrow. Any problems, give me a ring."

After replacing the receiver, Tanya had a panic attack. Just the thought of tending to her father-in-law was enough to send her stress levels rocketing. She paced the kitchen floor, trying to calm herself down. "Okay, okay. First things first … Tea. Make the tea"

She brewed a pot of masala chai and poured out two cups. She put them on a tray and carried them upstairs. Halfway up she suddenly realised she had the wrong cup; Satish always insisted on drinking his morning tea out of a special china mug, a blue-and-white affair with a gold rim. She hurried back into the kitchen, found the right cup, and transferred the hot liquid. She rushed back upstairs and went into the spare room. She gave Vidya her tea and told her about the district nurse.

"Oh dear," Vidya said with a sigh. "That means …" She could barely say the words.

"Don't worry," said Tanya. "I'll look after him. Now drink your tea and try to keep warm. If you need anything, just give me a shout." She left Vidya and walked along the landing, knocking politely on the master bedroom door.

"Come in!"

Tanya swallowed hard and entered the dimly lit room. Satish was sitting up in bed reading. When he saw her walking towards him carrying the tray, he froze. "What's going on? Where's Vidya?"

"In bed with flu. I thought I'd bring you this." She handed him the cup.

"What do you expect me to do with that?"

Tanya realised he couldn't hold the cup properly, so she leaned over the bed and raised it to his lips gingerly. She'd never been this close to him before. She felt herself blush.

He took a sip and turned his head away. "It's cold. Make me another."

Tanya was about to explode but managed to hold her temper. She took the cup and walked back towards the door. "Oh, by the way, the district nurse phoned. She won't be coming today."

Satish's mouth dropped open. "W-why? What do you mean?"

Witnessing the look of absolute horror on his face seemed to embolden her. It was she, after all, who had the power. She marched over to the window and flung open the curtains. "We're snowed in." Then, with an almost evil relish, she let him have it. "That means I'll be looking after you."

Five minutes later Tanya returned to the master bedroom. She gave Satish his scalding masala chai before saying, "Drink that, then I'll give you a wash."

It was bad enough having some white floozy flannel him down every morning. But this … this was unthinkable. "You will not! I'll see to myself!"

"Fair enough," said Tanya, revelling in his embarrassment. "I'll be downstairs if you need me." Before he had chance to speak, she turned round and flounced out.

Stunned, Satish glanced around the room as if searching for a way out. But there was no way out. His blood boiled. He'd be damned if he'd let that gold-digger touch him! The en suite wasn't that far. Surely he could make it if he tried? *Yes, just roll off the bed, shuffle onto the wheelchair and buzz into the bathroom. Easy.* After a few moments of struggling, he somehow managed to haul himself up and drag his tired body to the edge of the bed. Sweating, he took a deep breath and grabbed the side of the wheelchair. He could feel his heart pounding in his chest. Then disaster. He leaned over too far to his right; the wheelchair suddenly slid back, and he went crashing to the floor. Unable to move, he lay helpless on the carpet like a bull elephant brought down by a hunter's rifle. Suddenly he felt a draft; his pyjamas had slid down, revealing his hairy backside. For such a proud man it was the final indignity. An emotional dam broke within him, and he screamed out in frustration.

Tanya was in the kitchen when she heard a dull thud followed by a scream. "Oh God, no!" Blaming herself for leaving him, she rushed up the stairs, terrified Satish had had another seizure. She burst into the master bedroom and found him lying on the floor in a crumpled heap, weeping like a child. Relieved, she rushed over, sat him upright, and held him in her arms. "It's okay, *Papa-ji.* I'm here."

Astonished to hear her use such a respectful term of endearment, he slowly raised his head. It was the first time he had looked at her properly since she'd arrived. She had such a pretty face, with kind eyes and a warm expression. No wonder Rajesh had fallen for her. Wracked with guilt over the way he had treated her, he began to sob. "I'm a useless old man. Forgive me."

Cradling his shivering body, Tanya felt her heart wrench. "Shush. There's nothing to forgive. We've all been under a lot of stress. Everything's all right now."

He gripped her arm, his eyes red-rimmed. "I'm frightened, Tanya. I've … I've lost everything … my business, my dignity. My son treats me like an idiot …"

"Don't say that. Rajesh loves you. You're the one person in the world he respects most."

"It doesn't seem like it, the way he was boasting last night. Old-fashioned, he called me. Perhaps I am." He smashed the carpet with his fist. "Oh, what's the point of carrying on!"

Tanya looked at him firmly. "I'll tell you why." She took his hand and placed it on her stomach. "Your grandchildren, that's why."

Confused, Satish blinked rapidly. "Grandchildren?"

Tanya's eyes moistened. "Yes … I'm having twins."

"Twins!"

She nodded. "A boy and a girl."

Satish enveloped her in a hug. "Oh that's wonderful, Tanya! A boy and a girl! A boy and a girl!" He let go of her. "Does Rajesh know?"

Tanya shook her head. "No. I only found out on Friday, at the hospital. He never asked, so I didn't tell him. He was too full of his business deal."

"That boy needs a lesson in manners. He's a complete idiot sometimes. What about Vidya, does she know?"

"Not yet."

"Then we must tell her! Quick, get me up … please."

Tanya helped him into his wheelchair. They charged down the hall and went crashing into the spare room. Despite feeling ill, Vidya sat bolt upright in bed, an anguished look on her face. She had heard the commotion and was expecting the worst. She was amazed when a beaming Satish took hold of Tanya's hand, stroking it affectionately.

"Our daughter is having twins, Vidya! Twins!"

13

"Fuck me, you bastard! Fuck me with your rock-hard cock!" Bav wrapped her legs around Rajesh as he violently thrust in and out of her, scissoring him tightly.

He noticed her mouth, pursed with pleasure; the determined creases in her brow. The whites of her eyes rolled upward deliriously. "You like that, don't you?"

"Oh yeah, baby, yeah!" She willed him on. "Hurt me! Go on, hurt me!"

Rajesh kissed her savagely, biting her neck and tugging her hair. Drenched in sweat, he threw her over onto her stomach. "Kneel up," he demanded. "I'm gonna fuck you till you scream." He took his cock in his hand and slammed its full length into her, spanking her arse hard with each powerful surge.

"Oh yeah, that's gorgeous. Go on, harder!"

Rajesh glanced at their reflection in the mirrored wardrobe – side on they resembled an Egyptian tomb drawing come to life. "Look at us, baby. Look at us fucking."

On all fours like a tigress, Bav caught sight of herself. She swung her head wildly, her lustrous mane thrashing from side to side. Feeling his pace quickening, she gasped. "Come on my tits, baby. I want to feel your hot come all over me."

The invitation hastened his orgasm. "I'm coming!" Like trained acrobats taking up their positions, each knew instinctively what to do. As Bav rolled onto her back, Rajesh grasped his erupting volcano, holding back its creamy lava and jerking his hips so that his erect tool was inches above her bare breasts. Straddling her, he watched with intense pleasure as his pearl-white juice splattered her fleshy domes. "*Baby!*" He squeezed every last ounce out of himself, slopping her nipples in warm come. Panting, he collapsed onto the bed.

They lay there in silence, the sound of their breathing slowly lulling them back to reality. Bav reached across him matter-of-factly, pulling a handful of tissues from a box on the side table. He hadn't noticed the box before; it was a made of scrolled silver with an engraved top, the kind you see in those exclusive Mayfair shops. She sat up and wiped her breasts clean of him. Watching her, Rajesh felt slightly nauseated. He hated the nuts and bolts of life.

Bav got up, walked into the bathroom, and turned on the shower. After a few moments, she called out. "What are you doing at Christmas?"

A succession of images spooled through his mind like an MTV fast edit – the desolate pall hanging over the dinner table, Satish staring into his roast turkey, Vidya looking tense, Tanya running out of the room in tears. No, he wasn't looking forward to it one bit. "Spending it at home, unfortunately. You?"

"Same. I've not seen my mum for ages."

Sighing, Rajesh looked outside and noticed the snow falling. One good thing about snow, it gave him an excuse to stay overnight in London. "Fancy going to Rouge tonight?"

"Great!"

He looked at his watch – 10.45 a.m. These days he didn't set out for the office until at least midday. After wining and dining potential customers into the small hours of the morning in London's most exclusive bars and restaurants, he figured that normal office hours didn't apply to him. But today was different. The delegation from Spirito was due at midday. Patel would deal with them, but he wanted to be on hand just in case. He was the boss, after all.

Driving through central London, its main streets festooned

with yuletide decorations, he saw couple after couple doing their Christmas shopping. A gnawing guilt overcame him – Christmas was all about family, and he hadn't seen his for over a week. He made a mental note to go shopping later that day. He would make it up to them the only way he knew how – by showering them with expensive gifts.

Pulling into his dedicated parking space at S. T. Freights, he noticed Patel's old Ford Mondeo had been replaced by a brand-new BMW 5 series. *Good for him*, thought Rajesh. *Now the company's doing well, he's obviously splashed out*.

Instead of going straight to his office, he decided to visit the bonded warehouse – he'd not been in for a while and was curious about stock levels. Fearing a half-empty warehouse might put his Italian clients off, he entered the huge shuttered doors with trepidation. At moments like this, he chided himself for not being more "hands-on". Still, he couldn't be in two places at once, pulling off deals *and* keeping an eye on things. Not even his father possessed that ability. He needn't have worried. The warehouse was stacked from floor to ceiling with goods. As he walked around poking his nose into this and that, not really knowing what he was looking at but trying his best to appear knowledgeable, he noticed there were a lot of new faces. Patel had obviously fired the slackers and replaced them with eager new recruits, judging by their enthusiasm and efficiency. You had to hand it to Patel; he was an excellent number two.

When the Spirito delegation arrived – three sharp-suited Italians with jet-black hair – Rajesh had them shown into his office. Always keen to mimic the gestures and body language of foreign clients – Bav had taught him that – he rose from his desk like a grand dictator, throwing his arms out. "*Ciao, tuti!* Welcome to S. T. Freights!" Before they could ask any awkward questions, he immediately sent for Patel. "My man here will show you around. Ask him anything you want. Anything at all. Now if you'll excuse me, I have to take an important phone call." Careful not to be seen, he watched from his office window as Patel led them over to the bonded warehouse.

In less than an hour, Patel was standing at Rajesh's side, witnessing him signing the contract. It amused him how much his boss's signature had changed over recent months, becoming more ebullient and self-assured as each new contract was despatched with regal grandiosity; it had come to incorporate rococo swirls and dramatic slashes,

They toasted the venture with vintage port. Rajesh was in such a good mood he even allowed Patel a few sips before ordering him back to work. Before leaving, the *Spirito* delegation once again reiterated their boss's invitation to visit his house on the banks of Lake Como. Rajesh was delighted, promising he would do just that the next time he was in Milan. As a gesture of good faith, they presented him with a case of wine from the Rosica estate. Rajesh knew exactly what to do with the paint stripper. When the delegation had left, he called Patel back into his office and said, "Merry Christmas, Jainti Bhai. Here's a little something from me to you for all your hard work."

Later that night Rajesh and Bav drove through the snow-swept city. The view was magical. It was as if London's iconic skyline had been shaken and they were entering a giant snowglobe. As they drove into Mayfair, the streets were packed with revellers: office partygoers – drunken city types in large, boisterous groups. The festive spirit was everywhere. Sadly that was not the case outside Rouge. The bouncers were as intimidating as ever, barely cracking a smile as they acknowledged Rajesh's arrival by moving a set of traffic cones, allowing him to park right outside the canopied entrance. Lined up along the street was a phalanx of luxury autos – limos, Mercedes, Rolls – more than usual. *Regan must be throwing one of his famous VIP nights,* thought Rajesh.

Resplendent in one of her Milanese purchases – a tight-fitting metallic silver dress hanging by the faintest of straps, with dramatic slashes to both front and back – Bav sashayed in, her waitress days long since forgotten. With Rajesh on her arm, she was now part of the establishment. But even she was surprised by the warm welcome she received from Regan. After greeting Rajesh with a bear hug, he kissed her on both cheeks, complimenting her on how nice she looked. Rajesh was delighted; his mistress had finally been accepted.

Regan's entourage was out in force, hovering around his booth like butterflies. Regan pointed at two people Rajesh had never seen before. "You pair! Shift yourselves!" Room was made inside the inner sanctum. Mark Shearsbe was there, as usual, another busty blonde on his arm. So was Teddy the bulldog. As Rajesh took his place beside Regan, he felt strangely blessed. It had been a hell of a year so far. Providence was smiling down on him.

The atmosphere inside the club was electric; the dance floor and bar area were crammed with partygoers. It seemed as if the whole of London had descended.

High on coke, Regan proudly surveyed his mirror-balled creation. He leaned across and spoke into Rajesh's ear. "They're all in tonight – footballers, movie stars, you name it. We've even got a bunch of chinks in. Entrepreneurs. Loaded, they are. Flew in this mornin' from Beijing. That's where all the money is these days."

Rajesh turned to see a group of smartly dressed Chinese businessmen sipping champagne in the next booth. "Looks like they're enjoying themselves."

"Tell you what; they didn't half give Bav the eye when you two walked in. Randy bastards." He took a swig of brandy. "Listen, what you doin' Boxing Day?"

"Spending it at home, unfortunately."

That bad, eh? Only I'm having a bash at the house. Just a few close friends, that sort of thing. If you get bored, you're welcome to join us."

"Thanks, Uncle Joe. I'll keep that in mind."

"Mark tells me your business is doing well."

"Yeah. Great. He's a real asset."

"Hold on to him. One day that boy's gonna be governor of the Bank of England."

As the night wore on, Rajesh kept glancing over at the Chinese businessmen. He was intrigued by their inscrutable manner and waxwork demeanour. Nothing seemed to escape them. It was as though they were studying their surrounds in minute detail, nodding at one another and forming little cliques. What were they doing over here? What business were they in? His father used to say the Chinese would end up ruling the world. He was probably right. There were billions of them, their global trade empire expanding at an amazing rate. China fascinated Rajesh. He viewed the continent like the merchants of old – a vast treasure chest just waiting to be plundered. If he could only get a foothold in the country, it would make the deal with Spirito seem like chicken feed. He sat back and had visions of articulated lorries bearing the S. T. Freights logo thundering through the streets of Beijing and Shanghai.

Rajesh noticed one of the Chinese ogling Bav as she returned from the loo, and an idea formed in his mind. When she sat down, he ran it past her.

"Leave it to me," she said.

He could only watch in admiration as his mistress made eye contact with her Asian admirer before joining him at his table. She flirted with him expertly, laughing at his jokes, running her fingers along the sleeve of his jacket. She was a natural. Soon she had the whole booth spellbound. Rajesh noticed the atmosphere around the table change. The frivolity had vanished, replaced by a more business-like ambience. Bav chatted earnestly with the group. After half an hour she got up and exchanged business cards. She bowed politely and returned to Regan's booth.

"Well?" asked Rajesh eagerly.

Bav took a sip of champagne. "You've hit the jackpot. One of them owns a telecoms business, one of the biggest in China. He's looking to expand into the UK. I told him about S. T. Freights."

Rajesh could hardly control himself. *"And?"*

"Wait for it, baby. He asked me to set up a meeting with you."

* * *

"Twins?" It was Christmas Eve. Rajesh had barely walked through the door before Tanya ambushed him in the hall. One minute he was driving home looking forward to the meeting with Mr Li Jianguo in three days' time, and the next minute this! Gobsmacked, he put his briefcase down.

"A boy and a girl" said Tanya breathlessly "Look!" She handed him a grainy black-and-white photo taken at the scan. "Look at our little babies! Aren't they cute?"

Rajesh suddenly felt the weight of two unborn souls pressing down on him. For the next eighteen years they would be *his* responsibility. Not one child, but *two!* "Wow," he said, his features frozen and expressionless.

More surprises. Shocks. A beaming Vidya entered the hall pushing an equally delighted Satish.

"Wonderful news, eh?" said Satish, taking hold of Tanya's hand.

What the fuck's going on, thought Rajesh. *Am I in the right house?*

Vidya sensed her son's confusion. "Tanya, would you take Satish into the lounge?"

"Of course!" Gleefully she took hold of the wheelchair. "Come on, Papa-ji. That film you wanted to watch is on in five minutes."

Rajesh was stunned. *Papa-ji? I'm definitely in the wrong house!*

Vidya took Rajesh into the kitchen and told him about the week's momentous events. "Tanya's looked after your father all week. She's been a godsend. The district nurse couldn't get through because of the snow. Then I was ill for a few days. It was mayhem. But Tanya took care of everything. She cooked, cleaned, looked after us both. Isn't it wonderful? Your father's a different person."

"Why didn't you tell me you were ill?"

"I didn't want to bother you. Anyway, there was nothing you could do. We were snowed in."

"You could have at least *told* me!"

"Why are you angry? I thought you'd be pleased. Fate has brought Satish and Tanya together."

"I'm not *angry!*" said Rajesh. "You should have *told* me, that's all!" But he *was* angry. Fuming, in fact. This cosy little domestic scene had taken the gloss off his impending meeting with Mr Li Jianguo. He wanted to announce it over dinner and watch his father squirm. He wanted Tanya to appreciate what a successful businessman he had become. But she had trumped him with news of her own. Twins! For fuck's sake, *twins!* And now the house was one giant love-in! He much preferred it when everyone was at each other's throats. At least that gave him an excuse to be with Bav ... sexy Bav. He wouldn't see her now for a few days. *Fucking hell!*

When Rajesh woke up on Christmas morning, he decided to make the best of it. He couldn't wait for his parents to go downstairs so he could give them his present. But first he wanted to surprise Tanya. Lying in bed next to her, he turned over roughly a few times to wake her up. When she did, her pretty face broke into a smile. She sighed and snuggled up to him. "Merry Christmas, darling."

"Merry Christmas, Tans." He produced a large pink envelope from under the bed. It was wrapped in a green bow with "Harrods" emblazoned across it in gold letters. "Here's your present. Go on, open it."

Tanya yawned and sat up. "Ooh! What's this?"

"Open it and find out." Ever since he was a child, he had been impatient when it came to opening presents.

Tanya grinned. About to tear open the envelope, she suddenly remembered something. "Dad! I need to take him to the loo." She got out of bed and hurriedly put on her dressing gown. "He usually goes first thing in the morning."

"For God's sake, Tanya!"

"What?"

"My dad can wait! Bloody hell!"

"Okay." She rushed back to bed and opened the envelope. Inside was a glossy brochure whose front cover featured a beautifully decorated nursery. There was a large Victorian cot, a rocking horse, sash curtains, and painted shelves stacked with a multitude of toys – a calm oasis of childhood tranquillity that was picture-book in its perfection. Confused, Tanya looked at Rajesh. "What's this?"

Nodding smugly, he deigned to inform her. "I've hired the interior design team from Harrods to convert one of the bedrooms into a nursery. It's gonna cost an absolute fort—"

"Tanya!" A helpless shout came from the master bedroom.

Alert, Tanya stood up."Yes, Papa-ji!"

"Please … I need to go to the toilet."

Rajesh tutted and shook his head. "'Please'! What's come over him? Bloody hypocrite."

"Don't say that about your father."

"Listen to you! Last week you hated his guts."

"Rajesh! Things have changed. Isn't it better we all get on?"

"Suppose so," he said begrudgingly. "Anyway, what do think of your present?"

"Oh it's—"

"Please, Tanya, I'm dying to go."

"Coming!" She kissed Rajesh on the cheek. "It's a lovely present, Rajesh. Thanks. I better go and see to Dad."

He slumped back onto the bed. "For fuck's sake!" Once again his father had spoiled the moment.

But Rajesh got his own back later that morning when he gave his parents their Christmas present – two tickets for a world cruise. But this wasn't any old world cruise on any old ship; it was the *Queen Mary II*, Cunard's finest, and he had booked the most expensive state room, the Queen's Grill, costing £37,688 per person!

"Oh my God!" exclaimed Vidya. "How wonderful! It must have cost a fortune!"

Rajesh was dying to tell them just how much but resisted the temptation. It was enough to see the look on his father's face. Staring at a photo of the sumptuous state rooms, Satish looked as though he were facing a firing squad.

"Thank you, Rajesh," he said. "That's ... er, that's very kind of you." Satish remembered the one and only time he had taken Vidya on a cruise. It was a cheap ten-day affair around the Med on an obscure Greek liner called the *Sparta*. Aptly named. The facilities were basic and the food was terrible; half the passengers, including Vidya, came down with a mysterious diarrhoea and sickness bug midway through the voyage.

Rajesh could see his father mentally reliving the experience, so he went in for the kill. "Yeah, the Queen's Grill comes with its own butler and private dining room. Think of it, Maa, you'll have your own Michelin-starred chef cooking for you. The cruise lasts one hundred and six days and takes in the most glamorous places on the planet – Hawaii, Hong Kong, Rio, you name it. You'll be treated like royalty." Then came the coup de grace, guaranteed to make Satish cringe. "Let me put it this way: it's a lot better than that rust bucket Dad took you on years ago. Do you remember? What an experience *that* was! Talk about a Greek tragedy! Mind you, you get what you pay for." *Should I? Yes, I should.* He plunged the dagger in mercilessly. "This one costs thirty seven grand ... *each!*"

Despite Patel's best efforts, closing the deal with the Chinese telecom giant Jianguo Industries took longer than expected. The owner and chairman, Mr Li Jianguo, was a tough negotiator, skilled in the art of offer and counter-offer. One moment the deal was on, the next it was off ... only to be on again a week later.

It was now April, and negotiations had been dragging on for over three months. One morning a frustrated Patel complained to Rajesh, saying, "Bloody Chinks! I've never known anything like it! They want to know the ins and outs of everything. My God, they need a rocket up their backside!"

Concerned, Rajesh called Shearsbe into his office and told him about the delay.

"Don't worry," said Shearsbe laconically."I've done business with the Chinese before. It's always the same. They take things at their own pace. The worst thing you could do is to try and hurry them along. They're just a bit suspicious, that's all."

"Suspicious! What have they got to be suspicious about? We're a legitimate company!"

"Don't take it personally, Raj. That's just the way the Chinese operate. They need to know we're not hiding anything."

"Like what?"

"Nothing sinister. There's a lot at stake for both sides. They just want to be sure S. T. Freights is financially stable and won't go bust mid-deal."

"But we're a bomb-proof company!"

"You and I know that. But look at it from their point of view; they don't know us from Adam." He gazed out of the window towards the bonded warehouse; it was busier than ever, with forklift trucks zooming in and out. "The Chinese are careful people. They've had their fingers burnt with Western companies before."

Rajesh threw up his hands in frustration. "Fuck knows what I'm supposed to do!"

"Just be patient. Let them work at their own pace. Believe me, they'll respect your discipline. And besides, Patel's on the case. They trust him."

Sighing, he sat down at his desk. "I'm desperate not to lose the deal, Mark."

"You won't, mate; don't worry."

Easier said than done. The deal consumed Rajesh like a wildfire. When he was out of the office, which was most of the time, he would phone Patel at least three times a day for an update. The answer was always the same – no news yet. To alleviate the pressure, he threw himself into a world of hedonism, staying away from home for days at a time, much to the despair of Tanya, who was in the final stage of pregnancy. Bav was the only person he wanted to be with; she alone understood him. Night after night they went out partying – bars, restaurants, private members' clubs – a dizzying social whirl amongst London's glamorous elite.

One morning Tanya was brushing Satish's hair when a Harrods delivery van pulled onto the drive.

"What in God's name has he bought now?" exclaimed Satish. They were getting used to such deliveries.

Two large boxes were unloaded in the hall. They were full of designer baby clothes and accessories: Christian Dior floral babygrows, Ralph Lauren teddy-bear-print body suits, Chloe bobble hats and mittens, Armani cashmere baby blankets, two huge Paddington Bears, matching sheepskin woollen booties, and a limited edition set of Jemima Puddle-Duck cups and bowls made of bone china and signed by the artist, a well-known children's illustrator.

"Ridiculous!" said Satish.

Tanya shook her head in despair. "I'm losing him."

Her words struck a chord with Vidya. Rajesh had become a stranger. As Tanya carried the baby clothes upstairs, she felt the twins kick inside her womb as though they, too, were registering a silent protest.

* * *

The ungrateful cow, thought Rajesh, putting the phone down after speaking with Tanya. He had called to bask in the glory of his Harrods's delivery, only to be told, "I want your love, not your gifts." *Women!* Well, it was her lookout. Feeling guilty about staying away, he had planned to go home that evening. Not now. Shearsbe was throwing a party at his swish new apartment in Kensington, so he would go there instead.

Driving over to Bav's – he and Regan had just finished one of their legendary lunches in Sketch – he checked in with Patel. "Any news about the Chinese deal?" "Yes, sir-ji. I have just finished speaking with them. They confirmed they will sign the contract in two weeks."

Rajesh was elated. "Really? That's fantastic news! You've done a brilliant job, Jainti Bhai; I won't forget this."

"My pleasure, sir-ji."

Joy of joys! He slammed his Ferrari into fourth and accelerated along Belgrave Road, the throaty roar of the engine growling like a hungry predator. His whole body surged with adrenalin. China! China was opening its doors to him! The world's biggest economy! He felt invincible. Nothing could stand in his way. When he told Bav the news, she threw her arms around him.

He ravaged her with kisses, stopping intermittently, breathlessly. "I couldn't have done it without you … You're the one who charmed them. Remember?… Without you, it wouldn't have happened."

She responded with equal passion, "We make a great team, don't we?… Me and you … Fuck, we're good."

His was drowning in sensation – sex, money, success; the holy trinity. Millions would pour into his bank account. He began to spend it there and then – a brand-new apartment for Bav. On his way over he had seen a fabulous penthouse for sale in Chelsea; he would buy it for her and shower her in luxury. He might even treat himself to a house on Lake Como. Why not? Maybe his own vineyard? He'd show Roberto Rosica how to make wine. Anything was possible.

* * *

As he opened the door of his new duplex apartment, Mark Shearsbe was jubilant. "Rajesh! Bav! Come in! Come in! Fabulous news! I told you they'd sign in the end!"

"You were right, Mark. As always."

"Hey, what are friends for! Now come in and have some wine!" The entrance hall was packed with Rouge regulars. He grabbed three crystal glasses off a silver tray. "Let's get shitfaced!"

* * *

Tanya unscrewed a bottle of olive oil and poured a glug into her hand. She rubbed the thick, warm liquid onto Satish's shoulders, massaging them gently.

"Oh, that's nice … I really appreciate you doing this, Tanya; I've been in so much pain."

"That's all right, Papa-ji. The district nurse said it would help."

"I might be able to sleep tonight."

"I hope so. You're very tense."

"Yes."

When Tanya finished, Satish lay back on the pillow. He took her hand and said, heartfelt, "Thank you."

Tanya smiled modestly. "What are families for?" She plumped his pillow and turned off the light. "Goodnight. Sleep well."

A thin, reedy voice sounded in the dark. "Goodnight, betta."

She closed the master bedroom door and walked downstairs. Suddenly, shockingly, she felt a gush of water pour down her legs, followed by a massive contraction. Grabbing the banister rail for support she called out. "Mum! Mum!"

Vidya appeared from the kitchen and dashed upstairs. "What's the matter?"

"My waters have broke."

"But you're not due for two weeks!"

"I know. Please do something.

"Okay, okay. Now, don't panic. Let me get my car keys; I'll drive you to the hospital."

"What about Satish?"

"I'll ring Neelam and tell her to come over."

"Okay." Tanya felt the contractions increase. She took a deep breath. "I need to call Rajesh."

"Do it from the car."

Vidya put Tanya's coat on whilst leading her outside. Although it was spring, there was a chill in the air. They got into the car and drove off. Tanya scrolled down to Rajesh's number and pressed dial.

* * *

Rajesh was sprawled on the sofa, knocking back a glass of vintage brandy, when his phone buzzed. He fished into his pocket and looked at the screen: "Tanya". Patel had obviously told Satish about the deal and she was ringing to congratulate him. *Oh!* thought Rajesh, his ego tumbling out of control, *You're interested now, are you? Well, you know what* you *can do!* With a cursory snap of his thumb, he switched the phone off.

* * *

"It's gone to answerphone!" exclaimed Tanya.

"Leave him a message," said Vidya.

"Okay." She spoke into the phone frantically. "Rajesh! It's Tanya! I'm on the way to the hospital! My waters have broke … *Ahhhhhh!"* A searing pain tore through her body. "Please … come quickly!"

* * *

Through misted eyes Rajesh peered at the bedside clock: 2.46 p.m. What a night! He just about remembered getting into a cab at 3 a.m. and stumbling back to the apartment. He turned over in bed. His mouth felt papery dry; his head pounded mercilessly. Bav lay next to him comatose – she'd hoovered enough coke to satisfy the greediest Colombian cartel. Rajesh slipped a fragile foot out of bed. Yawning, he sat up and reached for his mobile. Eight text messages, one answerphone message. He scrolled through to "Listen".

"Rajesh! It's Tanya! I'm on the way to the hospital! My waters have broke … *Ahhhhhh!"*

"Oh my God"! In a millisecond he had sobered up. He leapt off the bed, scrambling around on the floor for his clothes. "Shit! Shit!"

The noise woke Bav. "What's the matter?"

"Tanya's gone into labour! I switched the phone off last night and didn't get the message! *Shit!*"

"It's not your fault … What are you gonna do?"

He jammed his shoes on. "What d'you *think* I'm gonna do! I'm going to the hospital!"

Suddenly Bav became insecure about Rajesh's urgent sense of responsibility towards his wife. She was used to being top priority in his life. "Calm down, honey. You had loads to drink last night; it'll still be in your system. Don't even think about driving. Have some coffee and make your way over later. There's nothing you can do right now anyway, so you might as well take your time."

She had barely finished speaking when Rajesh left the apartment and ran into the lift. Whilst dropping three floors he tried ringing Tanya's mobile, but it was switched off. He dived into his Ferrari and raced out of the underground car park. He then switched to Hands Free and called home.

A female voice answered. "Hello?" He didn't recognise it.

"Who's this?" *Shit, the traffic's bad!*

"It's Kate, the district nurse."

Approaching Marble Arch, he sped through a set of amber traffic lights. "Put my mum on. It's Rajesh – her son."

"I'm sorry, but she's at the hospital."

"Is my wife okay? Has she given birth?"

"I don't know. You see—"

"Put my dad on, then!"

"I'm afraid I can't do that. He's asleep. He needs his rest."

Rajesh wasn't used to being told no. "*Put him on, you stupid bitch!*"

"I beg your pardon?"

"Listen, if you don't put him on, I'll make sure you're sacked!"

"Don't speak to me like th—"

"*Fuck you!*" He ended the call and scrolled to the number of the hospital. Engaged. He punched the steering wheel in frustration. A dual carriageway loomed up. Overtaking a lorry, he narrowly missed an oncoming car by inches. Horns blasted. He aimed his Ferrari arrow straight and blistered down the twin-lane highway, weaving in and out of the traffic recklessly. He couldn't get Tanya's scream out of his mind. If anything had happened to her or the babies, he'd never forgive himself. Eventually he came to the sign for Gerrards Cross. Above a line of trees he could see the hospital. Only a hundred meters to go. Flashing blue lights appeared in his rear-view mirror. A police car. *Shit!* For a split second he thought about accelerating away and screw to the consequences, but he realised his life was complicated enough at the moment, so he pulled over.

A tap came on his window; it was a uniformed traffic cop, his face clocked in sarcasm. "Nice car, sir. Very nice. In a hurry, are we?"

"Er, yes, officer. My wife's just given birth."

"And you think that gives you the right to drive like Lewis Hamilton?"

"No, I er ..."

"Is this your car, sir?"

"No. It belongs to a friend."

"Do they know you're driving it?"

"Course they fucking do!"

"I'd watch that attitude if I were you, sir.

"Sorry."

"Now step out of the car."

"Look, I said I'm sorry!"

"*Step out of the car! Now!"*

Rajesh was led to the patrol car and made to sit inside whilst his story was corroborated. Eventually he was released with a speeding ticket. Officious bastards! Still, it could have been worse. They could have breathalysed him.

He parked his Ferrari in the disabled bay outside Casualty and sprinted into the hospital, massaging his throbbing temples as he dashed through the clinical surroundings: white coats, trolleys, that nauseating antiseptic smell. Upon finding the maternity ward, he rushed inside and saw his mother sitting by a bed at the far end. Tanya was asleep by the look of it. Most of the beds had cots containing babies. Not Tanya's.

"Hi, Maa."

Vidya looked at him bleary-eyed. "Shush!" She gestured

towards a sleeping Tanya. "Where the hell have you been? We tried to contact you?"

Rajesh was shocked by her tone. He had never heard his mother curse before. "Business meeting. Dragged on into the night. My phone was switched off."

"We've all been so worried about you. Why haven't you been home?"

He couldn't answer. His eyes darted to the empty cot at the end of the bed. "Where are the babies? She didn't lose them, did she?"

Her tone softened. "No, betta. They're fine. They're being fed by the nurse."

An overwhelming sense of relief flooded his body, followed by the crushing weight of responsibility that threatened his playboy existence.

"Do you want to see them?"

"Er, not now. I'll come back later, when Tanya's woken up."

15

Tangled vines, splintering sunlight. Rajesh was following a narrow path through the forest. The heat was unbearable. A cacophony of insects and chattering monkeys surrounded him, setting his nerves on edge. He strode on, deeper into the darkening glade. Soon the light dulled to a green, subterranean hue. The forest was closing in. Then he heard the dry snap of a twig. He looked round and saw the face of a tiger staring at him through the undergrowth. Blind panic. He set off running, crashing into low-hanging braches and densely packed shrubs. The tiger was gaining on him, its huge paws thrumming the ground like an executioner's drum. He vaulted over a fallen tree trunk and he found himself at the bottom of a gorge. The only way out was up, miles up, towards a swirl of vultures. He could hear his mother calling. Gasping for breath, he took hold of the rock surrounding him and tried to haul himself up. But the rock crumbled away in his hand and he fell backwards, crashing to the ground. Suddenly the tiger came bounding towards him, its powerful muscular body gaining stride by stride. It sprung forward ferociously, claws extended, teeth bared.

"*Ahhhhh!*" Rajesh sat bolt upright in bed, gasping for breath.

"What's the matter?" asked Bav, scared out of her wits.

He was covered in sweat; it took him a few moments to realise he was safe. "Oh, thank God. I've just had a terrible nightmare. It was awful. I dreamt I was being chased by a tiger."

Bav kissed him on the cheek. "You're all right now. Go back to sleep."

It was the morning after Tanya had given birth, and he still hadn't seen his twin babies. The truth was that he was frightened of setting eyes on them. He couldn't explain why, but it was as if the reality of their presence would somehow drag him back into his former life. He was *this* close to surpassing his father's achievements and living the life he had always dreamed, but two little souls had come into the world, millstones blocking his way. He sank back onto the pillow and stared at the ceiling. He couldn't put it off any longer. He had to visit Tanya.

Armed with flowers and a giant, oversized teddy bear, he walked onto the maternity ward as though approaching the gallows. When Tanya saw him, instead of being upset she smiled and gave him a hug. "It's lovely to see you. Maa said you've been busy at work."

"Er … yeah." She smelt of warm milk and baby sick. "How are you?" Through his peripheral vision he saw two shapes in the cot at the foot of the bed. Still he couldn't look at them.

"Oh, I'm a lot better now. The birth was terrible. It felt like my insides were being ripped out. It was worth it, though. Look." She pointed at the Perspex cot. "There they are," she said proudly, "our children."

Rajesh got up and walked to the end of the bed. There they were, all right. Finally. He stared at the wrinkled brown faces, the tiny quivering fingers – fruit of his loins. His – they were his. He wanted to run out of the maternity ward and never look back.

"Do you want to hold them?" asked Tanya.

"Er … better not. Scared of dropping them."

She sensed in his body language a distancing. She put it down to awkwardness. *Typical man; scared stiff of newborn babies. He'll soon get used to them.* "They said I can go home tomorrow."

Tomorrow? Shit! "Really? That's good."

She patted the bed. "Come and tell me what you've been up to. How's the business?"

Glad to change the subject, he sat on the edge of the bed and told her all about the mega deal with Jianguo Industries, his eyes darting now and then to the Perspex cot.

Tanya came home, and during the next two weeks Rajesh was as elusive as ever. He used S. T. Freights as camouflage, shielding himself from any form of parental responsibility. But no one in the Thakral household dared to complain. For years they had urged him to put his head down and work hard, so he was only doing what they had asked. The only real input he had was when he and Tanya got together one evening to choose the twins' names – Rishi and Maya.

* * *

"Big day today," said Rajesh, slipping on his brand-new suit; a single-breasted navy chalkstripe cut by Gieves and Hawkes of Saville Row. "Signing the Chinese deal. How do I look?"

Bav was sitting at the dressing table, putting the finishing touches to her makeup. She got up and kissed him on the cheek. "Rock star." She looked stunning in a two-piece Chanel suit made from embroidered ribbon tweed with fringe trim, her wrists embellished with resin bangles adorned with a diamante "CC".

He drank in his mistress. "You look gorgeous. Going anywhere nice?"

"Oh, out for lunch with Kim. You know, we met her at Mark's party."

Rajesh couldn't remember anything about Shearsbe's party. "Oh yeah. Kim. Well, have a nice time. See you later, yeah? I've booked a table at the Ivy to celebrate."

"Can't wait."

* * *

Driving through central London, past the steel-and-glass edifices of multinational companies, Rajesh had a vision of his own corporate headquarters: a vast modernist complex bearing the S. T. Freights logo. He mulled over changing the name to R. T. Freights, but then he thought that R. T. International sounded better. He pictured himself in his new office high on the fortieth floor, overlooking the city with endless views of the horizon … master of the universe.

He arrived at work and strolled into the outer office. Margaret was at her desk as usual. Strange, she looked tense. He put it down to the fact that a big deal was about to be signed and she was feeling the pressure.

"Morning, Marg." He rubbed his hands together. "Big day today."

She lowered her head, replying nervously, "Er … yes, yes. I suppose it is."

What the hell was wrong with her? He decided there and then that the grumpy cow was part of the old regime and would have no place in his new empire. He shrugged and walked into his office. The cheeky bastard was at it again! Often, Rajesh would catch Patel sitting at his desk, only for him to jump up and vacate the boss's chair. Not today.

Annoyed, Rajesh gave a sarcastic cough. "Shift your arse, J. P."

Patel raised his eyes slowly, a look of absolute contempt on his face. "I don't think so."

"You what?"

"I'm not going anywhere."

"What the fuck's going on? Move!"

"Listen to you; you're pathetic."

"What did you say?"

"You think you run this company? If it wasn't for me, S. T. Freights would have gone bankrupt months ago."

"Now listen, Patel. I don't know what the *fuck's* got into you—"

"No! You listen, you fucking wastrel! Do you know how many years I've had to put up with you? Eh? Do you? Demeaning myself – 'Yes, sir-ji; no, sir-ji' – just because you're the boss's son! And then you take over, without a clue how things work, and *I'm* expected to sit there and take it. *Me!* A loyal servant who helped build this company! Do you know what it's like having to sit there day after day, listening to a spoilt brat who doesn't know the first thing about business, flouncing in whenever he pleases, boasting about how *He's* going to build a 'global empire'? Global empire! You couldn't build a toy car!"

"*You're sacked! Now get out!*"

Patel simply shook his head and guffawed. "Go home, sonny, and change some nappies."

Rajesh flew at him, grabbed him by the lapels, and punched him the face. Patel hit floor with thud. He sat up, wiped a smear of blood from his lip and said, coolly, "Mark said you would react like that."

"Mark? What the fuck's Mark got to do with it?"

"We're partners; didn't you know?"

Rajesh felt the earth tipping. "Partners?"

"And if you don't do exactly as I say, you'll lose your house, your business, and you'll end up going to prison. And God knows what *that* will do to your precious father. The shock will probably kill him."

Rajesh stood there unable to move, his mind in turmoil. He glanced around the room, desperate for the sight of familiar things to calm his nerves. Yes, this was his office, but everything seemed to have changed.

"I see I've got your attention. Good." Patel got to his feet and walked over to the desk. He picked up a piece of paper and handed it to Rajesh. "Read this."

He tried, but his eyes just wouldn't focus. "What is it?"

Now it was Patel's turn to be sarcastic – a first, and boy did it feel good. "You still need your arse wiping, don't you. It's a VAT bill for twenty-one million pounds."

"How much?" Rajesh snatched the bill back and studied it. There it was, in black and white.

"Twenty-one point two million, to be precise," said Patel. "Problem is, the company can't afford to pay it."

"Bollocks! We can cover that!"

"You know that for sure, do you? You've seen the accounts?"

"No, but—"

"'No, but. No, but.' Idiot! Well I have, and there's no way we have that sort of money. Someone's been spending it. Guess who?"

"But, but all those contacts I brought in—"

"*You* brought in! You live in a fantasy world, boy. They've barely covered the running costs. But you wouldn't know about such dreary details, would you, out gallivanting with your whore every night, spending the company's money on her."

Rajesh began to panic. "You better tell me what the *fuck's* going on!"

"Simple. If we can't pay the VAT bill, the company will go bankrupt. And as the company have a debenture on all of your family's personal properties, including your home and the lavish lifestyle you all enjoy, they'll seize all your assets, your house, your cars, your little love nest in Pimlico – everything. They're ruthless. Your family will be out on the street. You won't have a pot to piss in."

"You're wrong! I'm signing the Chinese deal today! That'll more than cover the cost!"

"It would," said Patel, smirking, "but I'm afraid Mr Jianguo no longer wants to do business with you. Only I can bring the deal in."

"Bollocks!" Rajesh snatched the phone up off the desk. "Margaret, get me Mr Jianguo." As he waited for the call to be put through, his eyes came to rest on a photo of his father hung on the wall. He was dressed in a dinner jacket, receiving the

Queen's Award for Industry. "Hello, Mr Jianguo … Hi, It's Rajesh Thakral. How are you, sir? Good, good. Erm, I'm ready to sign the contract. What time can we expect you?"

In cold, clipped Mandarin tones, Mr Jianguo spelt it out. "No, no, that cannot happen, I'm afraid. Not if you are in charge of the company. You see, Mr Thakral, we Chinese are careful people. We simply cannot do business with a playboy. I have done my research on you. You are most unreliable. Mr Patel, on the other hand, is a solid businessman. We will deal only with him."

Rajesh felt the blood drain from his body. He let go of the receiver. It went crashing onto the desk.

Patel picked it up. "Hello, Mr Jianguo. I think he's got the message … Yes, see you later." As if to cement his hold over him, Patel sat behind his desk. He relaxed into the chair, coolness personified. "Now listen to me very carefully. You're going to hand control of the company over to me. I've been running it for months anyway, so it won't affect things. Don't worry; I'll find you a nice little job somewhere in the office." He smirked, his podgy face lighting up. "Nothing too taxing; I know how much you hate hard work. You'll still be head of the company – I'll need your signature on the contracts – but in name only. I won't deprive you of that."

"And if I don't agree?"

"If you don't?" He picked up the phone. "Then within in a month HMRC will wind up the company and put you and your affairs under investigation. The mighty Thakral name will be ruined, your precious father will die of shame, and your mother will no doubt follow him. You see, my child, you're dammed if you do and dammed if you don't."

Rajesh looked at Patel with utter hatred. "You've got it all worked out, haven't you?"

"I'm only taking what's rightfully mine. Your father should never have overlooked me when he put you in charge."

"Leave my dad out of this! You're not fit to polish his shoes!"

"Your anger is only to be expected. Take the rest of the day off. Cool down. I want you back in here first thing in the morning. Nine o'clock sharp. Now, if you don't mind, I have to prepare for some very important clients."

Visibly shaken, Rajesh left the office and closed the door. Only now did he notice the shiny new name plaque proclaiming "J.P. PATEL, CHAIRMAN". He stared at it, dumbstruck.

"I'm sorry, Rajesh."

He turned and saw Margaret sitting behind her desk, a tearful expression on her face. "That's all right, Margaret; it's not your fault. Don't worry; I'll fix it."

When he walked outside, the full force of what had happened hit him like a Tsunami. So Shearsbe was involved, was he? Right!

Rajesh hit the throttle and raced along Kensington High Street. A short distance from Harrods he turned left and screeched to halt in front of Shearsbe's new apartment set in a row of pristine Georgian town houses. His heart pounding, he climbed the steps and stabbed the doorbell impatiently. "Come on, come on, you bastard!" No answer. He took a deep breath, realising that if Shearsbe had answered the door he probably would have killed him on the spot. But maybe Patel had been lying about his involvement. Maybe he just wanted him out of the office. So much had happened that Rajesh didn't know what to think. *I know; I'll talk things over with Bav. She'll know what to do.* He climbed back into his Ferrari and headed to Pimlico.

Opening the front door to the apartment, he noticed Bav's Prada handbag sitting on the hall table. *Good, she's not gone out yet.* He walked into the lounge and was about to call her name when he heard a noise coming from the bedroom. Tilting his head he could hear moaning, as if someone were in pain. *Perhaps she is ill?* He opened the bedroom door. "Are you all right, Ba—" Inside he saw a tangle of naked flesh. Shearsbe was lying on top of Bav, his hips thrusting into her. "What the fuck!"

Instead of jumping off the bed, Shearsbe simply stopped, eased himself from between Bav's legs, and sat up.

Rajesh looked at them in disbelief, his eyes burning with manic intensity. "What the fuck's going on!" He noticed Bav smirking. "You fucking slut! How *could* you!"

"Ignore him, Bav. He's just upset because he's lost his business."

So Patel was right. "Y-you're in on it? I-I thought we were friends, you motherfucker!"

"Welcome to the real world, sunshine."

"Bastard!"

Rajesh had barely raised his fist when Shearsbe sprung from the bed and in one movement pivoted ninety degrees and smashed his foot into Rajesh's jaw, sending him crashing into the dressing table. After a few seconds Rajesh came to his senses and stood up. Grabbing a wine bottle off the floor, he noticed Shearsbe had readied himself in a martial arts stance by standing side-on with his left hand in front of his right, bouncing lightly on his toes à la Bruce Lee. Rajesh came at him again, bottle in hand. Shearsbe seemed to have all time in the world as he stepped expertly away from the path of the bottle, allowing it to pass before punching Rajesh in the biceps and then smashing his forearm into the side of his temple. As he fell to the ground a second time, Rajesh knew he was beaten. He looked up and saw Bav grinning. The heartless bitch.

Panting, Rajesh stood up, swaying slightly. "You're fucking dead! Wait till Regan hears about this!"

Shearsbe burst out laughing. "Regan! He doesn't give a shit about you! He's used you, you stupid little cunt. We all have."

The words seared into his brain. Shaking his head, he stumbled from the apartment, oblivious to the world around him. Somehow he found his way to his car. With trembling hands he opened the door and got in. He put his head in his hands and screamed. A voice inside his head told him to drive, drive! Like an automaton he started the engine and tore out of the underground car park

Day turned to night. Pulses of sodium yellow told him he was travelling along the motorway. He'd been on the road for hours, driving to clear his head. His mouth felt arid, his mind violated and abused, and his body bruised and drained. Then he saw a warm and familiar sign – Gerrards Cross. It was midnight when he eased to a halt in front of a set of metal gates that were so familiar. Home. He stared at the house as though through the bars of a cell. His family were in there, fast asleep – his wife, his twin babies, his father, his mother, the people he loved most in the world – all oblivious to the catastrophe that had befallen him. But it was his fault. Greed had caused his downfall. He had allowed himself to be flattered, sucked into a world of glamour by a gangster elite. What an idiot! He had made the mistake of "getting high on his own supply". *I don't need those wankers,* thought Rajesh. *I need to get my life back on track.*

Suddenly a light went on in his bedroom. A shadow flitted across the curtain. Tanya. He watched as the shadow moved back and forth. She was carrying a bundle of some sort. Of course, she was breastfeeding one of the twins. The sight tore his heart out. His stomach churned; his anxious heart pulsated. To think he had betrayed his loyal wife, the mother of his children, by having an affair with that greedy, self-obsessed whore. Choking with emotion, he began to sob – quietly at first, then howling uncontrollably. He looked down at the steering wheel and saw the Ferrari logo glinting in the moonlight; the ultimate symbol of glamour. He couldn't believe he had been seduced by such trinkets. He slammed his fist into the prancing horse. "Bastard! Bastard! Bastard!" He wanted to run inside and confess all to his family. He reached into the glove compartment for the key fob to open the gates. But something stopped him. No, he would start by returning the car to Regan.

* * *

Dawn. A pale mist hung over the fields. Rajesh drove past a succession of millionaire's mansions. He was exhausted after spending the night in his car. By the time he reached Regan's house, the sun was up. As he stepped out of the Ferrari, a cool breeze kissed his face. Silence. Everything was still, as though the earth had stopped turning. He walked towards the huge wrought-iron gates, his finger hovering over the intercom's call button. *Do it!* He pressed the button and waited.

A cockney voice thick with sleep crackled angrily through the speaker. "Who the fuck's this?"

"It's Rajesh, Mr Regan. We need to talk."

Without an answer, the gates swung open. Rajesh drove up to the house and parked the car outside one of the double garages. He noticed the front door had been left open. It took all his willpower to walk across the drive and enter the house. The hallway was curtained against the light, its grand staircase subdued in shadow. He remembered the last time he was here – the night of the orgy, when he had rushed up those very stairs with Bav. *The two-timing slut.*

A voice sounded from the lounge. "In 'ere, son!"

Rajesh swallowed hard and opened the door. Regan was sitting on the sofa wearing a silk dressing gown of teal blue, his hair stuck up in unruly tufts. By the look on his face, Rajesh surmised he was none too pleased to have been dragged out of bed.

"Thanks for seeing me, Mr Regan. There's no easy way of saying this … I want out."

Regan smirked. "Oh you do, do you?" His expression changed in a flash. "Do you think I'm a fuckin' idiot!? Do you think I'm gonna let you walk away just like that? After all the dosh I've spent on you? Oh no, sunshine, you're my investment."

"Investment?"

"Yeah, investment. What, you think I treat you like a prince because I *like* you? Fuck me, you're even more stupid than you look. There's no way out, cunt. Ever. You're in too deep. All those deals you've signed. You're mine, body and soul. So enough of this shit and get back to work; you've got a contract to sign."

Rajesh froze. "You're in on it with Shearsbe?"

"Shearsbe does what I tell him. And so you had better; otherwise, I swear to God I'll kill your parents, your wife, *and* those fuckin' kids of yours. Got it? S. T. Freights is a gold mine; there's no way I'm letting it go."

The door opened, and Rajesh turned to see Shearsbe and Bav enter the room. He watched in utter astonishment as Bav walked over to Regan, sat on his knee, and gave him a peck him on the cheek, "Hi, Uncle Joe; is this prick bothering you?"

"Not really, darlin'. I've just give it to him straight. We won't have any more problems."

We! It was as if the fog had cleared and Rajesh could see the whole stinking truth. Somewhere along the line Bav had sold her soul to Regan. On his orders she had lured him into a world of glamour, telling him how to dress, how to behave, and how to speak; she had even introduced him to certain clients. She had used her sexuality to corrupt and ruin him. "You fucking bitch!" He lunged at her with his fist, but Shearsbe grabbed his arm, spun him round, and punched him in the face. He fell backwards onto the marble coffee table, scattering a gold cigarette box. Regan leapt to his feet.

He rushed forward and kicked Rajesh hard in the stomach. Like an out-of-control pit bull, he crouched over him, snarling. "Still not got the message? Eh? You Paki bastard! Right, Mark, let's give him something to think about."

Regan and Shearsbe set about him mercilessly, kicking, punching, and gouging. Blow after blow rained down, a torrent of sickening violence. Just before he passed out, Rajesh heard Bav scream, "Kill him! Kill him!"

* * *

"You can see him now."

"Thank you, doctor."

Rajesh prised opened a swollen, bloodshot eye. Through a

hazy film of mucous he saw Tanya walking towards his bed. He had been lying unconscious in hospital for the past two days. Someone – God knows who, probably one of Regan's minions – had driven him there and left him on a trolley outside Casualty like an unwanted piece of meat. He recalled men in white coats standing ghostly by his bed whilst he drifted in and out of consciousness. Certain phrases stuck in his mind: "Fractured collarbone." "Ruptured spleen." "Broken wrists." Propped up on the pillow, he now resembled a mummified Pharaoh, his spirit long since departed. The look on Tanya's face said it all. What a mess.

Tearful, she sat next to the bed and took hold of his bandaged hand, stroking it gently. "Oh my God. Look at you. What happened?"

Rajesh spoke in a staccato whisper. "I-I've let everyone down, Tanya ... I trusted people I shouldn't have. We're ... we're ruined."

Tanya gripped his hand resolutely. "Hey now. Don't say that. Whatever it is, we can work it out."

Her angelic face floated above him, radiating goodness. The edges of his vision began to blur. "Tell Mum and Dad I've been mugged ... Just tell them that ... ... Please ... I don't want them to ..." Darkness closed in, and he blacked out.

During Tanya's next visit, Rajesh told her everything. In a faltering voice, he exorcised his soul, leaving nothing out. He confessed his adulterous affair, his reckless spending, his unbelievable naivety, the fact that one of London's most dangerous gangsters was now de facto head of his father's company, a company he had spent years building up.

"What have I done, Tanya? What have I done?"

Tanta just sat there listening. She realised it was pointless to judge him, that to do so would only compound the situation. After all, she had married him for better or for worse, and it couldn't get any worse.

Rajesh told her how the massive VAT bill had been

accumulated to oust him. He had no idea how this bill had been run up; normally the accounts department would flag up any problems before they arose. It was only when Tanya asked him who the chief accountant was that everything fell into place. In was none other than master of all trades Jainti Patel. The traitorous bastard had obviously been corrupted by Shearsbe, who in turn was answerable to Regan. But what kind of fraud were they running? With her legal background, Tanya realised that to get to the bottom of it she had to find out. Only then would she be able to fight back.

"Okay," said Tanya. "First thing you're gonna do is put the Pimlico apartment on the market. And Rajesh, don't ever mention that bitch's name to me again."

Rajesh nodded subserviently. "Yes, Tanya. Thank you, Jaan."

"No time for that Jaan stuff right now. We need to stay strong and focused"

Driving home from the hospital, she steeled herself for the battle ahead. That bastard Regan had no idea who he was messing with.

16

"Hmm, I can see why you came, Tanya. Extremely nasty ... extremely nasty indeed." Neil Acherson rose from his desk and walked towards the window. Dressed for court in his barrister's wig and robes, he looked the essence of integrity. He turned, the morning light profiling his aristocratic features. "When did this happen, you say?"

Tanya leant forward earnestly, flicking a rogue strand of hair from her face. "Two days ago. My husband's still in hospital." She had travelled to London to see her former mentor and visit her mother in Southall, leaving the twins with Vidya.

"You did the right thing coming to me. This Regan character sounds horrendous. Funnily enough, I remember him from your wedding. Rajesh seemed somewhat enamoured with him."

"Under his spell, more like. The guy's absolutely screwed him."

"Yes. Twenty-one million pounds is no small amount."

Tanya had contemplated this enormous sum for the past two days. But hearing it said out loud really brought it home to her, and she broke down. "I'm ... I'm desperate, Neil. Rajesh is suicidal. Broken. I-I need your help ... I don't know who else to turn to. Please, will you help me?"

Neil rushed over to her and placed a firm hand on her shoulder. "Don't cry. Of course I'll help."

She smiled, her eyes bloodshot and tearstained. "Thanks. I know how busy you are."

"Nonsense. I've always got time for my favourite intern. You're like a daughter to me."

His kind words calmed her. "That's so nice of you, Neil. What are my options?"

"Well, for starters you're a trained lawyer. Get back in the saddle. Use the firm's contacts with the police and fraud squad to find out all you can about Regan. In the meantime, I'll ring someone I know from Customs and Excise to see if they can fathom out what might be going on at S. T. Freights." He noticed a wave of hope break across Tanya's face. "I have to warn you, this doesn't look good for Rajesh. He's up to his neck in it by the sound of things."

"I know, I know. I just want to get the ball rolling. I feel so helpless doing nothing."

"That's perfectly understandable. But be in no doubt, Tanya; cases like these are extremely complex. Men like Regan have got an army of lawyers. You're really going to have to do your homework before you can even *think* about going up against him." He glanced at his watch. "Sorry, I'm due in court in half an hour – another city trader with his fingers caught in the till. Leave it with me. I'll ring you just as soon as I've heard back from my contact in Customs and Excise. And don't worry."

Neil left his chambers and headed for court. On her way out, Tanya popped into the main office to say hello to her former colleagues. She smiled bravely, telling them how wonderful married life was. "You'll be seeing a bit more of me. I'm doing some part-time work."

She took the tube to Southall. As she walked along South Road, the sights and sounds of her old neighbourhood seemed to lift her spirits. It felt good to be back home again, amidst the hurly-burly. She entered a covered market and bought her mother a bunch of flowers, lingering to enjoy the multicultural mayhem, the jabbering tongues and exotic smells of a world distilled into this small area of London. Then a face from the past appeared. When she exited the market, she saw a group of men arguing on the street. One of them was mouthing off threateningly. It was Mac. He hadn't changed, by the look of it, still playing the tough gangster. She remembered the last time she saw him; it was outside Madhu's the day he and Rajesh almost got into a fight, before that Range Rover pulled up and that ugly white guy separated them. That was the first time she had ever seen Mac back down. Whoever that guy was really frightened him. She put her head down to avoid being seen and crossed the road.

She spent the afternoon with her mother before taking the train back to Gerrards Cross. After checking on the twins, she drove to the hospital to see Rajesh. Halfway there, her mobile rang.

"Hi Tanya. It's Neil. I spoke to my contact in Customs and Excise. I told him the facts, and he was extremely helpful. According to him it sounds like some sort of carousel fraud's been taking place."

"What's that?"

"Search me. He didn't go into too much detail, but apparently it's something to do with non-payment of VAT."

"That fits."

"He told me it's better if you speak to him face-to-face, so I've made an appointment for you at his office at ten o'clock tomorrow. I hope that's convenient?"

"Brilliant, Neil! Honestly, I can't thank you enough."

"Always glad to help. Let me know how you get on."

Tanya arrived at the hospital feeling much more in control. The panic that had swept over her these past few days had now subsided, replaced by a feeling of optimism. She still had a long way to go, but at least the forces of the law were on her side.

Entering the ward, she suddenly remembered she had to wash her hands. She stopped at the dispenser and glugged out two squirts of antiseptic gel. As she glanced down the corridor, she saw a man walking towards her. He was dressed in a shell suit and had a huge cannonball head. The thing that caught her eye was the fact he was carrying an expensive leather briefcase. As he swaggered past, barging through the door without washing his hands, she was certain she had seen him somewhere before.

She strolled onto the ward and straight away noticed something was wrong. Rajesh was sitting up in bed looking pale, a frightened expression on his face.

"What's the matter?" asked Tanya.

Rajesh took a deep breath. His hands were shaking, his eyes darting back and forth towards the door. "I've just had a visitor ... Teddy, one of Regan's thugs."

"A bald guy in a shell suit carrying a briefcase?"

"How do you know?"

"He just walked past me on the corridor."

"Fuck me. He didn't he see you, did he?"

"No. I had my back to him."

"Thank God for that."

"What did he want?"

"He wanted me to sign some papers."

"You didn't, did you?"

"I couldn't." He held up both plaster casts. "Look at the state of my hands. He was really pissed off. He even asked one of the nurses when the plaster was coming off. Oh shit. Oh shit."

Tanya put her arm around his wounded shoulder gingerly. She had never seen him so terrified. The self-confidence, the chutzpah – everything that made Rajesh Rajesh – seemed to have vanished. "It's all right, baby. He's gone now."

"Yeah but he'll be back. You don't know him, Tanya; he's an evil bastard." He paused, glancing once more down the ward. "Actually, you've seen him before; that day outside Madhu's. Don't you remember? Mac and I were just about to go at it when he drove up in his Range Rover."

"I thought I recognised him! You never said he worked for Regan?"

"I didn't know it at the time. Well, he does, yeah. It's his right-hand man."

A light went on in Tanya's head, a flash of inspiration she kept to herself. She sat beside the bed and told him she'd been to see her mentor, Neil Acherson, and that he was convinced some sort of fraud was taking place at S. T. Freights.

Hearing the word "fraud" sent Rajesh over the edge. "What do you mean? What do you mean? I've done nothing wrong! Everything I've done is legal! Legal!" A wave of panic seized him. "Fucking hell, Tanya! What are you saying? It's bad enough I've lost control of the business without this! Oh God, what if Dad finds out? It'll kill him!"

"Shush, Rajesh. Calm down." Realising he was far too fragile to face the truth, she softened her words. "Nothing's certain. I just need to find out what's been going on first. Don't worry; it'll all get sorted."

He stared at her like a child emerging from a nightmare, his whole body trembling. "Will it? Will it? Promise me? Promise me?"

"I promise."

The next morning, Tanya was back in London. At 9.30 a.m. she took a cab from the station and drove to 100 Parliament Street, headquarters of HM Customs and Excise. Situated in the beating heart of Westminster, a short distance from the Houses of Parliament, the building was a colossal rectangle made of Portland stone. Everything about it, from its grand entrance to its rows of sturdy Georgian windows, exuded the power of the State. "We are in control," it said.

She gave her name at reception and was told to make her way to the second floor. At ten o'clock precisely, a thin, nondescript man in a grey suit invited her into his large oak-panelled office. He was middle-aged and spoke with a public school accent.

He pointed to a green Chesterfield sofa that stood beside a wall of leather-bound law books. "Do take a seat, Mrs Thakral. I'm John Harvey – head of Strategy. Very pleased to meet you."

Tanya shook his hand and sat down. Feeling intimidated, she stared at a collection of beautiful eighteenth-century oil paintings hung on the wall – views of the Thames, English country churchyard scenes. The office was neat and tidy, befitting a disciple of precisely calculated transactions, a man whose power was based not on violence and intimidation, like Regan's, but on the eternal principles of the law. She was glad he was on her side.

"Would you care for some tea, Mrs Thakral?"

"No, thank you."

Mr Harvey sat down next to her. "So you want to know about carousel fraud?"

"Yes, please."

He relaxed into the soft leather sofa. "Were to begin? Well, it's a sophisticated cross-border VAT fraud that involves tax evasion and theft. We're coming across it more and more nowadays days, especially amongst organised criminal networks, since the rewards are virtually limitless and the sentences, if a conviction can be secured, are relatively modest. What happens is, a fraudster obtains a VAT registration to obtain goods within the EU. Preferably they're small, highly valuable, and easy to transport – such as computer chips or mobile phones. Now, these goods can come from anywhere in the world, but in order for the fraud to work, they must pass through a European country. The goods are then sold on at a higher price, inclusive of VAT, with the fraudster absconding without paying tax. But that's just the start. The goods are held in a bonded warehouse and then sold on through a series of VAT-registered companies, who then re-export them to another EU country. Are you with me?"

"I think so."

"Good. Amazingly, the goods are then sold *back* to the original exporter, usually on the same day and at a reduced cost, over and over again, without the goods leaving the bonded warehouse. So not only does the original exporter get away without paying VAT, but the re-exporter *then* has the *nerve* to reclaim the VAT that wasn't paid in the first place! So the more trades, the greater the profit. And if two bogus companies are involved, the gains can be huge. It's costing HMRC billions."

"And if there are more than two companies involved?"

Mr Harvey shook his head at the sheer audacity of such a scheme. "Then the profits would be astronomical. Astronomical! To put it in laymen's terms, Company A sells a mobile phone to company B for £100, but VAT is zero-rated, as the transaction sits within the European Union, where VAT is exempt when trading between two EU countries. Company B then sells the mobile phone to Company C for £102 + VAT. Company C then sells the phone back to Company A for £104 but at zero rate of VAT. Company A has purchased a phone for £104 which it originally sold for £100, but company B will be holding the VAT that was paid when company C made the purchase. Are you still with me?" Tanya nodded intently. "Because company C eventually sold the goods for export, it will be able to reclaim the VAT paid to company B, which means that although the chain has lost £4 on the transactions, the net profit has been the twenty per cent accumulated in reclaimed VAT! The same goods will go around and around the system accumulating VAT – hence the term 'Carousel fraud'."

"Say I had my suspicions that a company was involved in such a fraud. How would I go about proving it?"

"Ideally you would need to infiltrate the company in some way. Place a mole on the inside to gather evidence – names, dates, bills, transactions; that sort of thing. It's terribly difficult. A lot of these bogus companies are good at covering their tracks. And if a gang of criminals are involved, it can be very dangerous."

Tanya thanked him for his time and left. Her next appointment was with a senior detective she had struck up a friendship with during her internship. Her name was Kath Tyler, a mother of two who had risen through the ranks of the Met with her tough approach to policing. Their off-the-record chat took place in a coffee shop in Soho. Kath was easy to spot. Six foot tall and athletically built, she dominated the tiny Turkish establishment with her Amazonian presence. She looked every inch the undercover policewoman in her sensible black trousers and dark duffle coat.

After exchanging pleasantries, Kath laid it on the line about Regan. "We've been after the bastard for years. You name it, he's involved in it: drugs, prostitution, racketeering, murder. But we've never been able to pin anything on him. I'm telling you, Tanya, what I wouldn't give to bust him. It'd mean instant promotion for sure." She took a sip of ink-black coffee and set the little cup down on its saucer with a satisfying clink. Fixing Tanya with an inquisitorial stare, she asked, "So, er … why the sudden interest in Regan?"

Not wanting to give too much away, Tanya baited the hook perfectly. "I might have something on him."

"Really?" Promotion! She could smell it! "Don't be shy; you can tell your old mate, Kath. We go way back."

Tanya found her a little patronising. "It's early days, but …"

Kath understood her reticence. "You don't want to go into too much detail. Totally agree. If you do find anything on him, anything at all, come to me day or night. Understand? Us girls have got to stick together."

Tanya smiled. Naked ambition had made Kath the perfect cop. "Why should the men get all the plaudits?"

"Exactly." Kath delved under the table and brought out a plastic folder. "Read this; it's a detailed file on Regan – business interests, known associates. It might come in handy."

"Thanks."

"And for God's sake, don't do anything stupid. Come to me the second you've got anything." She gave the café the once-over before whispering, conspiratorially, "Regan's a vicious bastard, so don't take any chances." Kath got up and slipped on the hood of her duffle coat, monk-like. She stared out of the window. It had begun to rain. "Facking weather. See you soon, Tanya … And be careful."

Tanya ordered another coffee. Over the next half hour, she studied the file carefully. Then she found what she was looking for. Staring up at her on a page titled "Known Associates" was a photo of Mac, his pockmarked face set in a grimace. Below the photo, he was described as a "foot soldier and general dog's body." Tanya was ecstatic. Here was a way into Regan, but she would have to use all her charm to activate the plan. When she turned to the last page of the file, she almost had a heart attack. There was a photo of Rajesh! Taken with a telephoto lens, he was pictured climbing into his red Ferrari outside Regan's mansion. This was serious. Tanya felt her knees buckle. Neil was right; Rajesh was up to his neck in it. She knew she had to act now in order to save him, and Mac was her only chance. She picked up her mobile, scrolled down to Mac's number, and pressed Call.

After a few moments, a rough, streetwise voice answered aggressively. "Who's this?"

"Mac, it's me."

"Who the fuck's me?"

"Tanya."

Suddenly the voice changed, gathering warmth. "Hiya, babes! Long time. How's that loser husband of yours?"

"He's okay."

"Should have married me, Tanya. You should have married me. Anyway, what's up?"

"Can we meet?"

"Sure, babes. Anything you say. I'm in Southall, where are you?"

"Soho. I'll grab a cab and come over. Where do you want to meet?"

"How about Madhu's?"

"Great. I'll treat you to lunch. See you there at twelve."

When she got to Madhu's, Mac was already there. Dressed in black Levi's and a hooded top, he was sitting in the corner, sipping an ice-cold Cobra.

He got to his feet and embraced Tanya affectionately, kissing her on both cheeks. "Tanya! Wow, look at you! You look great, girl!"

"You don't look too bad yourself." Although she wasn't attracted to him physically, she had always retained a soft spot for him. They went back a long way and had played together as children.

"Hear you've come up in the world. What you doin' slummin' it round here? Southall's a long way from paradise."

"I've come to see my mum. Besides, I'm still the same old Tanya." She had to broach the subject carefully. "How are *you* doing? Still hanging out with that dangerous crowd?"

"Business is business." A politician's answer. Typical Mac.

"Only the last time I was here, you got threatened by a white guy in a Range Rover."

"*That* scumbag!"

A chink of light. "He looked like a somebody to me."

"A 'somebody'! Do me favour! He's a shithead. Always giving me orders – do this, do that. Don't you hate the way whites come into our area and boss us around?" Even at school Mac had been a racist.

Right, hit him with the truth. "Actually, it's not him I've come about. It's his boss."

Mac spat his beer back into his glass. "What! You know Regan?"

"No, but Rajesh does. He's in a lot of trouble. I need your help."

"And what makes you think I'd lift a finger to help that prick?"

"Please. I'm begging you. We grew up together. You've always had a special place in my heart."

"Is that why you married Rajesh?"

"Come on, Mac, you know I've never felt that way about you. We've always been friends, always. Remember when you used to protect me at school? Well, I need you to do it again. If you ever felt anything for me, now's the time to show it. Be an uncle to my children. Please, for their sake, help us."

Mac couldn't help himself. The one true love of his life, a girl he'd worshipped for years, was asking for help. How could he possibly refuse? Besides, he had his own secret agenda. "Okay, Tans. You'd better tell me what all this is about."

Over lunch Tanya told him everything – how Rajesh's business had been taken away from him, how he'd landed up in hospital, courtesy of Regan. Inwardly Mac was pleased Rajesh had got his comeuppance. All his life the prick had got everything on a plate – money, good looks, Tanya – but now he had flown too close to the sun. It amused the hell out of Mac to think that Rajesh had got the shit kicked out of him. He only wished he'd been there to see it.

After Tanya finished talking, he took a sip of beer and asked, "So what is it you want me to do?"

"I want you to help me bring Regan down."

His first reaction was to laugh out loud and tell her not to be so fucking naive. *Bring Regan down? Do me favour!* The combined forces of the law had been trying for years without any success; what made her think *she* could do any better? But the germ of an idea began to grow; it was one he had harboured for a long time. "And how the fuck am I supposed to do that, exactly?"

"You work for him. You could give me an insight into his operation."

Typical woman. Betrayal comes easy to them. "What, rat on him, you mean?"

Tanya shrugged. "If you like. Then I can start to build a case against him. From what I've heard about Regan, he controls a huge crime network. Bring him down, and the whole rotten lot follows."

Mac was about to ask what was in it for him, but he knew exactly what was in it for him. If, by some miracle, she was to succeed, then it would leave a void in London's underworld and he could waltz straight in. And if she failed, which she was likely to, then at least he would come out looking like the hero. Heads he wins, tails she loses. Mac was streetwise enough to know that your enemies' enemy is your friend. "And what's Rajesh gonna be doing while I'm putting my life on the line? Sitting in his mansion in Gerrards Cross with his finger up his arse?"

"You always did have a way with words, Mac. No, he'll be back at S. T. Freights, gathering evidence."

"You've got it all worked out, ain't you, girl?"

"It's called planning. So are you up for it?"

Mac sat back and chuckled. The girl had balls, no doubt about it. "Yeah, why not."

Rajesh was discharged from hospital, and over the next few weeks he slowly began to recover – physically, not mentally; his wounds healed, but his spirit seemed broken beyond repair. He would sit in the chair for hours, staring aimlessly out of the window, his mind replaying over and over the events leading up to his downfall. Like an expert pathologist, he disseminated his former life in minute detail, examining each incident with microscopic clarity – situations, conversations – before shaking his head and moving on to the next. Conclusion – his rampaging ego had led him astray.

Surrounded by his family, he realised what a fool he'd been to put his trust in a bunch of glamorous strangers – strangers who had used and abused him. But the person he felt the most hated for was Bav. He had scooped her up from the gutter only to be betrayed in the most cold-hearted and callous way. He didn't deserve that. No way. Or did he? Watching Tanya go about her daily routine, putting everyone else before herself, he realised he did deserve it. Only a complete moron could have betrayed such a kind, loving wife. His days were filled with regret. One afternoon Tanya found him in the nursery leaning over the cot, tears streaming down his face. When she asked him what was wrong, he said he couldn't bear the fact that he'd let the children down, that because of him their inheritance had been squandered, their future made uncertain. Tanya tried to lift his spirits by telling him that when he was better he would go back to S. T. Freights and rescue the company.

Rajesh's concern about S. T. Freights was picked up by Satish, though for a different reason. Having swallowed the story of the vicious mugging, Satish was convinced his son's unhappiness was due to him not being back at work and in control of the business. To reassure him the company was in safe hands during his temporary absence, one morning, just after breakfast, he said to Rajesh, "To put your mind at ease I've invited Jainti Patel round to the house at eleven o'clock for a progress report. He's more than capable of running things while you're away. So you see, there's no need to worry."

No need to worry! Rajesh's jaw fell open. He couldn't believe his father's naivety. As the clock ticked round to eleven o'clock, a fear akin to a child's imminent visit to the dentist swept over him. He knew Patel would be at his grovelling best, giving his father no hint of his true personality. When Tanya heard about this, she decided she would stay around to meet this so-called loyal servant of the company. Having read Sun Tzu's book *The Art of War,* she understood the famous maxim "Know your enemy." She would play Patel at his own game, observing him closely whilst planning her strategy.

When the doorbell rang, Tanya rushed across the hall to let him in. She had tried to picture this scheming Machiavellian, imagining him to be a tall, stern-looking individual imbued with evil charm. But when she opened the door, she was surprised to find a balding, chubby little man standing in the porch, a sickly smile wreathed across his face. "Hello, Mr Patel. I'm Tanya. It's good of you to come."

Patel oozed his way in, bowing obsequiously. "Oh, thank you. Thank you. It is such an honour to meet you, Mrs Thakral. Rajesh has told me all about you. How is sir-ji, by the way? Well, I hope? His presence is greatly missed."

Patel was good. Very good. Tanya couldn't help but admire his supreme acting skills – skills that had propelled him to the top of the company. Behind the schmooze she detected a dangerous individual. Bred on a diet of envy, he was not to be underestimated.

She took him by the arm. "Rajesh is a lot better, thank you. It won't be long before he's back at work."

"Wonderful news!" said Patel, beaming. "The place isn't the same without him."

"I'm sure the company's in safe hands. I know how much he values your ability."

"You are too kind."

Leading him across the hall, she noticed his eyes darting here and there, taking in the luxurious surroundings. She could almost hear him thinking "Soon I will have a house like this." When they arrived at the door on the opposite side of the hall, Tanya said, "Rajesh and Mr Thakral are in the lounge. I'm a bit of an airhead when it comes to business, so I'll leave you to it."

When Rajesh caught sight of Patel entering the room, bowing and scraping, his stomach turned over. He couldn't believe the man's Judas-like audacity.

Satish swallowed the deception. "Jainti Bhai! Come in! Come in! You're a sight for sore eyes!"

"Thank you, Mr Thakral, sir. You don't know how good it makes me feel to see you looking so well."

"Do you hear that, Rajesh? We're so lucky to have such a loyal employee! Sit down, Jainti Bhai."

Patel sat opposite them on the sofa. He threw Rajesh a quick fox-like grin before his face descended into solemnity. "I heard about your terrible ordeal, sir-ji. Goodness me. The streets aren't safe nowadays. If I had my way, I'd hang every single mugger from a lamppost."

"Hanging's too good for the bastards who did this," said Rajesh, fixing him with an icy stare.

Patel raised an amused eyebrow. "Your wife tells me you will soon be back at work. I do hope so. There is much to be getting on with. Not that we've been idle since you've been away. Goodness me, no! The company has never *been* so busy!"

For the next hour Patel spun a fantastical tale of burgeoning balance sheets and healthy order books. Satish was enthralled. He kept glancing over at Rajesh, smiling and nodding as if to say, "Isn't Patel doing a great job!" It took every ounce of Rajesh's willpower to prevent him from launching himself onto the sofa and wringing Patel's neck. What sickened him most was the way his father was so taken in. Watching Patel weave his magic, he vowed there and then to get even with him. Whilst out of sight behind the door, taking notes, Tanya was listening to his every word.

When Patel finished, Satish thrust out his hand. "Well done, Jainti Bhai! You're doing a magnificent job! Magnificent! Isn't he, Rajesh?"

"Yes, Dad ... he certainly is."

Patel bowed. "It is nothing, Mr Thakral, sir. I'm glad to be of service." He glanced at his watch. "Now, if you don't mind, I have to be getting back to work."

"The man's worth his weight in gold! I wish all our employees were so conscientious! Rajesh, see him out!"

Rajesh escorted Patel to the front door. Once they were out of earshot, Patel's syrupy expression changed to one of granite-like truculence. "I want you back in the office first thing in the morning. Don't be late." Then, just as quickly as it had disappeared, his sickly sweet smile returned as out of the corner of his eyes he saw Vidya emerging from the kitchen carrying a Tiffin box. "Mrs Thakral! What a pleasure it is to see you!"

Vidya handed him the box. "Just a little something to show my appreciation for all your hard work – some homemade spicy *Mysore Dosa."*

Patel outdid even himself in cringe-worthy appreciation. "Oh! Mrs Thakral! What can I say? Such kindness. Such generosity! Rajesh has often told me what a wonderful cook you are." He hadn't. "If only my wife was as talented!"

Vidya blushed like a schoolgirl. Rajesh saw the glint in Patel's eye and imagined him already planning to ditch the current Mrs Patel and propose to his mother the second Satish's ashes floated serenely down the Ganges. The thought of Patel as his stepfather made him want to heave. "Jainti has to go now, Maa."

"Of course, of course. See you soon, I hope."

Patel proffered the cheesiest of grins, reminiscent of '80s Bollywood, winking outrageously at Vidya. "You may rely on it."

Unbelievable! The bastard really did have his sights set on his mother! In a flash Rajesh opened the front door. "See you tomorrow, Jainti."

Rajesh watched from the window as Patel walked to his car. He saw him take a backwards glance at the house, as if eyeing the property for himself. After Patel drove away, Rajesh went into the kitchen to find Tanya.

"I'm going back to work tomorrow, Tanya."

"Do you feel up to it?"

"No. But the sooner we do something about the situation, the better."

Tanya flicked the kettle on. "Okay. Sit down. I've got a plan."

18

At 8.55 a.m., Rajesh eased his Porsche into the car park at S. T. Freights. He hadn't been up this early for a long time. As though it were his first day at school, he felt tense, a ball of anxiousness spinning in his stomach. He drove up to his dedicated parking space but was shocked to find his name plaque had been removed. In the space marked "Chairman" stood Patel's BMW. Alongside was Shearsbe's midnight-blue Maserati GranTurismo. No space for Rajesh. He would have to park with the rest of the staff. The message couldn't have been clearer.

His humiliation was complete when Patel led him to a tiny windowless office at the far end of the corridor next to the Gents and said, "You'll be working in here from now on."

Formerly used for storage, the damp-smelling room had a Formica desk, a rickety chair, and a battered filing cabinet. On the desk was an ancient Apple Mac computer, its grubby keyboard a testament to thousands of stabbing fingers. Next to that was a pile of timesheets.

Rajesh looked at Patel quizzically. "And what is it you want me to do, exactly?"

"Go through each time sheet and input the data onto the computer." A cynical smirk spread across his face. "Like I said, nothing too taxing."

From dazzling chairman to lowly data imputer. Rajesh wanted to tell Patel to go fuck himself, but he remembered what Tanya had said about controlling his temper. So he simply nodded and took off his jacket.

"Come to my office in half an hour," said Patel. "I've got some papers for you to sign." As he was leaving, he turned back to face Rajesh. "And no more long lunches. You get an hour like everyone else."

Rajesh's mission was simple; he was to do as he was told, however demeaning, and in the process gather as much information as possible – receipts, emails, copies of contracts – anything that would lead back to Regan. Shearsbe and Patel were small fry, so if Tanya's plan had any hope of succeeding, they had to implicate London's top gangster. Mindful of Rajesh's fragile ego, Tanya likened the assignment to that of his hero, James Bond. He would in effect be a secret agent, working undercover to save S. T. Freights. That made him feel a whole lot better.

Number one on the agenda was making a detailed analysis of the goods stored inside the bonded warehouse. According to Tanya this was key to uncovering the carousel fraud; anything that remained inside the warehouse but was recorded as having been shipped out was evidence of malpractice. From there they could work out which companies were involved, follow the trail, and build up a picture of the magnitude of the fraud. But how to get inside the warehouse without arousing suspicion? Obviously Patel would be watching him like a hawk. Rajesh sighed. It wasn't going to be easy.

He sat down and booted up the computer. As he began the mind-numbing process of inputting data he realised how much his life had changed; less than a month ago he was feeling on top of the of the world. Now everything had crumbled.

An old saying came to mind: "Life is like a carousel – up and down, round and round." He smiled at such a delicious irony. But it worked both ways. He would make damn sure Regan and his crew took their turn on fate's rollercoaster.

At nine thirty Rajesh left his pokey office and made his way down the corridor. When he saw Margaret sitting at her desk, he gave her a friendly smile. The look on her face told him how uncomfortable she was with the situation. He thought about confiding in her; for years she had been a trusted employee. But no, after what had happened to him, he would never trust anyone outside his family again.

The intercom buzzed. "Is Rajesh there yet?" It was Patel, and he sounded impatient.

"Er, yes, Mr Patel. He's just—"

"Well send him in then!"

Margaret sighed. "You'd better—"

"Yeah," said Rajesh. "I heard."

He took a deep breath and opened the door. The welcoming committee couldn't have been more intimidating. Patel glowered at him from behind the desk, whilst Shearsbe, lounging on a chair, raised his eyes and smirked.

"Well, well," said Shearsbe, his voice dripping in sarcasm. "If it isn't the wounded soldier! How are you, mate?"

Somehow Rajesh managed to control his temper. Ignoring Shearsbe's jibe, he addressed Patel. "You wanted me to sign some papers?"

"He's a quick learner," Shearsbe said with a chuckle.

Patel motioned for Rajesh to come forward. "Yes." He handed him a pen and pointed to the bottom of a bulky contract lying on the desk. "Sign here … and here."

Rajesh noticed the other name on the contract – Mr Li Jianguo, of Jianguo Industries. "When's the first shipment due?"

"None of your business!" said Patel. "Now get back to work!"

"Don't be like that, J. P.," said Shearsbe. "It's his first day back. He's finding it hard to let go, aren't you, Rajesh?"

Rajesh shrugged. "Whatever." He turned and walked towards the door.

"Bav sends her regards, by the way."

Rajesh stopped, Shearsbe's words penetrating his skull like

tracer bullets. He gripped the door handle tightly. Without looking back, he opened the door and walked out. Boiling with anger, he stormed down the corridor, flung open the door to his office, and kicked over the rickety chair. "*Bastards! Fucking bastards!*" He paced the floor, gulping air like a drowning man. Gradually he calmed down. Tanya had warned him this might happen. But it was just the impetus he needed. He sat down, more determined than ever to get his revenge.

An hour later he came across an anomaly on one of the timesheets – a forklift truck driver had filled in the wrong hours. Rajesh tutted. *Can't the guy add up?* He glanced at the top of the timesheet and noticed the man worked in the bonded warehouse. It was just the excuse he needed to go poking around! He grabbed the timesheet and made his way across the yard, glancing up at his old office in case Patel was standing at the window.

After passing through security he walked towards the top end of the cavernous warehouse, where the electronic goods were kept. The section was packed with boxes containing mobile phones and computer chips, stack upon stack of them. Patel was right; business was booming! Keeping an eye out for anyone watching, he ducked behind a large pallet. Crouching down, he inched his way along, examining each of the shipping labels. After a few minutes he came across a pile of boxes whose labels were printed in Chinese. He peered closer. Beneath the Cantonese calligraphy, in tiny writing, were the words "Jianguo Industries." *Hold on,* thought Rajesh. *I've only just signed the contact! How come the goods are already here?* Suddenly he heard footsteps. *Shit!* If anyone caught him snooping around, he'd be reported instantly to Patel. The footsteps were getting closer. He held his breath. It was two men by the sound of it. They were standing on the other side of the boxes. Obviously someone had seen him and had come to investigate.

"When I got in," said one of the men, "the game had already started and I missed the first goal."

"I watched it on *Match of the Day*," said the other. "I'm fucked if I'm paying their fancy prices."

The men walked off cursing and swearing. Rajesh let out a sigh of relief. He'd been there long enough. It was time to leave. He stood up and squeezed between two pallets. As he was about to enter the main body of the warehouse, he suddenly caught sight of a label that set his pulse racing: "Élan Électronique" – the Swiss company he'd signed the very first contact with. But that was months ago! Then he remembered seeing a sales invoice for the exact same phones. It made no sense. If the goods had been sold, what were they still doing here?

"Thakral! Thakral!"

Patel! Shit! Rajesh composed himself and stepped out onto the main concourse of the warehouse.

Patel was standing about twenty meters away. When he saw Rajesh, he came rushing towards him. "What the hell are you doing in here?"

He held out the timesheet innocently. "I'm looking for Les Haines. He's a forklift truck driver. He made a mistake on his timesheet. I just wanted to speak to him about it."

Patel snatched the paper off him. "Let me see."

Rajesh pointed to the irregularity. "There. He put down eight hours of overtime, but the weekly total doesn't add up."

"Hmm, I see. The idiot obviously does not know his head from his arse! I'll deal with it. In future come to me if you have any problems."

"Sure."

"Now get back to work."

Patel marched off in the direction of the canteen. As Rajesh was making his way outside, he saw a black transit van being unloaded. The driver was leaning against the door, puffing on a cigarette. His face looked familiar. Then he remembered; it was the head bouncer from Rouge, one of Regan's most trusted employees. *What the hell is he doing here? And what is he delivering?* Careful not be seen, Rajesh skirted round the other side of the van and made his way back to the office.

Later that night, after changing the twins' nappies, Rajesh told Tanya what he'd discovered.

She listened carefully, making notes. When he'd finished she put her pen down and said, "Definitely sounds like a carousel fraud, the goods not leaving the warehouse like that. You'll have to give me a list of all the companies you dealt with recently. I bet every one of them is going to end up as the missing trader company. And try and get copies of the contracts if you can."

A terrible feeling of foreboding came over him. "The thing is, Tanya, my name's on all those contracts. If anything happens, I'll be to blame."

"Leave that to me."

"Why? What are you going to do?"

"Just leave it to me."

"Oh! I forgot to tell you, when I was leaving the warehouse I saw one of Regan's goons delivering something."

Tanya's ears pricked up. "Really? What was he delivering?"

"Couldn't see. Parcels of some sort."

"And you're sure he works for Regan?"

"Positive."

"Great. I'll tell Mac."

Rajesh thought he was hearing things. "Mac? *Mac!* What's going on, Tanya?"

"I was going to tell you … I went to see him while you were in hospital. He's agreed to help."

"I don't believe this! He works for Regan!"

"I know he does. And he hates his guts."

"He hates mine even more. Why the hell should he help me?"

"Because I asked him to. We go back a long way, remember?"

"Well, I don't trust him. How do you know he won't go to Regan?"

"He won't."

"You don't know that for sure!"

"He's given me his word."

"And you believe him? You're more naive than I thought, putting your trust in that dog!"

Tanya delivered her repost with calm, ice-cold clarity. "And you know all about trust, don't you, Rajesh? You're the expert."

She was right; after what he'd put her through, he was last person to talk. Chastised, he stared at the carpet. "Okay. But be careful. These people are dangerous."

The next morning, Tanya dropped Rajesh off at work. "Don't forget, try and get copies of those contracts."

"Easier said than done. Patel keeps them in his office – *my* office!"

"Do your best. See you later."

She gave him a kiss and headed into central London. The first of her three appointments was with John Harvey – head of Strategy at HM Customs and Excise. Armed with the list of companies given to her by Rajesh, she told him exactly what they'd discovered – the mysterious Chinese goods that had somehow appeared before the contract was signed, the Swiss mobile phones that had been sold but had never left the warehouse, the fact that a well-known gangster was seen delivering packages.

Mr Harvey listened intently. "Hmm. After what you've just told me, I'm convinced a major fraud is being perpetrated. This is serious. Really serious."

"I'm wondering if we could do a deal."

"Go on."

"It's about my husband ... I know he's not totally innocent, but I can honestly say he had no idea any of the deals were fraudulent. The people he got involved with duped him. Set him up. They knew his father owned an import–export business. They targeted him and flattered him, and like an idiot, he fell for it. I know he'll have to face the consequences, but I'd really like to save the company. His father built it up from nothing, you see. He's worked hard all his life; paid his taxes, supported the community. He's even won a Queen's Award for Industry! He doesn't know anything about this. He's been ill recently, and if he lost the business, it would kill him ... So please, for his sake, can't we do a deal to save the company?"

Mr Harvey couldn't help but admire Tanya's passion and commitment. "I must say, Mrs Thakral, your husband's a lucky man having you on his side. A very lucky man." He got up and began to pace the room. "What do you have in mind, exactly?"

"Well, if you could waive the twenty million VAT bill, then with Rajesh's help you could smash a major fraud – one that stretches across the whole of Europe by the look of it."

He was flabbergasted by the boldness of her proposal. "This is not an exchange bureau, where we can wave a magic wand and make twenty million pounds' worth of tax liabilities disappear! We are answerable civil servants and have to follow protocol and the law of the land! Taxes that are accumulated have to be paid or the consequences have to be faced. Do you honestly think that Her Majesty's Revenue can or would right off such a substantial amount of money for what is, in essence, titbits of information?"

Tanya could not mask to the feeling of being humiliated "The titbits, as you call them, that I am offering are names, places, documents, concrete evidence, guns, and the possibility of drugs seizures. How many man-hours of surveillance would it take to get this information, and what would it cost? And even if you did pour vast resources into it, what would be the guarantee that you would get a comparable result? I am gift-wrapping Regan and handing him to you on a plate. You will speed up Regan's arrest by years! And let's face it, how close has HMRC or any other authority ever come to putting Regan away? We both know that his operations are a lot more damaging and dangerous than twenty million pounds of hypothetical tax. It is tax accumulated by a paper fraud! It does not really exist! And now with the added revenue of the carousel empire, Regan will be unstoppable."

He thought about if for as moment. "Of course, it all depends if we can bring these people to justice. If we can, then I'm sure we can come to some arrangement."

"I can't thank you enough, Mr Harvey."

"Please, call me John."

Tanya's next appointment was with Detective Inspector Kath Tyler. They met in the same Turkish coffee shop in Soho they had met at previously. When Tanya told Kath about Mac's decision to turn supergrass, Kath's eyes lit up.

"*Really?* That's fantastic! We've tried every trick in the book to nail that bastard. Having someone on the inside's a dream. A dream! You've made my day, Tanya, you really have."

"How should we play this? I'm seeing Mac later and need to know how to handle him."

"Good. Good. Right, first thing he needs to do is find out if Regan's got any major drug deals in the pipeline – names, dates, locations, any information, anything that will lead back to him. We'll do the rest. If Mac plays his cards right, you can tell him from me we'll wipe the slate clean. Can't say fairer than that."

Tanya went on to explain she was working in conjunction with John Harvey from HM Customs and Excise.

"I've heard of him," said Kath. "The guy's a real bloodhound. Once he's on the scent, he never lets go, ever."

"Tell you what *would* be good, if you could liaise with him – bring the two investigations together."

"Yeah, he hinted at the same thing."

"Great. What I really want to do is link Regan to this fraud I'm investigating. That way he'll go down for longer. I know for sure one of his top men is involved, a guy called Mark Shearsbe."

Kath wrote the name down. "That's the hard bit. Regan's been linked with different criminals in the past, but he's always managed to come up smelling of roses. This time we'll have to make it stick; otherwise, he'll have us up for harassment and you and your family will be exposed."

"What a joke!"

Tanya's next stop was Southall. When she told Mac about

the immunity deal she'd managed to broker with DI Tyler, his pockmarked face broke into a wise-guy grin. "I could do with having you as my personal lawyer."

"You couldn't afford me, Mac. Seriously, it all depends on the quality of the information you can provide."

"How's this for starters. Word is that Regan's got a big shipment of coke coming in. Not sure when or where. I'll keep my ear to the ground."

"The thing is, Mac, we need something concrete. Something that'll lead right to Regan's door."

"Trust me, baby, by the time I've finished, Regan will be washing dishes to get by in prison."

"Is that a promise?"

"Solid gold."

Tanya could sense the workings of a devious mind and wanted to ensure that Mac would not derail her plans by going renegade with his overzealous ambitions.

"One last thing ... How about you and Rajesh meeting up? He reckons Regan might be storing illicit goods in the warehouse at S. T. Freights. Perhaps you could help him shine a light on it?"

"What! Me and Rajesh work together? Fuck me, wonders never cease!"

Tanya made light of the situation. "You love each other, really. Do you remember when he broke a window at school and you took the blame?"

"Yeah, and I've been taking the blame ever since!"

Tanya unfurled the cutest of girlie grins. "Pleeeeease, Mac. For me."

Mac paused and smiled. "Speak to him, and if he is willing, I will go along with it. But don't expect me to shake his hand or anything."

"Great. How about tonight?"

"You don't waste time, do you, girl?"

"No time like the present. Meet us in Madhu's at seven."

✲ ✲ ✲

Rajesh finished inputting the last of the data into the computer. He glanced at his watch – 4.58 p.m. He leaned back in his chair, stretching and yawing. *My God! Is this how ordinary people earn a living? Poor sods.* His previous life had been a dream compared to this. Still, it wouldn't be long before things were back to normal. Or so he hoped.

It had been a frustrating day. Patel and Shearsbe hadn't left the office, so he hadn't gotten a chance to go searching for evidence. As Tanya said, he would have to bide his time. But he didn't know how much more of this mind-numbing job he could take before he went insane.

When he joined the rest of the throng streaming out of the gate, Rajesh felt a strange kind of camaraderie. His brief time at the coalface had given him a newfound respect for his fellow workers. He realised there was more to a successful business than the man at the top.

To avoid being seen, Tanya had parked around the corner. When Rajesh climbed into the Porsche, he sighed frustratedly. "I've had a hell of day. Not stopped. Honestly, I don't know how people do it."

Tanya was about to say "Welcome to the real world" but thought better of it. Instead she indulged him, planting kisses on his cheek. "Orrr, poor baby. You look worn out."

"Oh, I am."

She started the car. "Hungry?"

"Starving!" Rajesh sat back. It was a change not to be driving. "Where are we going?"

"Thought we'd take a trip down memory lane. There's someone I want you to meet."

"Who?"

"You'll see."

A stranger to a hard day's work, Rajesh drifted off to sleep. When he woke up, it took him a few seconds to get his bearings.

Then he saw the old familiar frontage to Madhu's restaurant. "Don't tell me," he said, smiling, "Your sister's joining us. Great. I've not seen her for—" Tanya shook her head. "Your mum, then?" Another shake. "Well *who?* Come on, Tans, what's with the cloak and dagger?" When he said the word "dagger" he noticed her expression darken. He recalled just such an expression appearing on her face the last time he was here ... *Mac! No, it can't be.* The look on her face said it was. "Tanya! For fuck's sake! What planet are you on?"

"He's here to help."

"I'm not meeting that scumbag!"

"It's just as difficult for him, you know."

"I don't give a shit! I'm not going in!"

"Please, Rajesh. For me?"

"No way!"

Tanya exploded. "Right! Get the fuck out of this car now! Go on!"

"W-what?"

"You heard! Do you think I enjoy meeting petty gangsters!? I'm doing this for *you*, you stupid bastard!" She took hold of the ignition key and fired the engine up, revving it aggressively. "Just say the word and we're out of here! But I'm warning you, don't come crying to me when Regan's got your balls in a vice!"

As she moved to put the car in gear, Rajesh took hold of her hand. "Okay, Tanya. Calm down ... I'm sorry. You're right. I'm an idiot." He took a deep breath. "Okay, let's do it."

When they walked in Madhu's, Mac was already there. Sitting by the window, he had witnessed the silent argument that had taken place inside the car. *Typical Rajesh. Spoilt bastard.* It amused the hell out of Mac that finally Rajesh had come off second best. As Rajesh came walking towards him, the look on his face told him this was the last place he wanted to be. To exacerbate things further, Mac rose magnanimously from his seat, throwing out his arms. "Tanya! Baby! Great to see you again!" He gave Rajesh the briefest of nods. "Raj."

Rajesh remained stubbornly silent, staring at the tablecloth. Tanya elbowed him in the ribs, bringing forth a recalcitrant "Oh, er … yeah … Hi."

"There we are," said Tanya, as if to a child, "That wasn't too difficult, was it?"

Rajesh forced a grin and they all sat down. To oil the wheels Tanya ordered a round of ice-cold Cobras and a sweet lassi for herself. Both Rajesh and Mac gulped theirs down the moment they arrived. There was silence, both men looking anywhere except in the other's direction.

Tanya couldn't believe their juvenile behaviour.

. "Right. Rajesh wants to ask you something, Mac."

"Do I?"

"Yes, you do. You wanted to know if he—"

"Can't he speak for himself?" said Mac, obviously enjoying Rajesh's embarrassment.

"Too right I can!" said Rajesh aggressively, eyeballing Mac.

"Ooooh! The great man speaks."

Rajesh shot up from his chair. "Fuck this! You always were an arsehole, Mac!"

Mac grinned triumphantly. Tanya had to take control. "Sit down, Rajesh! And Mac, stop being an idiot! We're here to work things out, remember?!" Rajesh did as he was told and sat down. "Well go on, we haven't got all night!"

Rajesh began to mumble. "One of Regan's sidekicks delivered something to S. T. Freights the other day. He's the head bouncer from Rogue. I wonder if you know anything about it."

Being spoken to in a civilised manner by his nemesis made Mac feel superior. He relaxed into his chair, consultant-like. "When, exactly?"

"Last Wednesday."

"Like I told Tanya; Regan's expecting a huge shipment of coke sometime this month. He might be moving his stock around to prepare."

"*What!*" said Rajesh. "You don't think he's storing drugs in there, do you?"

"What better place than a secure warehouse."

Hyperventilating, he gripped the tablecloth. "Oh God! I don't need this! I do not need this!"

"Calm down, bro. Give me a couple of days. Let me find out for sure."

Rajesh made brief eye contact with his old enemy. "Thanks, Mac."

Tanya noticed a genuine spark of warmth flash between them. She fanned the embers. "Hey, it's just like the old days – all for one and one for all."

Both men laughed, a succession of childhood memories flitting through their minds.

Driving back to Gerrards Cross, Tanya felt triumphant. She had finally managed to broker what seemed an impossible peace. After that she felt she could tackle anything. The Arabs and Jews? No problem.

When they got home, she took a shower. Whilst she was in the bathroom, Rajesh dipped into her handbag and took out her mobile. He scrolled down to Mac's number. After entering it into his phone, he sent him a text: "Appreciate your help ... ... Rajesh."

Seconds later a text came back: "No probs, bro."

19

"Leave it with me," said Patel. Rajesh had brought him a bunch of timesheets that needed his attention. "I'll sort them out later." Patel opened a drawer in the desk and took out a key. He picked up a file and took it over to the safe, which he then unlocked. A quick glance told Rajesh the safe was full of contracts. If only he could get his hands on them! Patel placed the file in the safe, locked it, and then walked back to the desk and slipped his jacket on.

He must be going out! thought Rajesh. *Finally! Right, you bastard, put the key back in the drawer where it belongs.*

Patel was about to do so when he caught Rajesh staring at him. "That'll be all. Now get back to work."

As he turned to go, he saw Patel slip the key into his jacket pocket. Bastard! Rajesh left the office and made his way back to his rabbit hutch. Gutted, he sat down and scratched his head. Then he remembered something – his father kept a spare key to the safe taped beneath the desk! He had a habit of mislaying things – car keys, credit cards – and so he always kept another one handy. Rajesh shot out of his chair. Good old Dad! Slowly opening the door to his office, he peered down the corridor. He saw Patel leave and then heard him say to Margaret, "I'm going out for a few hours. Ring me on my mobile if anything comes up."

"Certainly, Mr Patel."

Rajesh walked slowly up the corridor. He peeked inside

Shearsbe's office. Empty. *Great.* He looked at his watch – almost ten o'clock. Margaret went on her coffee break at ten. Hiding behind the door, he stared at her reflection in the window opposite. After a few minutes she got up and made her way to the coffee machine. *Right.* He dived into the office and went straight to the window. He saw Patel standing in the yard, giving orders to a truck driver like he owned the place. *Officious bastard.* Rajesh got down on his knees and began a fingertip search beneath the desk. After a few moments of fumbling, he felt the outline of a taped-over key. *Bingo!* He peeled it away, got up, and hurried to the safe. With trembling hands, he unlocked the safe, took out a pile of documents, laid them on the floor, and began searching through them frantically. Filed away in a brown folder were the contracts he was looking for: Élan Électronique, Spirito, Jianguo Industries. He took the first and last pages of each contract and laid them on the carpet next to one another. These were the important pages, the ones with all the details. He took out out his mobile phone and began to photograph each page.

Patel opened his car door. As he was about to climb in, he suddenly remembered he'd left his mobile on the desk. Annoyed, he slammed the car door and trudged back towards the main office.

Rajesh had just finished taking the last of the photos when he heard Margaret's voice outside the door. "You're back early. Mr Patel." *Shit!* He scooped up the documents, shoved them back in the safe, and hurriedly locked the door.

"Forgot my mobile."

"Er, Mr Patel. I wonder if you could look at this."

Like a hunted animal, Rajesh scanned the room for a place to hide.

"Not now, Margaret. I'm late as it is."

Rajesh saw the doorknob turn. Just in time, he dived behind the filing cabinet and pressed himself up against the wall. He heard Patel enter the office, walk towards the desk and pick up something. Rajesh held his breath. That's when he noticed the safe. Through a slit between the filing cabinet and the wall he could see the key sticking out of the lock; in his haste he had left it in there! If Patel saw it, he was finished. Patel's mobile suddenly rang.

"Oh, hello, Mr Regan … Yes, Mr Regan. Yes, yes, I'm on my way."

To his relief he heard Patel scurry out of the office and close the door. So Patel was in direct contact with Regan, was he? The idiot obviously had no idea who he was dealing with. Rajesh waited for a few moments before easing himself out. He peered through the window and saw Patel get in his car and drive away. *Oh no!* Shearsbe was hurrying across the car park towards the main office. Rajesh began to panic. He was trapped. He couldn't leave, because Margaret would see him. And if she did, she was bound to report him … But would she? He'd always got on with her and treated her kindly. But maybe Shearsbe had corrupted her and she was now one of them? He couldn't wait to find out. Shearsbe be would be there any moment. He had to trust in fate. As he pushed open the door, his eyes met Margaret's. He looked at her pleadingly and then hurried down the corridor. Halfway along he stopped, his pulse racing. He heard Shearsbe ask, "Hi, Margaret. Anything happen while I was out?"

"No, Mr Shearsbe."

"Good, good. Er, Rajesh behaving himself, is he?"

"I think so. I've not seen him all morning."

Rajesh was touched by Margaret's loyalty. When he left for home later that day, he caught up with her in the car park. "Thanks for not giving me away this morning."

"That's all right. It's an absolute scandal what's going on. I'm not happy about it one bit. If there's anything I can do to help, just let me know."

At last he had an ally, someone he could trust. "Thanks, Margaret. I won't forget this."

"Say hello to your father from me."

"I will."

When he got home, Rajesh downloaded the photos from his iPhone onto Tanya's laptop. Tanya studied them carefully. "Well done! Now we're getting somewhere!" She downloaded the photos onto an attachment and emailed them to John Harvey at Customs and Excise.

The following day, mid-afternoon, John rang Tanya with some news. "We've done a check; all three companies listed on the contracts are bogus. I've liaised with my European counterparts, and it seems there's a highly organised criminal connection."

"Great!" said Tanya. "That means you can arrest Regan!"

"I'd love to, Mrs Thakral, but I'm afraid there's nothing in those documents that links him to S. T. Freights. All we have is your husband's signature on the contracts and his word that Regan is involved. Of course we believe him, but that's not evidence. We need something concrete before we can charge him."

Tanya felt as though Christmas had been cancelled. "I understand, John."

"Don't be too downhearted. Keep at it. You're almost there."

Tanya thanked him and ended the call. She needed time to think, so she put on her coat and went for a long walk around the lanes. Half an hour into her walk, she got a phone call from Mac.

"Hi, babes. Hot news about Regan; I've found out when that shipment of coke's coming in. And you'll never guess where he's planning to store it."

Tanya knew the answer. "S. T. Freights."

"Good girl! Are you physic or something?"

"I wish." She needed to act, and fast. John's words came back to her: "Keep at it. You're almost there." Suddenly a plan coalesced in her mind. "Let's meet at Madhu's tonight."

"Great. What time?"

"Half seven." She paused. "Oh, and Mac ...?"

"Yep."

"You don't mind if I bring DI Tyler along?"

Secretly Mac was thrilled at the thought of meeting the enemy.

After all, it wasn't every day you got up-close and personal with a high-ranking member of the filth. It would give him an opportunity to assess her for future reference. "Fine by me. Don't you trust yourself alone with me?"

Whilst driving over to Southall later that evening, Tanya broke the bad news to Rajesh about the contracts. "There's still not enough evidence to link Regan."

Rajesh exploded. "What do they want, a signed confession?"

"Something like that."

"Do you know how hard it was to get hold of those contracts? I almost got caught!"

"Don't worry; I've got a plan."

To the casual observer, the four people gathered around the table at Madhu's looked an unlikely alliance. There was Mac, hooded, cocky, and arrogant, throwing sideways glances at DI Tyler, who in turn was not only eyeballing Mac but also giving Rajesh the once-over. For his part, Rajesh felt extremely uncomfortable, so he was relieved when Tanya finally got down to business.

"Okay, Mac, tell DI Tyler what you told me."

In hushed tones, Mac gave her the lowdown on the shipment of cocaine. It was due to arrive in the country by cargo vessel in a week's time. The ship would dock at Tilbury, and from there the contraband would be driven to up London, where it was due to be stored in the bonded warehouse at S. T. Freights.

When Rajesh heard this he almost fainted. *"What?* Fuck me!"

"Hmm," said DI Tyler. "My guess is Regan's using the company to launder drug money."

Rajesh threw his arms up. "Oh that's brilliant! Fucking brilliant! He's turning the place into Mafia central!"

"You've got to hand it to Regan," observed Mac, full of admiration for his boss's audacious scheme. "If the warehouse gets busted, his hands are clean. Involving a third party like that is pure genius." He took a sip of beer and looked at Rajesh. "They've stitched you up good and proper, bro."

Rajesh stared beseechingly at DI Tyler. "You know when the shipment's coming in! Can't you just arrest whoever picks it up at the docks?"

She shook her head. "Small fry. We want Regan. We've been after him for years. We're sick of arresting his minions while he gets away scot free."

"There must be *some* way to get him! The guy's as bent as they come! Hang on, I've got an idea. What if I testified against him in court?"

"His barrister would rip you apart in cross-examination. Believe me; we've gone down that route before."

"This is different! We've got him on two counts – carousel fraud *and* this drug shipment thing. Surely that's enough to send him down?"

"Not without hard evidence."

"Got it! How about Mac going to court and testifying?"

"No way!" said Mac. "Not if you want to see me in a body bag!" He threw Rajesh an indignant look. "I ain't takin' the rap for you again, brother. I did that enough at school."

Rajesh let out a sigh of defeat. "So that's it, then; I'm fucked."

"Not necessarily," said Tanya. "There *is* a way we can get him."

DCI Tyler was overwhelmingly intrigued. "Go on."

* * *

Rajesh looked at his watch – 9.59 a.m. Margaret would be on her way to the coffee machine. He left his pokey office and walked down the corridor. Passing the door to Shearsbe's office he overheard a snatch of conversation: "About two point two mil. Minimum." In the outer office he found Margaret extracting a cup of coffee from the machine. He had to work fast. Glancing behind him, he asked, "Can you get hold of the latest accounts file and let me have a copy? You said you'd help me."

"I'll do my best."

"Brilliant." Suddenly he heard a door open behind him. Expecting to see Patel he was relieved when one of the IT managers walked past clutching a piece of paper. "Morning." When he'd gone, Rajesh continued. "Also, could you go into the database of the bonded warehouse and get me a list of all the deliveries in the past two weeks?"

"Sure."

Rajesh pecked her on the cheek. "You're an angel."

Margaret blushed, a stream of red moving from her neck to her cheeks. "I wouldn't say that."

Two hours later, on the pretext of bringing him another pile of timesheets, Margaret entered Rajesh's office. He was expecting her to hand over the information he'd asked for, but his heart sank when she said, "Bad news, I'm afraid. I tried accessing both the accounts file and the bonded warehouse database. It wouldn't let me in. Mr Patel musts have changed the passwords."

Rajesh's face visibly crumpled. "That's all right, Margaret. At least you tried."

"Sorry." And with that she plonked down another pile of timesheets. "Sorry."

When she'd gone he put his head in his hands. He looked at the mountain of work in front of him, hour upon useless hour of it. Fuck it! He took out his mobile and dialled Regan's number.

A familiar cockney accent reverberated in his ear. "Rajesh! Hello, sunshine! Long time no see. What can I do for you?"

Fear had dried his throat to sandpaper. "I … I wonder if I could come and see you."

Regan sensed a defeated man on the end of the line – just the way he liked them. "Orrr, sounds like you miss your Uncle Joe?"

"Yeah."

"Thought so. Come over to the house tonight. We'll have a nice cosy chat. Let's say eight o'clock."

"That's great. See you then."

When Rajesh got home, he was so nervous he could hardly eat. After dinner, whilst Tanya was helping Vidya with the washing up, he went upstairs and changed the twins' nappies. The task took longer than he had expected. Both Rishi and Maya were screaming their heads off. Then he noticed the time. He was late. He grabbed his mobile and phoned Regan. "Hi, Uncle Joe."

Regan could hear the twins caterwauling. "Blimey, listen to that! The joys of married life, eh?"

"Something like that. Just phoned to say" – before he could go any further, Tanya walked into the room – "I'll be over as soon as I can."

"No problem." Regan then heard Tanya explode. "You're not going out, are you?"

"Too right! I'm sick of this!"

"For God's sake, I thought you'd changed! Don't go, Rajesh. *Rajesh!"*

Suddenly the line went dead. Regan chuckled to himself. "Dear oh dear."

Rajesh arrived at the house within the hour. Crestfallen, he trooped into the hall. Regan noticed how tired and stressed out he looked. "Someone could do with a drink."

"Better make it a large one."

"Come into the lounge."

They walked into the lounge, the scene of Rajesh's beating, and he collapsed onto the sofa. He shook his head woefully. "I'm not cut out for married life."

Regan handed him a large brandy. "I could have told you that. I said to Shearsbe at your wedding, 'I'll give it six months.'"

"You were right." He sighed and gulped the brandy down in one. "What a mess."

Regan sat next to him. "I understand, son. She trapped you.

Fuckers, women. You marry 'em and they start thinkin' they own you. Scheming bitches. What are you gonna do?"

"I don't know … To be honest, I miss my old life."

"Once a playboy, always a playboy, eh?"

"It's not just that. I miss doing business deals. I miss the buzz."

Regan took a sip of whiskey, the tinkling ice cubes breaking the silence. "You want back in?"

Rajesh looked at him gratefully. "You don't know how happy that makes me feel. You should see the job they've got me doing! A monkey could do it."

"Yeah," Regan said with a laugh. "Patel told me all about it. A bit cruel seeing as you used to own the company."

"Say that again. First thing I'm gonna to do is sack that bastard—"

"Whoa, whoa! Hold your horses! I run S. T. Freights now. Patel's a good worker. Solid. Does as he's told. No, no, son. Before any of that, I need to know I can trust you." He got up and strolled to the drinks cabinet, where he refilled both glasses. "Are you up for a little job to prove your loyalty?"

"Anything's better than the data inputting."

"That's what you get when you make an enemy of me."

"I don't want to be your enemy anymore."

"Good, Rajesh. That's good … D'you know what? I've missed you."

"I've missed you, too. We had some good times together. Speaking of which, I've got this deal lined up—"

Regan cut him dead. "Do you think I'm gonna let you waltz back in and start doing deals as though nothing's happened? What do you take me for, a fuckin' idiot? No, you're gonna have to prove yourself, sunshine. You let me down once, remember?"

Cowed, Rajesh nodded. "So, er … what's this job you want me to do?"

"Piece of cake, really. Teddy and his crew are driving down to

Tilbury Docks tomorrow night to pick up a load of Charlie. I want you to go with them."

"Cocaine! I'm not a drug smuggler; I'm a businessman."

"Don't fuck me about. You said you wanted in."

"I do. But not this! I've pulled off some great deals in the past. That's what I'm good at. If I could just—"

"Shut the fuck up! You either do the job or go home to your wife and brats. Simple as."

Rajesh weighed up the options. "Okay."

"That's better."

Rajesh tipped down his brandy and got up from the sofa. "Right, what time do you want me tomorrow night?"

"Where d'you think you're going?"

"Find a hotel. I can't go home, not after the row I've just had."

"No need for that. You can stay the night."

"I don't want to put you to any trouble."

"No trouble. And don't worry about going in work tomorrow. I'll ring Shearsbe and tell him the score."

Rajesh spent most of the next day relaxing by the pool. He didn't see much of Regan, who left just after breakfast. Every now and then a member of staff would emerge from the house to ask if he needed anything. This was better than sitting in his pokey office taking orders from Patel. A strange thing, though – his mobile phone had gone missing. He was sure he'd brought it with him. In fact, he was certain.

Regan appeared a little after 7 p.m. "Get ready. Teddy will be here soon."

Rajesh went upstairs to the guest bedroom, the same bedroom where he and Bav had enjoyed their ménage à trois with that slut Donna. As he was getting changed, he heard a vehicle pull up. Glancing out of the window, he was surprised to see a white transit van bearing the S. T. Freights logo. Surprise turned to shock when Teddy and his two cohorts jumped out. Rajesh couldn't believe they were using a company vehicle to ferry drugs. Still, it made sense. No one at the docks would even think about stopping a van belonging to an import–export company. Regan had thought of everything.

As he made his way downstairs, a howl of laughter went up. Teddy, his two sidekicks, and Regan were standing in the hall, pissing themselves laughing.

"What?" asked Rajesh, completely bewildered.

"Look at the fuckin' state of him!" said Teddy. "You'd think he was going for a night out at Rouge!"

Rajesh saw what the others were wearing – dark blue overalls and baseball caps. He glanced at his own attire – a bespoke Saville Row suit. "Oh, yeah. Sorry. I didn't bring any clothes with me."

"That's all right," Teddy said, chuckling. "There's a spare boiler suit in the van."

Regan caught Teddy's eye. "We'll make a smuggler of him yet." He handed him an envelope. "Right. Teddy, the ship's called the *Southern Star*. All the details are in there. You know where to take the stuff, don't you?"

"S. T. Freights."

"Good boy. When you get there, Patel and Shearsbe will be waiting for you. Off you go."

They left the house and got in the van. Teddy threw Rajesh a boiler suit. "Get in the back and put that on."

Rajesh slipped on the boiler suit and wedged himself between a stack of pallets. They drove through leafy Essex, eventually joining the M25. The traffic was light. It wasn't long before they saw the sign for Tilbury Docks. Rocking from side to side in the back of the transit, his backside aching, Rajesh recalled his former modes of transport – silky smooth Lamborghinis and first-class air travel. Those were the days.

"All right in the back there?" asked Teddy, his piggy eyes flashing in the rear-view mirror. "Only you look as though you're about to shit yourself."

His two cohorts cackled.

"I'm fine," answered Rajesh, petrified.

Leaving the M25, they pulled onto the dock road. Rajesh could see the sprawling complex of warehouses dominated by huge dockside cranes, their crisscrossed silhouettes ink-black against the russet Kent sky. The sun was about to set, bathing the docks in a hellish glow.

Teddy stopped at the gate, flashed a piece of paper at the security guard, and got waved through. Piece of cake. He'd obviously done this before. Turing right, they headed along the wharf, passing myriad cargo ships being loaded and unloaded. At the far end of the dock stood a massive warehouse.

Teddy pulled up outside. He switched off the ignition and turned to Rajesh. "Okay, Raj, me old mate." He opened the envelope given to him by Regan and handed him a sheaf of documents. "Go in there and hand these in at reception. Once they've checked them out, they'll open the doors and wave us in. Got it?"

"Me?" asked Rajesh. "You want *me* to do it?"

"Mr Regan's orders! Now stop fucking about!"

Rajesh climbed out of the van and walked towards the warehouse. He noticed the entrance was bristling with CCTV cameras, each one pointing his way. It suddenly dawned on him why Regan had sent him; it wasn't only a test of his loyalty but also an insurance policy that if anything went wrong, he would be roped in with Teddy and his crew. No wonder the police had never managed to pin anything on him!

He pushed open a steel door. Directly in front of him was the reception desk, manned by a formidable-looking security guard. Rajesh handed him the papers.

The guard stared at them quizzically. "Wait there."

Another bank of CCTV cameras captured Rajesh sitting down on a white plastic chair. He tried reading a magazine but couldn't. His stomach churned over; his palms ran with sweat. He kept glancing at the door anxiously. Eventually the guard returned and handed the papers back. He pressed a button on the desk.

"Area B. Bay seven." A large set of roller doors screamed open, and Teddy drove the van inside. Rajesh climbed in, repeating the guard's instructions.

They followed the signs and found the correct bay. A warehouseman dressed in baggy brown overalls pointed to a stack of boxes marked "Ethical Coffee". Coffee was known to put even the finest sniffer dog off the scent. You had to hand it to Regan.

"Right," said Teddy. "Load the van."

"What?" said Rajesh. "Aren't you going to help?"

Teddy shouted through the van window, loud enough for the warehouseman to hear, "It's your stuff! You load it!"

Fuming, Rajesh went back and forth, loading the boxes into the van. After half an hour's back-breaking work, he slammed the back doors shut and climbed into the cab. "Thanks for that! Fuck me, you could have given me a hand!"

Teddy started the engine. "Stop moaning!"

"Hey! Just a minute!"

Teddy froze.

The warehouseman came rushing towards the van. "You've not signed for them!" He held out a clipboard and pen,

"So he hasn't," said Teddy, relieved. "Go on, Rajesh; give the man your signature."

He took the clipboard and signed for sixty-two large boxes of Ethical Coffee.

They drove out of the warehouse, Teddy and his crew whooping and cheering. As they headed up the M25 towards London, Rajesh sat in stunned silence; he had just imported God knows how many kilos of cocaine into the UK.

It was dark by the time they got to S. T. Freights. Teddy flashed his lights three times, and the gates swung open. A shadowy figure pointed them in the direction of the bonded warehouse. Rajesh closed his eyes, thinking, *If my Dad could see me now, delivering drugs to his own company, he'd die of shame.*

The van stopped, and they all piled out. Rajesh could see

Shearsbe and Patel standing beneath one of the security lights. Both of them were staring at him, smirking. Patel disappeared inside the bonded warehouse and opened one of its huge doors.

Shearsbe strolled nonchalantly over to Rajesh. He couldn't resist baiting him. "Who'd have thought it, eh? Rajesh Thakral, a drug dealer. I said to Regan I didn't think you'd have the balls to go through with it."

Suddenly the area came under attack. Sirens blazed as a dozen vehicles smashed through the gates. A helicopter hovered overhead, its powerful searchlight illuminating the front of the warehouse. "Police! Stay where you are!" Before anyone could move, a group of officers surrounded the van.

Now it was Rajesh's turn to smirk. "Oh, I had the balls all right." A look of confusion spread across Shearsbe's face. As the officers moved forward, guns in hand, Rajesh showed him a tiny button camera attached to his lapel. "Smile; you're on *Candid Camera*."

20

Two days later Tanya arrived at Paddington Green, London's high-security police station. Because of the secrecy surrounding the raid, she had only been told earlier that morning. An excited DI Tyler called and said to her, "We've finally got the bastard, Tanya! We've got him!"

Built to hold terrorist suspects, the cells at Paddington Green were now full to capacity with Regan and his gang. Operation Pinto had netted the entire top tier of his organisation. Rajesh was amongst them, but because he had cooperated with the authorities, he was held in a less secure part of the building. He still had to face charges, though of a less serious nature – Tanya's deal with Customs and Excise had seen to that.

DI Tyler arranged for Tanya to visit Rajesh in his cell. When she walked in, he was lying on his bunk, unshaven, unkempt, and tired looking. He sat up and said, wearily, "We did it, Tans."

She rushed in and threw her arms around him. "Oh, Rajesh! I'm so proud of you! You were really brave. If Regan had found that camera on your lapel, God knows what he'd have done."

"You needn't have worried; Special Branch were outside recording the whole thing. If he'd have discovered it, they'd have gone in all guns blazing." He grinned. "Tell you what, that idea of yours – letting him hear us arguing on the phone before I left – was pure genius. He never suspected a thing after that. As soon as I got to the house, he started admitting to all sorts. Kind of threw me a bit when he ordered me to go to Tilbury Docks with

Teddy and pick up the coke. I was just about to hit him with the business idea thing your Mr Harvey had cooked up, but I didn't get the chance. Still, it's all worked out, hasn't it?"

"Wonderfully." Tanya hesitated. "You'll still have to go to court, though."

"I know. I know ... But at least the company's safe."

"Yes, your father is so relieved."

Rajesh looked stunned. "You ... You've *told* him?"

"I had to. It'll all come out in the newspapers anyway when it goes to trial. I'd rather he heard it from me first."

"So he knows everything, then?" Tanya nodded. "How's he taken it?"

"Not good, Rajesh. He's devastated. He said you've let everyone down."

"He's right."

Tanya could see Rajesh's mood turning black, so she changed the subject. "You're gonna love this. When DI Tyler went Regan's house to arrest him, she said he just stood there cocksure, saying, "Fuck you, where's the evidence?" She said the look on his face when she played him the tape was priceless. He's only been inside for a few days and already his empire's crumbling. According to DI Tyler, now that Regan and his top lieutenants have been locked up, its left a power vacuum on the street. The likes of Mac are making their play to fill it."

"Probably the only reason why he helped us in the first place," said Rajesh cynically.

"I wouldn't say that. Deep down, he likes you. He sends his regards, by the way. He said he really admires you for having the guts to go undercover like that."

"That's nice of him. What's happened to Patel?"

Tanya's face broke into a smile. "This is the best bit. Soon as they arrested him, he started blabbing – names, dates. He couldn't wait to hand over files about the carousel fraud. Not only that, he led the police to a secure room in the bonded warehouse.

You'll never guess what was in there: guns, false passports, stolen jewellery, drugs – a real Aladdin's cave."

"You're joking!"

"They've got so much evidence against Regan, DI Tyler said that he will never taste freedom again."

"Let's hope so … What about Shearsbe?"

"He's in just as deep. When they searched his house, they found a gun that was linked to the murder of a policeman."

"Really? Fuck me!"

"So we can write him off too."

"Thank God." He sighed. "To think I got mixed up with that lot! I must have been mad."

* * *

The trial was held at the Old Bailey and lasted for six weeks. Regan was found guilty on four counts of fraud, money laundering, drug smuggling, and theft. He was sentenced to thirty years and twenty-five years concurrently. All his assets were seized, including his Essex mansion, two apartments in Marbella, a luxury yacht moored off Cadiz, and his prized supercar collection. Shearsbe was sent to prison for a total of thirty-five years, whilst the rest of Regan's gang received sentences between fifteen and twenty-five years. Despite pleading guilty and cooperating with the police, Patel got eight years. When the judge sentenced him, he cried like a baby. As for Rajesh, during the trial he was kept apart from the other prisoners and sentenced separately. The judge took into consideration his part in the undercover operation and the fact that he'd been duped into facilitating the VAT fraud. He was given a nine-month custodial sentence to be served in an open prison. John Harvey from Customs and Excise kept his word and wiped off the twenty-two-million-pound VAT bill from the S. T. Freights account. Thanks to Tanya, the company was safe.

After Rajesh was sentenced, he was transferred to Ford Open

Prison near Arundel, West Sussex. His fellow prisoners were mainly white-collar criminals and petty offenders. The regime was strict but fair, concentrating on reintegration into society rather than punishment. The inmates could choose from a variety of tasks, from working in the prison garden to vocational training in one of the many workshops. As it was approaching summer, Rajesh chose to work on the prison allotment, figuring that growing vegetables would be good for the soul. He shared a room with a former city trader convicted of insider dealing. At night they would sit and reminisce about the good times, when London was a jewel just waiting to be plucked.

Tanya came to see him once a week. They would go for long walks around the prison grounds. On one such walk, a month into his sentence, he asked her about S. T. Freights. He was surprised and delighted when she said, "I go in three mornings a week and report back to Dad. He's giving me a crash course in the import–export business. Margaret's a big help. We sort of runs things between the three of us. It's a challenge, but I really like it."

"Has Dad forgiven me yet?"

"I won't lie … He said it'll take a long time before he can trust you again."

"I don't blame him. The more I think about what I did, the more I can't believe it. That's the thing about prison; it gives you time to think. How's Mum?"

"She's fine. She loves looking after the twins. It's made her feel young again. She said she'll come and see you next week."

"Look forward to it. Ask her if she'll bring me a flask of masala chai and some homemade dosas, will you? The food in here's shit. I can't tell you how many times I've lain in bed at night thinking about the food at our wedding." Memories of that day came flooding back. He recalled how beautiful Tanya had looked and the heart-stopping moment when she walked down the aisle. To think he'd almost lost her. Choking back the tears, he stared into her eyes and said, "I'm sorry for putting you through all that. I love you more than anything."

"I love you, too."

Rajesh said goodbye and walked her to the gate. He gave her a kiss and stared out beyond the prison. "Funny, you don't appreciate your freedom until it's gone."

She took his hand. "You'll be out soon; don't worry."

* * *

Over the next few months, Tanya threw herself into the running of S. T. Freights. It wasn't long before she started to make decisions, though of course not without liaising with Satish. She became more and more fascinated with the workings of the company. At night, after putting the twins to bed, she would sit up talking with Satish, offering ideas about how to improve the company's performance. Satish was thrilled. He remembered what Rajesh had been like when he first took over the company; all he was concerned about was outdoing his father, whereas Tanya was just the opposite. She wanted to build rather than destroy. Slowly he came to realise she had become the son he never had.

After nine months, Rajesh was finally released from prison. Tanya drove over to West Sussex to pick him up. Emerging from the gates at eleven o'clock in the morning, he looked so different from the cocky Rajesh of his youth. Prison had taken its toll. When he got home, Vidya was waiting for him at the front door. Close to tears, she ran down the drive and clasped him in her arms. It was an emotional moment for everyone. The first thing he did was run into the house and hug the twins. "I won't let you down again," he said, covering Rishi and Maya in kisses. He stood up and looked round. "Where's Dad?"

"He's in his study," replied Vidya nervously.

"Oh … I better get it over with, then." It was the moment he had dreaded. He crossed the hall and tapped sheepishly on the study door.

"Who is it?"

"R-Rajesh. It's Rajesh."

"Come in!"

Satish was merciless in his onslaught. He gave it to him straight, accusing him of being an arrogant fool whose actions had brought shame upon the family. He had let down not only himself but the whole family, who, thanks to him, were now pariahs in the Indian community. It would be a long time, if ever, before he could trust him again. Rajesh took his punishment like a man, never once interrupting, and even nodding his head in agreement.

Finally the storm blew over. Rajesh looked at his father and said, "I'm sorry, Dad. You're right. What more can I say. I've been a fool."

His son's genuine contrition took Satish by surprise. He was convinced he would trot out his usual line of bland excuses. Satish decided to go easy on him. He'd served his time, after all. "Right, we'll say no more about it. I want you back at work as soon as possible. Best thing for you, hard work."

Rajesh was touched. "Really? You want me to go back to S. T. Freights?"

"No one else will have you! But don't think you'll be running the company. You'll have to start at the bottom, like you should have done in the first place."

That night Vidya poured her heart into cooking a sumptuous dinner. It was wonderful having all the family around the table again. Even the twins were well behaved, gurgling at each other in their high chairs. Satish opened a bottle of Château Lascombes to celebrate. His son had been a fool, yes, but deep down he was glad he was home. During the meal Rajesh noticed how close Tanya and his father had become. He closed his eyes and thanked God he was back in the bosom of his family.

After a week's recuperation, Rajesh was ready to go back to work. Before he left the house with Tanya, Satish called him into his study. "I want you to assist Tanya in the day-to-day running of the business. She'll tell you what to do."

"Yes, Dad."

They drove in to work together. Rajesh was glad to see the old place again. Business was booming, judging by the amount of trucks zooming in and out of the gate. Tanya parked the Porsche in her dedicated parking space.

As they walked into the main office, Rajesh suddenly lost his bearings. "What's happened to the Accounts Department?"

"I've moved it upstairs," said Tanya brusquely. "It's a lot more efficient having it next to the IT Department."

"Yeah, yeah … Good idea."

Margaret was in her usual place. When she saw Rajesh walk through the door, she got to her feet and nodded. "Nice to see you back, Rajesh."

"Nice to see you, too. I was just thinking—"

Before he could go any further, Margaret handed Tanya a file. "Good morning, Mrs Thakral. Here are those figures you asked for."

"Thank you, Margaret … Oh, when you get chance, could you get me Alan Beresford on the phone."

"Certainly, Mrs Thakral."

Tanya breezed into Satish's old office. She took off her jacket and sat down behind the desk. Rajesh noticed she'd had the room completely redecorated. The tatty blue carpet had been replaced with a polished hardwood floor, the austere white walls repainted an efficient steel-grey. Pride of place was a large photo of Satish smiling down benignly.

"Who's Alan Beresford?" asked Rajesh.

"Chairman of Beresford Electronics. They're a small company from Leeds, but I get the feeling they're going places."

Rajesh nodded. He stood there, arms dangling by his side, unsure of what to do next. "So, er …"

"Oh, yes! Sorry, Rajesh. I've got you an office next door. Margaret will show you what to do."

"Right. Thanks." He noticed Tanya boot up her laptop. "I'll, er … I'll leave you to it, then."

"Would you? That'd be great."

He turned and walked out. Closing the door behind him, he noticed the highly polished name plaque: "Tanya Thakral, CEO."

"Oh, Rajesh?"

He opened the door a slither. "Yes, Tanya."

"*Ek chai.*"

About the Author

Rajeev Rana is a serial entrepreneur who has had success in restaurants, catering, construction, and the care industry. Although successful in business, he has always felt a burning desire to validate his success by becoming a published author. This has been a personal journey, as Rajeev was forced to leave school at the age of fifteen and assume the role of head of the family after the death of his father. The mission of completing and publishing this book has become a replacement for the academic qualifications that he would have received in school.